Sensitivity Statement

WISTFUL WHISPERS INCLUDES EMOTIONALLY sensitive themes such as the loss of a child and references to past family addiction. The story also explores personal body image struggles, complex reputational dynamics, and how professional boundaries can be tested by desire, public perception, and workplace scrutiny. These elements are woven into the broader narrative with empathy and care as part of the characters' emotional and ethical journeys.

wistful WHISPERS

KAYLENE WINTER

Prologue – Eight Months Prior

THE PRE-OP ROOM IS quiet.

Humming with the weight of too many emotions in too small a space.

I'm nearing the end of my third year in my neurosurgery residency at University of Washington Medical School so I've been here before.

It never gets easier.

Especially when a patient is so young and vibrant.

Miranda Black sits on the exam table, her scrawny legs swinging like a metronome of nervous energy, oblivious to the gravity of what's about to happen. She's twelve—too young to shoulder the dread etched into her parents' faces.

Instead, she looks at me with big, brown eyes, radiating a kind of trust which makes my gut twist. This little girl should have a long future ahead of her. Filled with childhood memories. Sleepovers and scraped knees, awkward kisses and graduation caps—everything she deserves but might never get.

I'd burn down the goddamn world to give her a shot at all of it.

"You ready for your big day, superstar?" I crouch slightly so we're at eye level.

She grins. "Ready as I'll ever be. Will I be able to feel it?"

"Nope." I shake my head. "You'll be asleep the whole time. When you wake up, all those nasty tumors will be gone, gone, gone."

Miranda giggles and Myra, her mom, makes a choked sound behind her. I glance up, meeting Mrs. Black's eyes. They're rimmed red. Her fingers are clenched so tightly her knuckles have gone white. Beside her, Miranda's father, Daniel, stands rigid. His face is carefully blank and his arms are crossed like they're the only thing holding him together.

How I conduct myself now is, in my opinion, the most important part of a critical case like Miranda's. Her family deserves hope. Trust. Honesty. We want to give them their daughter back. It's important to coach them through what to expect.

I gesture to Layla, the nurse practitioner. "Can you take Miranda into the children's waiting room and give her one of the iPads? We need to chat with her parents."

"Sure." Layla winks at me and leads Miranda from the room, looking over her shoulder with a distinct nod toward the exit sign.

Yeah. I've been there. Not going back for seconds.

My longtime mentor, Bryce Caldwell, clears his throat from the other side of the room, reminding me he's in charge.

"Mr. and Mrs. Black. We'll be using MRI-guided laser interstitial thermal therapy." He doesn't see the benefit of being soft—a point of contention between us on occasion. "Lasers make this surgery minimally invasive, and our goal is to remove as many of the tumors as possible while preserving healthy brain function."

Myra sucks her bottom lip over her teeth. "What are the risks, again?"

"Either way, they're severe." Bryce doesn't sugarcoat. "The tumors are deep. Near the brainstem and the motor cortex. There's a significant risk of bleeding, swelling, and neurological damage. Surgery is our best option."

"Which means there are bad options." Mr. Black chokes back a sob.

Bryce barely inclines his head. "Leaving the tumors in will make life agonizing. Along the way, Miranda will endure debilitating headaches. Seizures. All sorts of complications. There are always risks in neurosurgery. In my opinion, this operation is the *only* option."

Jesus. He's like a robot. I step in before the conversation turns completely mechanical. "We've gone over Miranda's case extensively. Dr. Caldwell is the best. I'll be assisting every step of the way." I meet their eyes, my voice steady. "We'll take care of her like she's our own."

Mrs. Black bursts into tears. "Do you promise?"

Something clenches in my chest. "I promise we'll do everything we can."

It's not the answer she wants.

It's the truth.

The OR is cold, sterile, and humming with focused energy. I feel at home here, in a room where nerves don't exist.

Where they *can't* exist.

Miranda looks impossibly tiny on the table, her head secured in a rigid frame. I've assisted in dozens of surgeries. Something about this one feels different. Maybe it's her age, maybe it's the way she looked at me before they wheeled her in here.

Maybe it's because I need this to go well—not for her. For me. For my career.

For my *sanity*.

Bryce stands at the head of the table, his presence commanding. Movements deliberate. He's been in the game forever. His reputation borders on legendary. I'd be lying if I said I wasn't grateful to be learning under him.

There's always an unspoken tension between us—the unmovable old-school mentor and the ambitious resident who embraces a new way of patient care, yet still has to prove himself.

"LITT system ready?" Bryce peers over his glasses.

"Ready," I confirm, my steady hands poised and prepared.

The MRI monitor glows, displaying the biggest tumor in real-time imaging. It's invasive, nestled dangerously close to critical structures. Not unbeatable, though.

"Target locked." I focus in. "Ready for ablation."

Bryce activates the laser. The heat burns through the tumor, destroying the cancerous tissue while sparing the surrounding brain tissue. It's delicate, precise work, and I watch every movement with fascination as I do everything he asks of me.

This man is an artist.

For the first hour, everything goes according to plan. The tumor is responding, shrinking under the guided heat. Until—

"Pressure's rising," Kendrick Lyon, the anesthesiologist warns. "Intracranial pressure is up to 25."

I glance at the monitor and panic buzzes where my breath should be. This is way too high. We've been monitoring for swelling, however, this spike is dangerous.

Lethal.

Bryce's expression doesn't change, he remains calm under pressure. "Thank you, Kendrick. We need to manage the swelling. Seamus, please adjust the laser. We need to move faster."

I nod, adjusting the fiber carefully and quickly. The pressure *has* to come down. We can't afford a rupture.

Then something shifts—something Bryce obviously doesn't see. A shadow on the monitor. Small. Unmistakable.

A blood vessel. It's too close.

I hesitate, my instinct and training screams at me to slow down. To reassess. Bryce is already moving, already increasing the intensity.

"Dr. Caldwell—" I bark.

"I see it," he snaps. "Keep going."

Except he doesn't see it. Not really. At least, I don't think he realizes...

Before I can finish my thought, it happens.

A rupture.

Blood floods into the surgical field, the dark-red liquid pooling fast.

Too fast.

"Shit," Bryce mutters. "Suction, now."

I react instinctively, grabbing the tube, working to clear the blood. It's not enough. It's not working. The pressure keeps climbing.

Miranda's brain swells despite our every effort to control it.

"We need to back off. *Now!*" I cry out urgently.

"*No,*" Bryce snarls. "We keep going."

My pulse pounds. This isn't right. We've got to do something.

The monitors blare an alarm.

"We're losing her," Kendrick croaks.

"Goddamnit. I *know,*" Bryce bites out, his hands moving fast.

It's too late.

My stomach twists. I want to push back—except I'm not the lead surgeon. I'm the resident. I assist. I follow.

Even when I don't agree.

Bryce finally makes the call. "We need to close. Now."

The weight of what's happening slams into me. I manage to keep my hands steady as we work quickly to close the incision, stabilizing Miranda as best we can.

I know the truth before we even step back.

The damage is done and the ICU is quiet in the worst way.

I sit next to her bed. Miranda is still. Machines now do the work her body no longer can. The rhythmic beep of the monitor is the only sound filling the room.

Through the window, I can see Bryce is speaking to her parents. I offered. He insisted. I don't have to hear the words to know what he's telling them.

"The surgery didn't go as planned."

"We did everything we could."

"The swelling was too severe."

"She's in a state of unresponsive wakefulness."

Mr. Black is frozen. Mrs. Black crumbles to the ground.

I look at little Miranda, who doesn't move. Doesn't react. Doesn't wake up.

Never will again.

I should walk away. The job is done. I can't, though. My ass stays planted, my hand clutching hers.

Could we have stopped it? If I'd spoken up sooner, would it have made a difference?

I don't know. It's too late now.

All I know is this little girl trusted me to make her better.

The sharp pull of failure settles deep in my chest.

I don't think it'll ever leave.

One

Eight Weeks Later

FINNEY COOPER ISN'T A law firm.

It's a war machine.

We're the lawyers you call when you're done playing fair and ready to ruin reputations.

I didn't claw my way to partner in a firm like this by being nice.

I did it by winning.

By making damn sure no one questions whether I belong here.

Despite my confidence in the courtroom, I stand in front of the full-length mirror in my office, buttoned into a bespoke power suit—tailored, sharp, commanding—wishing I could shrink myself to fit a world built for someone else.

I feel rage simmer beneath the surface. Rage at every sideways glance, every softened smile. Rage at the way the world measures worth in inches.

Even more rage at the part of me who still cares.

I smooth my hands down the silky fabric and adjust my blazer. I can see the way the fabric pulls at my hips and doesn't quite cover the bulge of my stomach. Despite the custom fit, my ample curves always make everything feel a size too tight. If I didn't wear constrictive shaping undergarments, I probably couldn't even zip up my skirt. My thighs would rub together and chafe.

I know I'm objectively attractive. I have a face people notice—sharp cheekbones, full lips, long, brown hair gleaming in the right light. I take care of myself. I buy the expensive skincare. Go to the finest salons. Never miss a mani/pedi. Work out at the gym three times a week with a trainer.

I put in the effort.

Yet, I'm still a big girl. Alone. Thirty-seven. No prospects. Haven't had sex in two years.

Let's be honest, I'm past my prime.

A knock at my door snaps me back. I exhale sharply, forcing my lifelong insecurities down and locking them where I keep all the things I don't have time for.

Deep, deep inside of me where they can't be touched. I call out, "Yes?"

My assistant, Cora peeks in, all efficiency in her crisp navy dress. "The Blacks are here."

Showtime.

I stride down the hall to the conference room, my heels clicking against the polished floors. My spine is straight and my expression is deliberately composed. The weight of the case and what I'm about to ask these grieving parents to relive, settles over me. I don't let it show, though. This is about them, not me.

Pushing open the door, I step inside and immediately see Myra and Daniel Black sitting stiffly at the conference table. Their hands are clasped together, fingers knotted so tightly it looks painful. Myra's eyes are puffy. Exhaustion lines her face. Daniel's jaw clenched so tightly it looks like he's going to grind his teeth to dust.

Their grief and anger twist together in the space between them, raw and festering.

God, there's something about parents in situations like this—the way they hold on to each other like it's the only thing keeping them from falling apart. It breaks my heart and reminds me why I became a lawyer in the first place.

They may not want to be here.

To receive justice, they *need* to be.

I offer them a steady, reassuring nod as I sit across from them and open their daughter's case file in my laptop. "Mr. and Mrs. Black, I'm Marcella Delgado. I'm so incredibly sorry for what you're going through. It's too much for any parent to endure."

Myra swallows hard, her fingers grip and regrip her husband's. "We don't know what happens next."

"I've reviewed the medical records, and based on what I've seen so far, you have a strong case. What happened to Miranda never should have happened." I make sure to look at both of them, they need to trust me to seek justice for their daughter.

Daniel exhales sharply. "It doesn't change anything. How can we be sure we'll win? Going through a lawsuit might be more than we can endure right now."

"You're right to weigh your options." I tread carefully because I won't ever make promises I can't keep. "Medicine is complicated. Surgeons can argue sometimes, even when they do everything right, bad outcomes happen. My job is to prove Dr. Caldwell failed to uphold the standard of care."

"Dr. Caldwell..." She winces, the mere mention of his name is like an open wound she's still pressing down on. "He didn't even seem sorry."

I've done my research. He wouldn't.

Over the past decade, I've gone up against doctors like him many times before—always men. They walk into a room expecting me to believe they're godlike. Infallible. Hell, I get it. They've built entire careers on being revered.

None of it matters when I tear them apart. Reduce them to sniveling shells of their former self.

Ooooh. Now, I feel it—beneath the surface—the same hunger I always get when I'm about to dismantle someone brick by brick.

It's the fuel driving me and my tank is full.

"He probably isn't sorry," I say simply. "Surgeons at his level rarely engage in self-reflection."

Myra blinks rapidly and her lips press together.

Daniel shifts beside her. "There was another doctor in the room. A younger guy. He was the one who talked to us before the surgery and made it seem like…" He trails off, his free hand curls into a fist. "Like this would never happen."

"Do you remember his name?" I'll subpoena the records, of course. At the same time, it's always helpful to get as much information as possible now.

"Dr. McGloughlin." Myra's eyes soften. "*Seamus* McGloughlin. He was *so* kind."

There's something almost guilty in the way she says it, like she wants to be angry at him but isn't sure she can be.

"He sat with Miranda before the surgery," she continues as I type his name into Google. "Talked to her like she was a person, not just a patient. Told her she was a 'superstar.' She adored him." Her voice breaks on the last word.

The search loads, and suddenly, I'm staring at him. He's young. Younger than me, at least by a handful of years.

Overwhelmingly handsome in a way making my stomach twist and awakening something dormant deep inside of me.

Against my will, my pussy clenches and my clit begins to pulse.

Holy mother of God, Seamus McGloughlin exudes sex. The kind of man who makes my breath stutter.

He's big—broad shoulders and strong arms. A body built for capability. For endurance. Light-brown hair falls past his shoulders. It looks like it's been raked through a thousand times by impatient fingers. Stubble frames a too-perfect mouth.

Good God, his eyes stop me cold.

Blue. Deep. Soulful.

The kind of eyes you want to trust. Eyes that make you believe you're safe. That promise he'll fix whatever's broken.

There's something else. Behind the warmth, the strength. A sadness, maybe. A weight he carries, hidden beneath the surface...

Oh. Hell. No. These thoughts are wildly inappropriate.

I force my gaze back to Myra and Daniel, ignoring the way my pulse is suddenly in my ears. "He was in the operating room?"

Daniel nods, his expression unreadable. "Yeah. I don't know if he helped or if he was another part of the lie."

I flick my gaze back to his face on the screen—strong, striking, capable.

For the first time in my career, I yearn for something entirely off-limits. Something impossible.

I do my best to keep my composure. "Dr. McGloughlin is a resident. He wouldn't have been the one making the final decisions."

"He was there. He was part of it. She's—" His voice chokes off, his grief slamming into the room like a physical force.

I let the silence stretch for a beat, giving them the space to breathe through it. Then I sit forward slightly. "We're going to hold the right people accountable. Dr. Caldwell was the lead surgeon. He made the calls. If Dr. McGloughlin played a role, we'll uncover it."

Daniel nods tightly, tears stream freely out of the corners of his eyes.

"Will we have to go to trial?" Myra manages to utter through her sobs.

"Most cases settle before we see a courtroom." I fold my hands neatly on the table. They need to be able to trust me to hold things together. "Washington law requires mediation before trial which means, even after we file, we'll have a chance to settle. This is when I'll take their depositions, to see how strong our case is. Make no mistake—I prepare every case for trial. When we sit at the negotiating table, we'll be ready no matter what."

Daniel exhales. His features pulled tight though his expression loosens a fraction. Like he's choosing to believe I can give them justice for Miranda. "What do we do next?"

I meet his gaze, steady and unwavering. "From here, I'll do a deep dive into the medical records, file an initial claim, and start the process of gathering evidence including interviewing the doctors involved, as well as the hospital itself, to assess their defenses and strategy." I pause, letting my words settle. "Once we have a clearer picture, we'll decide on our next move—every step will be taken with your best interests in mind. Sound like a plan?"

Myra nods quickly, desperate for something—anything—to hold on to. "Yes. Please."

I stand, and they follow. As I walk them to the front, they thank me profusely, their gratitude thick with exhaustion and something close to hope. We finalize the engagement letter, formalizing what they already knew the moment they stepped into my office.

They need me to fight.

I will.

This is what I do. I seek justice for parents like Myra and Daniel.

Once they're gone, the firm's hallway swallows the sound of their retreating footsteps. I turn and head back to my office, my own heels sharp against the floor. A rhythmic reminder about the work ahead.

I close the door behind me and sink into my chair. The room is silent. A type of quiet seeping into your bones making you think even when you don't want to.

I should be focusing on strategy. On how I'll break Caldwell apart.

Instead, Seamus McGloughlin's face permeates my thoughts. I let myself imagine what it would feel like—his strong hands on my skin. Mouth against mine. The quiet, steady way I instinctively know he'd hold me.

Like I was something worth keeping.

My fingers trail over the polished surface of my desk. All I want to do is shove them down my panties and rub myself to oblivion.

It's ridiculous. I don't even know this man, yet I can't shake the way Myra said his name, like she couldn't possibly believe he fucked up.

The thing is, he might have been kind to Miranda and he probably made her parents believe she could be saved.

Now she's in a hospital bed, locked inside herself. The image of her helpless body knocks some sense into me. I shake my head, dismissing my stupid sexual fantasies about some cocky resident because I'm lonely.

It doesn't matter who he is. If he was part of this, I'll find out.

This isn't about me. It never is.

Seamus McGloughlin is a distraction I can't afford.

Loneliness doesn't win trials.

Miranda's parents are counting on me to burn the system down.

I intend to light the match.

Two

SEAMUS

A Few Day Later

The lab hums.

Postdocs whispering, machines blinking, breakthroughs on every screen, neural mapping and AI-assisted decision-making models.

None of it touches me.

Not since...

I used to believe I could change lives.

Now I sit during my R4 research year watching data scroll by, wishing I could go back in time.

Wondering, as I do every day, if I'd done something—said something else.

Goddammit. I feel so fucking useless.

Nothing holds my attention the way it should. Months ago, when I submitted my research proposal, I thought I'd be thrilled to step away from the brutal pace of residency. To immerse myself in something groundbreaking.

Nope. I can't bring myself to give a shit.

Each day I stare blankly at the ECoG data in front of me, watching brain wave patterns light up on the screen. Cortical representation of fine motor movements—important work, as it relates to alcoholism, supposedly.

I'd hoped it would be a distraction. A way to keep myself from thinking about the one person I failed so spectacularly.

Miranda Black.

Her name has been carved into my brain since the moment I walked out of the OR and her parents looked at me with shattered eyes, begging for an explanation I didn't have.

How is this fair? Me staring at neural pathways while she lies in a bed somewhere, locked inside herself…

Fuck.

I scrub a hand over my face, exhaling hard.

"What's with you today?" A familiar voice jolts my attention to the present.

I glance up. Sarah Patel, one of the postdocs I work with on a daily basis, stands in the doorway, arms crossed.

"You've been staring at the screen for an hour," she scolds. "Either you've figured out the secrets of the universe or you're slowly losing your mind."

I smirk, though there's no real humor behind it. "The latter."

She leans against the desk, looking at me a little too closely. "You know, when you presented your research proposal last year, I thought you'd actually be interested in it."

"I was back then," I say glumly.

Sarah folds her arms across her chest. "What changed?"

Everything.

She doesn't know about Miranda. Few people do. Surgeons lose patients every day, it's not even a normal topic of conversation. We're trained to compartmentalize and move on. I rub my temple with my thumb. "Eh—a little distracted."

"Hmmmm." Sarah studies me for a beat before shaking her head. "Try not to burn out so soon." She pushes off the desk. "We need you on the fMRI analysis later."

Annoyed, I wave her off and watch as she disappears down the hall.

She's not wrong, though. I am burning out. Not on the research—on my life.

I used to know exactly what I wanted. I came into medicine to study the brain. Originally, it was about addiction, about understanding what had turned my father into the man who nearly destroyed my family with his alcoholism and violent temper.

When I was ten, he punched my brother Liam and knocked him unconscious. Nearly put my other brother, Padraig, in the hospital. I've never understood why my mother stayed and kept us in danger. She has her reasons, I guess. At least he's been sober for a while now and our family seems to have healed, for the most part.

Once I started pre-med, I buried myself in research to understand TBI and alcohol's effect on cognitive function. I presented my findings at the UWSOM Fall Poster Symposium, thinking I'd dedicate my life to this research if I was lucky enough to be a neurosurgical candidate.

When my nephews, Torin and Tristan, were born—holding them. Helping my brother, Connor and his wife, Ronni watch them. Something clicked.

I didn't want to study the brain. I wanted to fix it.

To save kids.

It seemed so noble. With overachieving brothers, I wanted to matter.

Now, after Miranda, I don't know if I do.

Or, if I ever will.

She's still in the hospital bed.

Every time I close my eyes, I see her hooked up to the tubes keeping her body alive even though her brain will never function again.

It kills me. I need to do something to get the fuck out of my head. I need to find a woman. Make her come. Get myself off too. It's been too long. Nearly two years.

No wonder I'm so wound up.

I manage to make it through the rest of my shift by going through the motions and letting the numbers blur into meaningless distractions, all while plotting out my next move. By the time I step out of the lab I know exactly what to do.

My foolproof way of handling my, um, needs without getting roped into something permanent.

Hospital staff.

They work the same hours, understand the stress of life and death and generally—if I'm crystal clear with my boundaries—are down for a quick, uncomplicated mutually beneficial situation with no attachments and no expectations.

I don't have time for relationships. Dating. Feelings.

There's a reason I've earned the nicknames I pretend I don't know about.

I've learned the art of the female orgasm.

It started during anatomy lab in medical school.

At the time, I didn't have much—any—sexual experience outside of hearing about my brothers' endless conquests. I was too quiet and focused on my professional goals and the notion of fucking random women without any emotional connection turned me off.

Until one day when I overheard two of my female classmates while we were reviewing the clitoral structure. They joked about the men in our class and it stuck with me.

Tara Milan muttered, *"You know half these guys are going to ace this exam and still treat the clit like it's a rumor."* Priya Desai snorted. *"Doesn't matter how many diagrams they memorize. None of them care if a woman actually comes."*

It was a holy shit moment. I decided then and there, if I was going to learn about the female anatomy, I wasn't going to treat it like trivia. I read everything I could get my hands on—nerve maps, clinical studies, arousal theory.

I wanted to understand it fully. Not just the parts, but the whole system.

Not long after, Priya caught me in the library. I was sitting in a remote area at a table piled high with my "research." Once I explained myself, she convinced me to practice on her. Then told Tara about it and we started our own practice sessions.

So, my first real sexual experiences were in the library stairwells, learning exactly how to implement my book knowledge into action. Getting blowjobs in return.

Of course, word got out and things snowballed from there. I could barely get through the day without being propositioned.

By R2, the library stairwells became the hospital stairwells and it all became too much. Things were uncomplicated when orgasms were essentially transactional. Now, women seemed to be in competition for my attention, which was weird. Eventually, one woman became a little too obsessed.

It was a wakeup call. The last thing I needed was some sort of sexual harassment lawsuit when I'd put my personal life on a backburner to focus on my career.

So I stopped. Doesn't mean I still don't get propositioned, though.

Today? I'm feeling so low I don't give a shit about risk. I need to forget and feel something to dull this ache in my body.

As luck would have it, I head into the locker room and Cecily walks in. She's an ER nurse, one of many who've made it clear they're DTF. She's pretty enough—blonde hair, bright smile, curves in all the right places.

Perfect. It's been too long. My cock stirs as she approaches.

"Hey, Shay," she purrs, soft and teasing. "You look like you could use a quick break."

I glance at her briefly and return to the text I'm tapping out to my brother, Cillian and begin the game. "I prefer Seamus."

"Well, *Shay*-mus, I'm off the clock and..." She steps closer, her hand brushing against my arm as she raises her eyebrows suggestively. "I need something to *relax* me if I'm going to get to sleep tonight...what about you? Is the Orgasm Whisperer back in business for me tonight?"

Yeah. Didn't take any effort whatsoever. "What do you have in mind?"

Cecily's hand slides down my arm until her fingers intertwining with mine. "Come on," she whispers. "I'll suck you off and you make me come. I know the drill. We don't fuck. There are no strings."

I hesitate, now having second thoughts when she puts it so bluntly. I shouldn't do this. I *know* it. Despite my lapse of judgement a few minutes ago, I'm not particularly proud of my behavior. It's a little—juvenile.

On the other hand, fuck it. I'm tired. Lonely. Is it so wrong to want to feel something other than the weight of my responsibilities?

I let her lead me down the hall to the stairwell.

The dim, echoing cavern of concrete and flickering fluorescent lights is a place where many of my bad decisions have been made. Cecily presses me against the wall, her hands furiously tugging at the waistband of my scrubs. I let my head fall back against the wall and close my eyes when Cecily's mouth engulfs my cock.

She's enthusiastic, I'll give her props. The sensation is immediate, electric, and I can't help the low groan escaping my lips. Her tongue swirls around my crown, teasing and deliberate. My body responds, hips jerking slightly as she takes me deeper.

Cecily's hands move to my hips, holding me in place. Her mouth continues to work me with such skill I should be losing my mind.

Instead it starts to wander.

I can't stop thinking about Miranda. Or the way my mentor, Bryce Caldwell, seems to be completely unbothered by his fuck-up.

"Mmmmm," Cecily hums around my cock, snapping me back to the present. The vibration sends a shiver up my spine. Her hands are planted on my hips. Nails dig into my skin.

Shit. I should be enjoying this.

I'm not into it. At this point, my dick's reaction is pure biology.

She pulls back slightly, her tongue flicking against my balls. My breath hitches. I'm close. I want to get this over with. Her hands move to my ass, pulling me closer, and I push back into her mouth because it'll get me there faster.

Getting off is easier than admitting this isn't what I want.

I feel the pressure building. Tension coils in my gut. Even as my body responds and I shoot my load down her throat, I'm teetering on the edge of sanity.

I can't shake the guilt of giving in to temptation. Or the emptiness flooding my system.

This isn't who I am. Or, at least, it's not who I want to be.

Ah, hell.

What's done is done. I'm not going to leave her high and dry. I'd never dream of taking without giving.

Without warning, I pull her up and spin her around, pressing her against the wall. Cecily's breath hitches. She looks at me over her shoulder, her eyes wide with surprise as my body pins hers in place.

From this point forward, it isn't about me. It's about her. I know exactly how to make her forget everything for a moment.

My hands move with practiced precision, tracing the curve of her hip before sliding between her legs. She's trembling already, her body responding to my touch. I start slow, my fingers teasing her through the fabric of her scrubs, and she moans softly, her head falling back against my chest.

"Seamus." Her voice quivers with need.

I don't say a word. Instead, I slide my hand down the front of her scrubs, finding her soaking and ready. I know exactly how much pressure to use, how to circle my thumb on her clit and when to slow down to tease her. Cecily's breath hitches as her body arches against mine. She spreads her legs slightly and thrusts against my fingers.

I slide a finger inside her, my thumb still circling her swollen little nub and she gasps, her palms are clenched in fists against the wall. I locate the sensitive area on her inner walls and I press against it with constant, deliberate strokes until she's writhing uncontrollably.

Her cries grow louder, more desperate, and I know she's close.

"Oh God," she keens, grinding against my hand. "Don't you dare stop."

I keep the pressure steady, my thumb circling furiously as my fingers work inside her. I can feel everything. Her body stiffening, inner muscles clenching around my fingers.

Good. She's about to fall apart and I can get outta here.

When she comes, her hips jerk against my hand and her moans echo in the stairwell. This is where the magic happens. The reason why hospital women seek me out. Using my learned techniques, I'm able to draw out orgasms over and over until she's barely able to stand up.

My signature.

By the time I finally relent, she's breathless and disheveled. My scrubs are still around my ankles when she collapses back against me, her breath coming in short, eager gasps. "You're...amazing," she pants. "How do you it?"

I don't answer. Instead, I pull my hand away, fingers slick with her arousal, yank up my pants over my softening cock and tie the drawstring. Cecily turns to face me. Her face is flushed and I can see the flicker of hope in her eyes.

The hope *this* might mean something.

Hope she might mean something to *me*.

It doesn't.

She doesn't.

So I mutter out some shit about needing to get back to work and leave her there.

Forget all about Cecily the second the door shuts behind me.

Three

MARCELLA

Three Weeks Later

LUTHER YOUNG'S SMUG FACE flashes onto my screen—slick hair, steel eyes, the grin of a man who thinks he's already won.

I hope he chokes on it.

God, the mere sight of him makes my teeth grind.

"I see you wasted no time serving Dr. Caldwell." He leans back in his chair like this is a casual chat between colleagues instead of a battle line being drawn.

I match his energy, tilting my head slightly. "It's a strong case."

"Not as strong as you think." Luther exhales through his nose. "Neurosurgery is high-risk. Poor outcomes don't always equal malpractice."

"I'm aware. I also know the difference between an unavoidable complication and a preventable mistake. After reviewing the file, I'm confident Dr. Caldwell's decisions will show deviation from the standard of care." My eyes bore into his for emphasis.

He's unbothered, which pisses me off. "You're jumping the gun, Delgado. You won't have a single expert opinion back your claim. You're filing first and looking for proof later."

"You're dead wrong. The proof is in Miranda's medical records." My lips curl into a smug grin. "I also have an independent review from an outside neurosurgeon who already sees red flags. I have a devastated family who was assured by your client this was the best course of action. Let's set up Caldwell's deposition and figure out a fair settlement."

Luther taps his pen against his desk, unimpressed. "Well, it's going to be awhile before my client's available. He's one of the most coveted neurosurgeons in the region and has an intensive schedule. You know how disruptive litigation is to a physician of his caliber who's in the business of saving lives. The earliest he can do it is three months from now."

"Three months is unacceptable." I don't even blink.

He disgustingly sucks some remnant of food through his teeth. "It's not up to you."

"No. It'll be up to the judge when I file a motion to compel. When I argue you're deliberately obstructing discovery." I purse my lips.

Luther narrows his beady eyes.

"Dragging this out won't change the facts," I continue, my voice cool as ice cream. "It won't change the fact a twelve-year-old girl went into the operating room expecting to get better and instead will never wake up. It won't change the fact her parents are clinging to the hope she'll somehow recover. It won't change the fact I'm coming for Dr. Caldwell with everything I have to make sure Miranda has justice."

"Mediation may be *required*," he reminds me as if I don't know. "Why don't you spare me the theatrics and cut the bullshit. Give me a number and I'll take it to my client."

"I *never* settle before mediation." I wave my hand dismissively.

Luther sighs. "Then I guess we're going toe to toe."

"Guess so." I give him a tight smile before clicking out of the meeting.

I sit in silence for a moment, fingers tapping against my desk, staring at the blank screen where Luther's smug expression had been seconds ago. He thinks he's won the first round. I know how he operates—stalling and obstructing and dragging cases out, hoping his adversary will lose momentum.

He is forgetting something critical.

I *don't* lose momentum.

Leaning back in my chair, I exhale slowly. The fight doesn't usually bother me—this is what I live for. What I've built my career on. The strategy. The battle. The win.

I've gone up against some of the most powerful attorneys in Seattle, and I've beaten them. I'll beat Luther too.

I glance at the clock. It's later than I thought, and my stomach twists—not in hunger. More like a familiar gnawing sensation I've grown used to following aggressive conversations. Still, given my schedule, I need to get something to eat now before my afternoon full of meetings.

By the time I step into the Finney Cooper cafeteria, the lunch rush has passed, leaving a steady hum of conversation and the rhythmic clatter of utensils. I pick up my usual grilled chicken salad and chamomile tea, an order so ingrained I don't even have to think about it.

It's the safe choice—healthy and something no one will give me a side-eye for eating. Despite my regular workouts and dedication to a constant calorie deficit, I've gained two pounds this month, and I feel it, in the way my sweater rides up over my stomach. How the sleeves of my blouse feel tighter on my upper arms.

It's depressing.

With lunch in hand, I take a seat near the window alone and attempt to shake off my gloomy mood by reading on my iPad. Halfway through pushing my food around my plate, a familiar voice pulls me from my thoughts.

"Mind if I join you?"

I glance up, startled, to find the founder of the firm, my law partner, Joe Finney, hovering over me with a fresh coffee in hand.

Immediately, I slam my iPad shut and gesture to the chair across from me. "Of course."

"I had to conflict out of a potential client this morning," Joe says as he sits.

My eyebrows furrow, confused. *"Okay?"*

"A young neurosurgical resident, Seamus McGloughlin." His gaze narrows indecipherably.

I blink. I wasn't expecting to hear his name. *"What?"*

Joe watches my reaction, carefully. "He was referred by his brother and is looking for representation for any potential exposure he might have on a malpractice case. It didn't take long to realize it's the same lawsuit you filed against his mentor."

"Why is he preventatively worried about liability?" My hackles are up. This is strange. Did he do something in the operating room that contributed to Miranda's condition?

Joe tilts his head slightly. "Considering his background and some of the legal shit his family's been through, he's not stupid. He knows how this works."

"I don't understand." I exhale, shaking my head. "Sure, I might bring him into the suit if I learn something relevant during discovery. As far as I can tell, Caldwell is the one who made the surgical decisions and anything McGloughlin did would fail under vicarious liability. The fact he called, however, makes me think I should reconsider."

Joe hums, sipping his coffee. "Have you looked into him yet?"

"I have." I don't say how I really feel for obvious reasons.

Seamus McGloughlin isn't merely good-looking. He makes you imagine his hands all over your body before you can stop yourself. His eyes...

God, his eyes.

Deep, blue, kind in an unsettling way. I've known men like him—they look trustworthy and make you believe you have a future. Then you learn the hard way—you don't.

Good thing he's off limits. Too young. Eight years younger than me.

Eight years. Jesus. Back then, I was clawing my way up in this firm, desperate to make partner. Seamus has his whole future ahead of him. He's a baby. The way my body reacts when I think of him feels...inappropriate. For so many reasons.

"Marcella?" Joe leans back as I cycle through my thoughts. "You need to be aware of something else. Seamus isn't some doctor caught in the crossfire of your case. His family has deep ties to some of our most high-profile clients."

Shit.

I frown. "How deep?"

Joe's mouth twitches like he was waiting for this specific question. "His brother, Connor, is the bass player for Less Than Zero."

My neck stiffens. I knew his last name sounded familiar.

Joe continues, "Connor is married to the actress, Ronni Miller. She's one of our biggest estate clients. Then there's Tyson Rainier—also in Less Than Zero. His wife, Zoey, used to work here. She now runs The Rainier Foundation, also our client."

I exhale slowly, my pulse picks up. Am I going to get conflicted out of a potential goldmine of a case?

"There's something else you may not know," Joe arches a brow, "a year or so ago, Seamus is the reason Alex Deveraux survived an emergency surgery. Jace Deveraux is Less Than Zero's drummer."

I do remember hearing something about it, of course I had no idea Seamus was involved.

Joe watches as I absorb the information. "You see the conundrum here?"

I nod slowly, my thoughts spinning.

"You're a win-at-all-costs kind of lawyer. It has made you extraordinarily successful and I'm proud to call you my partner. The thing is, it seems there's more at play here. Collectively, these clients bring in a ton of revenue for the firm. More importantly, these people trust us with their reputations. I'm not telling you how to run the case, I'm asking you to be smart."

"I will." I roll my shoulders back as he stands. "Thank you for all of the insight."

As I watch him leave, I feel annoyed. Angry, maybe. I can't help but wonder, would Joe instigate the same conversation with a male partner under similar circumstances?

Do I *really* need to tread carefully?

The problem is—I don't know how. My career is my entire life. Winning is my only priority. I've clawed my way to the top, sacrificing everything to get here. I want to take Bryce Caldwell down for what he did to Miranda.

I sit in this too-big cafeteria as my tea grows cold. Seamus McGloughlin permeates my thoughts. He's young, talented and has a bright future in front of him. If he had a part in Miranda's demise, though...

This situation blows.

Whenever a case is this tough, a part of me wonders if I chose the right career path.

I've sacrificed too much to question any of it now.

The girl I used to be would barely recognize this version of me.

I don't know if it makes me a fighter...

Or a coward.

Four

SEAMUS

A Few Days Later

THE NOISE SHOULD FEEL like home.

Voices layered over one another. Traditional Irish music in the background. The smell of Ma's cooking in the air.

I sit at the edge of it—watching, not quite inside it, but steadied by it anyway.

These people know me. They always have.

Even when I don't know myself.

Growing up with my brothers was pure ruckus—fights left bruises. Never bad blood. Sports always ended with someone injured. I've endured slagging so ruthless it could break a lesser man. As the youngest, I didn't have the luxury of keeping up—I had to survive.

There are so many things about my childhood I miss.

A lot I'm glad is behind me.

Now, the little kids tearing through this house are my wee nephews and luckily, they have amazing parents who won't put them through some of the hell we experienced.

I'll admit, I love the sound of little feet pounding against the hardwood floors. The hum of overlapping conversation. The clatter of dishes as Ma moves around the kitchen like a general directing Ronni, who's trying to help.

Despite my ongoing sorrow about Miranda, the comfort wraps around me like an old, familiar jacket.

Right now, I'm half bent over in the living room while Torin and Tristan use me as their personal climbing apparatus. My oldest brother, Connor, lounges in the recliner, watching with amusement as I brace myself under the weight of the boys.

"Uncle Seamus is a mountain!" Tristan giggles as he latches on to my shoulder.

"A mountain?" I grumble dramatically as I shift them higher onto my back. "I thought I was a very serious doctor."

"You don't *look* serious." Torin grabs two fistfuls of my hair.

Connor smirks. "Because he lets the two of youse climb him like a jungle gym."

I huff, straightening and holding both boys under their arms before swinging them through the air. They squeal in delight before I plop them down onto the couch next to my brother.

Connor gives them a mock-serious look. "Alright, lads, wash up before dinner."

"We don't know how." Torin furrows his tiny brow.

Connor snorts, shaking his head. "Aye, right. You've only been alive four years and haven't figured out the art of washing your own hands."

Ronni appears in the doorway holding Teagan against her chest. "Nice try, boys." She lifts her chin toward me. "Seamus, will you help them? I need Connor to grab the diaper bag out of the car."

I groan in feigned annoyance, scooping up the twins and carrying them to the bathroom like a pair of wriggling sacks of potatoes while they giggle and shriek. They're barely any help at the sink, sending water splashing everywhere. I make sure they're at least somewhat clean before herding them back into the dining room, where Ma is setting the last of the dishes on the table.

The smell alone makes my stomach growl—roast lamb, the crispy edges glistening, mashed potatoes rich with butter and cream, roasted carrots and parsnips and a heaping plate of golden, flaky soda farls and fresh brown bread.

After a week of living out of a vending machine or drive-thru window, Sunday is when I can count on a filling, nutritious meal.

We take our usual seats. The moment I get settled, my gaze drifts to the empty chair where Cillian should be sitting.

He hasn't joined us for weeks—no, months.

Ma doesn't say anything at first. I see the way she sucks her lips over her teeth as she ladles food onto Da's plate. The way she keeps glancing at the door like maybe he'll walk through it.

Usually, we sweep this shit under the rug so I'm surprised when she speaks. "Cillian didn't even text me back this time."

Connor exhales, shifting a sleeping Teagan against his shoulder so he can eat. "Anyone talked to him?"

I don't answer immediately, cutting into my lamb instead. I feel my brother's eyes on me. He *knows*.

Finally, I decide to answer. "Brennan and I tried to talk some sense into him a few months ago."

Da, who's been quiet, looks up at me. His blue eyes—our blue eyes—narrow slightly.

"And?" Connor's fork is poised in mid-air.

I hesitate, then sigh. "He kicked us out."

"What?" Ronni's head snaps up.

"We wanted to check on him." I wince at the memory of what we found. "He stood us up for dinner and we were worried. For good reason. He could barely form a sentence and there was an empty whisky bottle on the counter. We tried to reason with him. He didn't want to hear it."

Ma exhales slowly and takes a drink of water. Looks off into the distance.

"Sounds familiar." Da sets his fork down and shakes his head.

His words settle like a weight over the table. Because we've all seen this before.

Lived this before.

I glance at Da, expecting him to tense up, to shut down and clam up like normal.

Instead, he looks...defeated. "This is my fault."

Ma immediately shakes her head. "Rory, ach, no—"

Which pisses me off. She's always letting him off the hook. If the man wants to take accountability, he should. He spent years putting the family through hell and while he's been sober for a long time now, it's rare to hear him apologize.

"Look. I failed Cillian." He looks at each of us in turn. "I failed all of you. He's got my genes..."

A lump forms in my throat. I love my brother. I can't bear to see him throw his life away.

"Da, you've come a long way—" Connor reaches for Ronni's hand. "We've forgiven you, so we have."

Of all of us, Connor sacrificed the most. Nearly giving up every one of his dreams to run the family business and make sure all of us made it through school. If Cillian hadn't wanted to take over McGloughlin Construction, Connor may have never pursued his dreams of becoming a rock star.

"You shouldn't." Da's voice cracks slightly. He drags a hand down his face. "I let the drink take me. I let it make me a man I never wanted to be. I see Cillian now, and I know what his road looks like. I know where it leads." He glances at Ma, regret carved into every line of his face. "I keep wonderin' if I was a better man back then, would he be strugglin' like this now?"

No one speaks for a long moment.

Then, Ma reaches out and takes his hand. "You came back to us. You changed. If you can do it, so can he."

Da nods, pain etched in his eyes.

"I should've followed up with him." I swallow thickly.

Connor shakes his head. "Your focus should be on your residency. I'll check on him."

"No." Da slaps the table. "You have a wee baby and two beautiful boys to love. Cillian needs me and I intend to get him back on the right track if it's the last thing I do."

The conversation shifts and Ma fills us in on Brennan's big deal for his company, CognifyAI down in Silicon Valley. Ronni excitedly gets us up to speed on her latest project. Connor gushes about Liam and Padraig's tour and lets us know the dates for LTZ's upcoming Seattle shows.

I listen, nodding along, though my mind keeps drifting back to Miranda.

Connor hands Teagan to Ronni when Ma goes into the kitchen to fuss over dessert. He leans toward me. "So, Joe Finney can't represent you?"

Instantaneously, the magic of tonight dissipates. I drag a hand through my hair. "No."

"Because?" He frowns.

I press my lips together. "He claims there's a conflict. Which means they're representing Miranda Black's family."

"Christ, Seamus," Connor swears under his breath, setting his glass down a little too hard.

"Yeah." I stretch my neck and roll my shoulders back. "I'm trying not to freak out."

Connor watches me closely.

"I mean, Bryce hasn't said anything about a lawsuit." I clasp and unclasp my fingers. "Not one word. If Finney Cooper won't take me on because of a conflict—" I swallow, the realization thick in my throat. "He's fucked. It's only a matter of time."

I don't have to tell my brother what malpractice means.

I'm barely hanging on by a thread about what happened—about Miranda, about her family, about the fact no matter how many times I replay the surgery in my head, I can't change the outcome. Now, on top of everything else, I have to wonder if my career is about to be blown apart before it even properly begins.

Connor rubs his beard. "Alright. First thing you do is find another lawyer. Someone good. I'll help."

I nod with a distance, my mind is already running through worst-case scenarios.

"Are you good, then?" he prompts.

I don't answer.

Because I don't know.

By the time I step outside an hour later, cool night air washes over me. I stare up at the dark sky, letting the sounds of my family still echo in my mind.

Cillian's falling apart. Brennan's burning out. Da hasn't forgiven himself in decades.

As for me? I'm not sure who I am without my white coat.

If I fail here—if I'm not who I thought—I lose more than a title.

I lose the only future I've ever let myself dream of.

Five

MARCELLA

One Month Later

There's a certain stillness before battle.

My office hums with it—pages turning, keyboards tapping, tension sharp enough to slice through glass.

We're preparing to depose Dr. Bryce Caldwell.

He's not a typical opponent.

I've deposed some of the best. He's different.

Dr. Caldwell isn't another neurosurgeon. He's *the* neurosurgeon. A man whose techniques have reshaped the field. Whose innovations have set the standard for modern brain surgery. The director of neurosurgery at University of Washington Medical Center. A pioneer. Researcher. Respected educator...and a living legend in his field.

The exact type of defendant juries love.

Someone who doesn't make mistakes.

Yet, he did.

And, here we are.

I flip through a stack of papers, skimming the highlights of his career—a staggering list of achievements, groundbreaking innovations, and accolades which, taken as a whole, make him practically untouchable.

"He's been continuously funded by the NIH since the nineties," I murmur, more to myself than anyone in the room.

"His research has changed how neurosurgeons approach tumor removal," adds Ethan Reyes, one of the associates, his eyes brimming with reluctant admiration. "Caldwell essentially pioneered intraoperative imaging guidance *and* developed new drug delivery systems for targeted chemotherapy. The man is a genius."

I don't argue.

I know he's a genius.

I also know none of it matters. He failed Miranda Black.

"Genius or not," I set my stack of documents down, "he deviated from the standard of care. He took an unnecessary risk and he's still liable for what happened to Miranda."

The slight hesitation in Ethan's posture tells me he's conflicted. Skeptical about how we're going to have to sell this to a jury. A man like Caldwell commands instant respect. Convincing twelve people a world-renowned surgeon made a catastrophic mistake won't be easy.

That's where I come in.

I'm going to teach these young lawyers how to win.

Ethan and Natalie Cho, the other associate, are whip smart and ambitious—the same way I was at their age. I catch Natalie chewing on the end of her pen. Fidgeting. Worried.

"Let's focus on strategy." I flip to the next section of my notes. "I want to start with his career—set the stage. Walk him through his credentials, his accomplishments. Establish how important he thinks he is."

Ethan smirks. "You want to inflate his ego before you take a scalpel to it."

"Something along those lines." I peer at him over my reading glasses.

At the other end of the table, Natalie scrolls through a document, then suddenly stops. "Wait. I think I found something. In multiple interviews, Caldwell describes himself as a visionary in neurosurgery." She looks up. "That has to mean something, right?"

Ethan leans back in his chair, tapping his pen against the table. "A visionary?" He exhales sharply.

"Wow...bold." His eyes flick to mine. "What does his monster ego say about him?"

I decide to let them puzzle it out. "Think about it. What kind of person calls themselves a visionary in a field where precision and humility are everything?"

"An asshole?" Natalie's brows furrow.

I laugh. "True. How can we use this?"

"Focus on the arrogance." Ethan snaps his fingers. "He doesn't think he can fail."

"He probably hates criticism." Natalie's rolls her eyes. "Takes unnecessary risks because he believes his own bullshit."

I nod, pleased. "Exactly. A surgeon who sees himself as untouchable is more likely to push boundaries and take risks without fully considering he could be responsible for the consequences." I smack my palm on the table for emphasis. "When those risks backfire? Children like Miranda pay the price."

A slow grin spreads across Ethan's face. "So we paint him as a man who was so convinced of his own genius he ignored the warning signs?"

"We're presenting the facts as we see them," I remind him. "And, yes. You're getting it. Let's make sure Caldwell and his legal team understand they're not in the driver's seat—we are."

Natalie leans back in her chair. "So what's your plan?"

"We chip away at him. Start with the basics, work in the accolades and let him feel comfortable. Once we get into Miranda's case, I want to walk him through every decision he made in the operating room. Every step." I glance at Ethan. "When we get to the complication?"

"We make him defensive," Ethan finishes.

I nod. "It works pretty well with self-important guys."

At least I hope it will because it's not enough to know what happened. Not enough the Black family knows what happened.

Bryce Caldwell has to admit it and explain why he did it.

If and when he does, I'll be ready.

"What do we have on the rest of the surgical team? I know Seamus McGloughlin assisted; I wonder if Caldwell will try to pin it on his protégée?" I glance at the clock. It's pushing eight p.m. We need to wrap this up so I can get some sleep.

There's a beat of hesitation before Ethan clears his throat. "Right. So, uh, about him..."

I glance over, catching the silent eyeball exchange between him and Natalie and recall what Joe Finney warned me about. Did he say something to Ethan and Natalie?

"What's going on with the looks?" I gesture between them.

Natalie sighs, setting her tablet down. "Well... He's not some random resident, Marcella. He's, um, kind of a thing at the hospital."

"A thing?" I frown.

"I mean, we started pulling research on him after you flagged his name for deposition prep." Ethan smirks. "Let's say, people talk."

My brow arches. "People talk about what?"

"I might as well tell you...my college roommate is in medical school. She did a surgical rotation or something last year. I mentioned I was working on a case involving Dr. McGloughlin, and she practically swooned through the phone." Natalie waggles her eyebrows. "Apparently, he's the guy every woman at the hospital covets..."

I steel my expression because—gah.

Ethan snorts. "C'mon. Call it. His body count is through the roof."

"Excuse me?" I blink rapidly, knowing how I must seem to these young lawyers. A fat, middle-aged spinster who gets embarrassed talking about sex. They probably think I'm a virgin.

"True. Apparently, it's not only about how he looks—though, I mean..." She waves a hand to fan herself. "You've seen him."

I grit my teeth.

Yes, I've seen him. I know exactly how ridiculously handsome he is.

I've nearly burnt out the battery on my vibrator while picturing the man. Though, I'm not confessing this to anyone. Ever.

"Everyone says the same thing—he's the nicest guy you'll ever meet. Kind, funny, easygoing..." Natalie pauses dramatically. "He has a nickname." She looks at

Ethan and then me, her cheeks pinkening. "The man is actually known as '*The Orgasm Whisperer*.'"

Ethan bursts out in laughter and I can't help it when my jaw hits the floor. "What do they mean?"

"It means he's strictly a fuckboy. Doesn't date. No relationships. If the stories are to be believed, the good doctor has an encyclopedic knowledge of female anatomy." She covers her face with her hand.

I pinch the bridge of my nose because this is the last thing I expected to be discussing tonight and I need to steer the ship on course. "So you're telling me Seamus McGloughlin is a walking HR violation?"

"More like a walking, talking hospital legend." Ethan grins like the man is his hero.

Jesus.

"Well, all of this is very interesting." I exhale, rolling my shoulders back. "Except, I don't care what he's doing when he's not holding a scalpel. I care about what happened inside the OR." I glance at Ethan. "Regardless of what Caldwell does tomorrow, we should get his deposition scheduled."

Ethan nods and looks down at his laptop.

"I know it's inappropriate, Marcella, so forgive me. How do you prep to sit across from a defendant for hours knowing what his nickname is?" Natalie blushes.

I narrow my eyes. "It's called professionalism. You can giggle and gossip about this in your free time. *Not* in the workplace. You should know better."

Despite myself, I feel the shift in the air.

Caldwell is the enemy I trained for.

I know how to disarm arrogance, crush ego, win with blood on my heels.

Seamus McGloughlin?

He's not a fight.

He's a distraction who might cost me everything if I'm not careful.

Six

Two Weeks Later

THE HOSPITAL CAFETERIA SWELLS with voices, trays clattering, forks scraping, and low music bleeding through the overhead speakers.

It's always packed at this hour. Residents inhale food before rounds. Nurses in scrubs lean in, laughing. Surgeons cluster at their usual tables, locked in case talk and quiet power plays.

I hover near the entrance, scanning for Bryce.

He asked me to meet him for lunch.

Unusual.

We've always been transactional—master, student.

Silence never surprised me before. Bryce isn't the debrief type. Decades in neurosurgery trained him to cut, decide, move on.

Now he wants to talk. Obviously, considering I'm mostly in the research lab this year, I knew immediately what this was about.

It's taken him long enough.

In my years of training with him, he's never been a bedside-manner guy. Or someone who second-guesses himself. I figured after thirty years of risky procedures, he's learned to compartmentalize his emotions when things take a turn.

I'm different. There's no way for me to pretend her tiny body isn't still lying in a hospital bed while her parents wait for a miracle. I'd love to comfort them. Try to explain. With a potential lawsuit pending, though, I can't.

It sucks.

Once they've gone home for the evening, though, I find comfort sitting by Miranda's side where I apologize for not being able to save her. Ask for forgiveness.

Cry.

If I manage to complete my residency, I'm going to be different than Bryce.

Until yesterday when he asked to meet up, I'd started to wonder if he even remembered her name. I guess a lawsuit is a good reminder.

Fuck, I'm not looking forward to this. Exhaling sharply, I shift my weight to the other foot. I hope he's on time. Connor managed to find another lawyer, so I'm scheduled to go into her office in a couple hours.

A familiar voice rings out over the crowd, distracting me from my thoughts. "Well, well, well. Look who it is."

I barely have time to turn before Abby, one of the night-shift trauma nurses I worked with as an R1, materializes beside me. She looks me up and down and her full lips curve into a knowing smile.

She tilts her head, auburn waves cascading over her shoulder. "It's been a while."

"Hey, Abby." I nod, keeping my expression neutral. Polite.

Before she can say another word, another voice I know calls out, "Shay-mus, hi-yee!"

Good god. I don't even have to look.

Lani.

Petite, blonde and—if memory serves—flexible, she sidles up to my other side with a look in her eye both playful and deadly.

Fucking great. How in the world do my rockstar brothers do it? Keeping up with multiple women is exhausting.

"I've missed our little stairwell dates. I heard you might be back in action." Abby scoots in closer in to squeeze Lani out.

"Dates. *As if.*" Lani sniffs and holds her ground. "Whatcha been doing, Shay?"

This is torture. If my future weren't at stake I'd bolt the fuck outta here. The truth is, I haven't seen either of these ladies in over a year and I don't care if I ever see them again.

There's no need to make them feel bad, though. I only have myself to blame. "You know how it is. Residency. Long hours. No free time."

"Honey, men have *needs*." Abby tilts her head, her smile a little too knowing. "I'm down for a repeat."

Lani scoffs. "Sounds like someone's a little desperate. *Cringe*."

For fuck's sake.

Territorial posturing. It's wild. Did I cause this? I've always been upfront about what my boundaries were. Everyone knows the drill.

"I didn't know you two had a thing." Abby lifts a brow.

Lani crosses her arms. "We did and you're not part of it."

I resist the urge to rub my temples. Things have clearly gone pear shaped. "Alright, let's—"

"*McGloughlin*."

The voice is commanding. Direct.

I turn to see Bryce approaching, his usual confident stride carrying him across the cafeteria. His expression is unreadable at first and changes when his gaze flicks between Abby and Lani—flattening into something unmistakable.

Disapproval.

Shit.

The two nurses scatter, murmuring half-hearted goodbyes before disappearing back into the crowd.

Bryce stops in front of me, arms crossed, giving me the look. The one he's given me a dozen times before. Half-bemused, half-irritated.

"Jesus, Seamus." He shakes his head.

I sigh, already tired. "Let's eat."

Bryce turns and heads into the cafeteria. I follow, grabbing a sandwich and coffee, barely paying attention to what he chooses. We settle into a corner, away from the noise.

It's about two point five seconds before he looks me over and points a fork in my direction. "You have to cut this shit out."

"Cut what out?" I stop mid-chew.

He gestures vaguely toward where I was standing with the nurses. "The...*sideshow*."

"I wasn't flirting." I huff a quiet laugh.

"No. You probably fucked both of them in the stairwell," Bryce scoffs. "Come on, McGloughlin. Everyone knows what's going on."

I take a slow sip of my coffee without answering. His words take me by surprise, though. Is it true? Are my secret extracurricular activities not so secret?

"You've always been the charming one. The golden boy." He leans forward slightly. "Charismatic shit only works for a while, son. I must tell you, I'm concerned. You're gonna fuck up your career before it begins. Please decide what kind of surgeon you want to be." He shakes his head. "No one's going to take you seriously with the way you're carrying on."

Carried on. I swallow the irritation rising in my chest. Aside from Cecily, it's been nearly two years.

There's something heavier in his voice. Foreboding. Like my casual flings are a personal annoyance to him.

I lean back. "Are we here to discuss my personal life?"

"No. We're here because I got served." A vein pops out on Bryce's forehead..

I stare at him for a beat. "Miranda? Should I be worried?"

"You ask if *you* should be worried when I was sued for malpractice a couple weeks ago? Fuck me, McGloughlin. *Probably*. Her parents moved fast. Hired a woman named Marcella Delgado from Finney Cooper, the biggest firm in town." He spits her name out like it's a curse. "She's ruthless and plays dirty. Apparently, has never lost a case. My lawyer warned me I'm going to get dragged through the mud."

"Shit. What can I do to help?" My mind races. Do I tell him I already know about the lawsuit? Would it piss him off to know I'm already preparing for the worst?

He exhales, rubbing his temple. "Look. I tried to keep you out of it. Unfortunately, I'm not sure she'll leave you alone. The goddamn woman is determined to make my life a living nightmare, and anyone else who was in the OR with me."

"How?" Hell. This is worse than I thought.

Something in his voice changes. Something I don't like.

"Well, like I said. I was trying to keep you out of it. Yesterday, I was deposed. She was a fucking bitch," Bryce seethes. "Fat. Smug. Nasty piece of work. Thinks she can outsmart me? *Please*."

I go still. Bryce doesn't notice—he's too caught up in his own anger.

"Chubby little pit bull," he sneers. "Trying to pin something on me she doesn't understand. You know how some women are. They get a little power to make up for the fact they can't get a man."

He lets out a low, humorless chuckle.

My stomach turns. I knew Bryce had an ego. I knew he had a temper. This is something else—my instincts at preparing for the worst were spot on.

"Do they have a case?" I press my lips together.

Bryce waves a dismissive hand. "One hundred percent bullshit. They've got nothing. I stand by every single move I made."

My mind reels. He made the decision to keep going...

His eyes darken. "So should you."

I stare at him. For the first time since I met Bryce Caldwell, I don't recognize him.

"So, have you been contacted?" He watches me closely.

I hesitate because I'm confused. Should I tell him I've hired counsel? Can I trust him?

"No." I decide to play my cards close to my vest. Because the truth is—no. I haven't been served yet. Technically, I know nothing. No subpoena. No lawsuit.

I haven't been involved in any legal capacity. "How can I help?"

"Lay low. Stay out of trouble." He stands and claps my shoulder. "Focus on your work. For God's sake, don't fuck hospital staff in the stairwell. Stop giving people ammunition to use against you because it'll look bad on me."

Selfish prick. Whatever happens next—I have to take care of myself.

I nod slowly, looking up at him. "Will do."

Bryce exhales, looking briefly relieved. "Good. We need to be on the same page here."

"I've got to go." I finish the last of my coffee, glancing at the time. My meeting is in twenty minutes, and suddenly, I feel like I need protection more than ever.

The thing is—I'm not sure I want to work with him ever again, no matter what happens. I know who he is now and I'll never be able to trust him.

I push back my chair. Bryce waits for me, something sharp in his gaze. "You sticking with me on this?"

His question hangs in the air, tainted and heavy.

"Of course," I say. The lie scrapes my throat raw.

When I turn away, it isn't guilt curdling in my gut. It's shame.

The sick truth I might sell myself out to survive.

Seven

MARCELLA

Five Weeks Later

Seamus slams me against the stairwell wall, one hand fisting my hair, the other dragging my leg around his waist.

His mouth crushes mine—biting, breathless, desperate.

I moan into it. Grind against him.

I need more. Need *everything*.

He growls low in my ear, "You want it?"

I nod, shaking. I'm wet with anticipation.

"Say it, Marcella. I need the words." He cradles my ass, pulling me against his cock.

"Yes," I breathe. "Touch me, Seamus. Please."

He groans, pushing up my skirt. His hands skim the sensitive skin of my inner thighs, stopping shy of where I ache for him.

"You're so soft," he rumbles. "Spread wider for me, baby."

I allow my legs to fall open, baring myself. His appreciative growl sends a thrill through me. He traces the damp cleft of my panties. "Ah, you're soaked. Because of me?"

"Yes," I whimper as he rubs me through the drenched fabric.

Unbutton your blouse," Seamus commands, his voice low and raspy. "I want to see those gorgeous tits."

With shaking hands, I obey, revealing my lacy, black bra beneath.

"Now take them out," he orders. "Let me see you."

Tugging the cups down, I free my heavy breasts. He fills his hands, squeezing and plumping my soft flesh. I watch him work my nipples between his fingers, pinching and rolling, until they're furled and pebble-hard.

"Look how pretty they are, baby." He licks his lips in approval. "Luscious brown berries, all tight and puckered for me."

Seamus ducks his head, sucking one into the wet heat of his mouth. I cry out, sparks shooting straight to my core as he nibbles and laves the sensitive bud. He moves back and forth, suckling and gently biting them until I'm writhing, desperate for more.

"*Ohmygod*," I keen shamelessly.

"Can I lick your pussy?" Seamus's blue eyes plead as he feathers a finger back and forth along the soaked crotch of my panties.

I suck in a breath. I'm thirty-seven years old and no one has ever asked me this question, they've taken what they've wanted from me. "Uh...yes?"

He yanks my panties aside, baring me to him. "Fucking hell, you're perfect." He dips his head, giving me a long, slow lick. "You taste like heaven," he groans, tracing his tongue around my clit. "Do you like me tasting your pussy, baby?"

I can only nod, pleasure stealing my voice. He swirls the tip of his tongue around my sensitive bud, flicking it gently. My hips begin to buck against his face.

"Yes. Fuck my face. I love how responsive you are," he purrs against me. "I'm gonna make you come so hard."

Seamus laps through my folds, alternating between spearing into my entrance with his tongue and sucking my clit. I'm pulsing and contracting as pressure builds throughout my core.

"*Mmmmm.* You're getting close, aren't you?" he growls. "I can't wait for you to come all over my face."

I'm lost to the most incredible sensations. Mindless with bliss. Seamus holds me at the edge expertly.

"Rub your clit against my tongue," he coaxes, grabbing my hips and showing me what to do. "Take what you need, beautiful."

I rock into his mouth, allowing myself to let go. Pleasure crests and crashes over me when I topple over, gushing my release against his lips. He moans in satisfaction, lapping up every drop.

Seamus rolls to my side and pulls me into his lap. His rigid erection presses against my sensitive pussy, wrenching a whimper from me at the thought of having him inside me.

"Do you feel how hard you've made me?" He thrusts up against me slowly. "I'm gonna fuck you so good. Fill you up with my come. Would you like me to?"

I bury my face in his neck, tears pricking the corners of my eyes at the intensity of the experience. He holds me close, stroking my back soothingly.

"Shh, I've got you," he murmurs. "You're doing beautifully, Marcella. I'm so proud of you."

The sharp buzz of my phone jolts me awake, ripping me out of the last traces of my dream—Seamus, the stairwell, his mouth on my skin. My body is still warm from it. My pulse thrumming too fast.

I sit up, untangling the sheets from my legs, and blink at the screen. My mother.

Exhaling, I swipe to answer. "Hey, Mom."

"You sound half-asleep," she chastises.

I glance at the clock. 6:57 a.m. "I was."

"Chellie, it's nearly seven. What are you doing in bed?" Her voice softens with concern. "Are you sick?"

I rub my face. "Sleeping. Like a normal person."

"You're working too much," she says automatically, and I swear I can hear the disapproving shake of her head. "When's the last time you took a break? Or better yet, when's the last time you came to see us?"

Guilt pricks at me. I don't need to answer. We both know it's been months. "I've been super busy."

"You know, the restaurant doesn't feel the same without you sitting at the bar on Saturday," my dad shouts from the background.

My parents own Costa del Sol, a Spanish restaurant on the Tacoma waterfront. It always smells of saffron and garlic. My dad makes every guest feel like family and my mom runs the show with unshakable authority.

My younger brother, Lucas, now manages the business side, always in a pressed button-down, juggling spreadsheets and supplier calls. Our youngest sister, Rosa, runs the kitchen—commands it, really—turning out the best food in the city, if not the whole damn state. I should know, I've got the hips, thighs, and ass to show for it.

I used to be here every weekend until I let my career swallow me whole.

Mom continues, her voice gentler now. "Rosa says if you don't come soon, she's taking paella off the menu to spite you."

"She wouldn't dare." I suck in a breath.

"Oh, she would," Mom insists. "You know how she can be."

Ugh. Mom is probably right.

I lean back against the headboard, closing my eyes. "I'll try to make it soon. I need to get through this trial."

Mom exhales because she doesn't believe me. She's heard it before. There are always other cases.

"Please don't work yourself into the ground, Chellie," she says softly. "Your job might be important, *mija*. Living a balanced life matters more."

I swallow past the lump in my throat. "I love you, Mama."

When I end the call and sit there in my barren apartment, staring at the open laptop on my nightstand, I wonder—what the hell is my end game?

Whoa!

I'm alone. My pussy is threatening to dry up.

My love life has come down to dreaming of a potential defendant—albeit the best-looking man I've never met—going down on me in the stairwell?

For the fourth time in a week?

Yet the dream lingers, curling heat in my stomach. My body is still thrumming with an actual orgasm I had in my sleep. Maybe the most powerful of my life.

My mind screams *nooooooo*.

Jesus Christ.

It's getting ridiculous. I can't go on like this.

Breathe in. Breathe out.

It was a dream. Just a dream.

My body doesn't seem to know it, though. My skin is too tight and my thighs squeeze together before I can stop myself. My panties are soaked.

It's time to get up. I swing my legs over the side of the bed and stare at the floor, grounding myself.

Tomorrow, I'm going to sit across from the man I've been fantasizing about and I cannot—will not—let this nonsense affect me.

I force myself to shower, drink coffee, and shove the dream into the deepest, darkest part of my brain where it belongs.

Then I go to work.

Ethan and Natalie are already in the conference room when I arrive, hunched over Bryce Caldwell's deposition transcript. The table is covered in legal pads, highlighted passages, and evidence binders.

I set my bag down, rolling up my sleeves. "Tell me we have something useful."

"Not useful. Definitely interesting." Ethan pushes a page toward me.

I scan the text, recalling this part of the deposition. Caldwell didn't distance himself from what happened in the OR—he tried to erase himself from it.

"He's framing it like he had no control," Natalie mutters. "Acknowledges McGloughlin's warning. Claims it was distracting. He ignored it, though."

I shake my head, tossing the transcript onto the table. "Utter bullshit."

"Big time." Ethan tosses his pen to the table.

"Look. Caldwell was in control. He was lead. The responsibility was his." I flip through the notes, scanning the details of Caldwell's history. Two prior malpractice suits in the past fifteen years. Two dismissals. Settled before trial, buried before they could make a dent in his reputation. I lean back in my chair. "Did he have a resident assisting in either of these cases?"

Natalie's fingers fly over her keyboard as she pulls up the old filings. "Looks like—yes. In both, the resident was named but not personally sued." She glances up. "Caldwell shifted the focus to them, argued their actions played a role in the poor outcomes."

My lips press into a firm line.

"So this isn't new for him," Ethan mutters.

"No." I glance at Natalie's tablet. "It's his pattern."

She leans back. "So, where does it leave us with McGloughlin?"

"It's not about him. Not really. We don't represent Seamus. He has his own lawyer and his career is his problem, not ours." I pick at a chip in the table when I realize I inadvertently called the man by his first name. "We only need one thing from him—the truth."

Because if we can prove Caldwell saw the blood vessel, he knew the risk and proceeded anyway, then he'll settle. Big. Money.

"Remember. Tomorrow's deposition isn't necessarily about pinning anything on McGloughlin," I remind them. "It's about figuring out what he knew. Did he see the rupture coming? Did he try to stop it? Did Caldwell ignore him?"

Ethan nods slowly. "What if he backs up Caldwell's version?"

I sip my coffee. "Then we go after him too."

"I doubt he'll be manipulated blindly." Natalie flips through the medical records. "The surgical notes don't lie. From all accounts, he's not some reckless intern—he's a fourth-year resident with a golden reputation in the OR."

I glance at the two of them. "Reach out to the residents from Caldwell's previous cases. See if they're willing to talk."

Ethan nods. "Good idea. If McGloughlin isn't forthcoming tomorrow, knowing he's not the first might shake something loose."

"Exactly." I stack up the papers. "If Caldwell has done this before, McGloughlin deserves to know he's not special—he's the latest in a long line of scapegoats."

Natalie frowns. "What if he didn't know what was happening was wrong?"

"A demonstratable failure in Caldwell's leadership. The hospital still pays." I stand and move toward the door. "Anything else? We can reconvene later."

Natalie and Ethan shake their heads.

"Tomorrow, we should know the easiest path to get the Blacks their settlement."

I need to remember why I'm doing this.

Forget my sex dream.

Justice doesn't care about attraction.

It demands precision, not distraction.

Tomorrow, I'll look him in the eye and do what needs to be done.

Count on it.

Eight

SEAMUS

The Same Day

SARAH MAHONEY DOESN'T SMILE. Doesn't blink.

She asked for coffee, but I don't think she tastes it.

She has no time for charm. No space for mistakes.

The woman's a shark. Exactly what I need. Even if I hate needing it.

I knew it in the first five minutes of our initial meeting and I believe it even more now, sitting across from her in a sleek downtown office, my fingers wrapped around my own cup of coffee I haven't touched.

She's direct, sharp-eyed, and doesn't waste time with pleasantries. Which is good, because I don't have time for them either.

Sarah leans forward, her eyes sharp. "Walk me through it. From the moment you entered the OR to the second it went wrong."

I exhale, running a hand through my hair, which is way too long. "We were removing Miranda's tumors with the laser. Caldwell was leading, I was assisting, everything was going to plan—until I saw the blood vessel."

"And?" She motions with her finger to keep going.

I press my palms against my knees. "I hesitated. Something felt off. I tried to slow down, to warn him." My throat constricts. "He kept going."

"Did you explicitly tell him to stop?" Sarah nods, her voice even.

"I said, 'Dr. Caldwell—'" I hesitate, trying to remember exactly what happened. "He said, 'I see it. Keep going.'"

She shakes her head in disgust. "You're sure?"

"Positive." I nod.

Sarah slams her laptop shut. "That moment is everything, Seamus. Caldwell overrode you. He dismissed a clear concern. This isn't your mistake."

I rub my eyes with my fists, the memory playing over again. The flicker of doubt. The push forward. The catastrophe. Does it really matter whose fault it is? Miranda's the one who's paying the price.

Sarah watches me. "When Marcella Delgado asks you about it tomorrow, don't hedge. Don't guess. Just tell the truth exactly like you told me."

I let out a slow breath, meeting her gaze.

There's one problem. The truth might not save me.

Not if it buries Caldwell, my mentor. The man who controls my future in neurosurgery.

"What's wrong?" Sarah's gaze is unyielding. "You're hesitating."

I grip the arms of my chair, my pulse hammering. "It's not so simple."

"It *is* simple." She's deceptively calm. "*Seamus*. You saw the warning signs. You hesitated for a reason. Caldwell ignored you."

I look out the window. All of this is moving so fast.

She exhales. "What if I told you you're not the first?"

The revelation causes me to snap my gaze back to her.

"Caldwell has done this before. Twice. Two other residents." She shoves a couple of files toward me. "Two other cases. Same story. They trusted him and stayed quiet. Then paid the price. Their careers suffered. Their patients suffered."

My stomach twists.

Sarah clamps a hand on my wrist. "If you don't speak up now, Seamus, you're not protecting Caldwell. You're letting this happen again."

Staring down at the files, I know she's right. The question is—am I ready to break the pattern?

"Both settled out of court. No trial, no testimony. The matters were quietly wrapped up once Caldwell made it very clear the complications weren't on him." She lets go of my wrist and waits.

I bury my face in my hands. This is too much. "Do you think he's doing the same to me?"

"I don't think, Seamus. I know." She flips through the files. "I talked to both of them. You need to read these."

I hesitate, then pick up the first file.

Case One: Dr. Matthew Lee, Third-Year Neurosurgery Resident.

Fifteen years ago, Lee assisted Caldwell in a high-risk spinal tumor resection. From what Sarah dug up, he had the same kind of mentorship with Caldwell I do—*did*. He looked up to him. Trusted him implicitly.

Until things went wrong.

I scan the details and feel nauseous. "The patient had an unexpected hemorrhage?"

"A small vessel Caldwell didn't anticipate." Sarah nods. "By the time he realized how severe the bleed was, the patient had lost too much blood. She survived—with nearly two years of recovery."

"Let me guess." I swallow. "Caldwell blamed Lee."

"Not directly." She tugs at her sleeves "He framed it in a way where it was hard to ascertain. Textbook diversion. He positioned himself as the experienced surgeon who was focused on the task at hand and Lee as the overeager resident who didn't spot the blood vessel. It was his first malpractice lawsuit."

I press my fingers to my temples. Despite his gruff disposition, Caldwell isn't merely a great surgeon—he's been such a cherished mentor. He leads neurosurgery. His reputation is for building careers, not destroying them.

Why the hell would he be so ruthless? Why would he let his own residents take the fall and stall their futures to protect himself?

The answer creeps in, cold and bitter.

Because his career matters more. He's spent decades cultivating his reputation and he's not about to let anyone—not even the people who trust him most—jeopardize it.

Sarah points to the second file. "Case two. Dr. Adrian Park."

Part of me doesn't want to read it. I already know what I'm going to find. Nevertheless, I can't bury my head in the sand.

Park assisted Caldwell on a pediatric brainstem glioma resection. Park also hesitated before a crucial step after seeing something on the imaging. Caldwell dismissed it.

"Let me guess," I murmur, "when things went sideways, it was Park's fault."

Sarah leans forward. "Caldwell went on the record stating Park's retraction placement was 'imprecise.' Inferred he was the reason the patient ended up paralyzed. The kicker?" She motions to the paperwork. "The surgical notes don't reflect any of this. Caldwell rewrote history."

The nausea morphs into the possibility of dry heaves. It's exactly what happened in the OR with Miranda. I saw the blood vessel. I knew it was too close. I hesitated.

Caldwell kept going. Probably knowing if he succeeded he'd be the hero. If he failed, it would be my fault. Either way, he'd walk away unscathed.

I force myself to meet Sarah's gaze. "Matthew and Adrian—what happened to them?"

"Matthew left neurosurgery entirely. He switched to radiology after his reputation took a hit. Adrian managed to finish residency. Gave up his fellowship. He ended up in a small private practice, nowhere near the career he was headed for." She bites her lip.

I grip the edge of the desk.

He buried them.

Now he's coming for me.

Sarah studies me. "Still think he won't throw you under the bus?"

"I—I can't believe it." I shake my head, slow and heavy.

Not Caldwell. Not the man who always pushes me to do better. *Be* better. Who said I had the hands and mental stamina of a surgeon. Who believed in me. These two examples aside, his history of ongoing mentorship to his protégées is legendary.

I blow out a breath I hadn't realized I'd been holding. "The deposition. It's me and the Black's lawyer, right?"

Sarah hesitates.

My stomach drops.

"Seamus," she says carefully. "You're not only facing Marcella Delgado tomorrow."

I feel the shift before she even finishes the sentence.

"The hospital's legal team is sending their own counsel."

I fight the urge to scream. "They think I'm a liability."

"My guess is their insurance company knows someone has to take the fall," she corrects. "Since Caldwell is the hospital's star surgeon and head of the department, guess who's the easier option?"

"Jesus." I let out a bitter laugh. "Fucking perfect."

"Listen to me. They'll try to corner you. To box you in with Caldwell's version of events and make it sound like you acted on your own." She emphasizes each point by slapping the table.

It's jarring. It snaps me to attention, though. I nod.

"Marcella wants the truth. She needs it for the biggest settlement." She tones down her delivery a bit, which I appreciate. All of this is incredibly stressful.

I run a hand down my face.

The truth.

The truth is: *I knew.* The truth is: *I tried to slow down.* The truth is: *it didn't matter.*

I was a resident, and Caldwell was Caldwell.

He's throwing me under the bus to take the hit.

Sarah leans forward, steady and fierce. "You are not going to be another Matthew Lee or Adrian Park, Seamus."

"You can't give me a definitive guarantee." I shake my head sadly.

She lifts a brow. "The hell I can't."

There's steel in her tone and in the way she looks at me. Like she's already gearing up for war.

"I know how this plays out. I know how hospitals protect their cash cows and let the rest burn. Not this time. Not you." She clasps my shoulder. "Caldwell isn't going to win."

I swallow hard and think about the sacrifices I've made for so many years. About Miranda Black, still lying in the hospital bed on life support. The entire McGloughlin clan, who are all so proud to have a doctor in the family.

"You're not alone in this," she says firmly. "No matter what happens in the deposition room tomorrow, I will fight for you."

For the first time since this nightmare started, I almost believe her.

Hospitals bury the innocent to protect the powerful.

Sarah knows it. So do I.

She says I won't burn for this.

Tomorrow will prove if she's right.

Nine

MARCELLA

The Next Day

I WAKE UP GASPING.

Flushed. Breathless. Pillow shoved tight between my thighs.

It takes a second to remember—my bed. My condo. No one's here.

Except for the ghost of him.

Seamus McGloughlin.

Again.

I press the heels of my hands into my eyes, trying to scrub the dream away.

Impossible.

It clings to me—hot, vivid, and absolutely inappropriate.

His talented hands had been everywhere. Mapping the curve of my waist. Pressing into my thighs. Tangling in my hair as his lips dragged over my pulse, down my collarbone, lower—

I whimper in frustration and throw the pillow to the floor.

What the hell is wrong with me?

This isn't some random guy. This is an adversary. A man eight years younger than me. Worse—a man whose mentor I'm actively trying to hold accountable in a multimillion-dollar malpractice suit.

Today, I'll see him in person for the first time. I'll sit across from him, stare him down, push him until I get the truth.

Why does my stomach roil at the thought of it?

I stand abruptly and head straight for the shower. Make sure the water is hotter than necessary. I tell myself I need to get my head on straight. Sex dreams about Seamus McGloughlin are my body playing tricks on me. The attraction isn't real.

Deep down, I know better.

Thirty minutes later, as I drive toward the office, my phone buzzes—*Rosa*.

I sigh and press the button on my steering wheel, connecting the call through the car's system. "Hey, I was going to call you later."

"*Mmm-hmm*," Rosa hums knowingly. "Sure you were. Too busy being a badass lawyer to call your baby sister back?"

I smirk despite myself. "Something along those lines."

She huffs. There's warmth in it, though. "I won't keep you, just wanted to check in. We all miss you, you know? Papa—he won't say anything. I can tell he's feeling it too."

"I know." My fingers tense on the steering wheel. "Work's been insane. I'll come down soon."

"You said you'd come home two months ago." There's no accusation in her voice, only quiet understanding. "I get it, Chellie. I really do. You're allowed to take a day off and let your people take care of you sometimes."

The lump in my throat is unexpected. I swallow it down. "I will. Tell them I love them, okay?"

"Maybe you should tell them yourself." Her voice softens. "We miss you. I know you miss us too."

"Yeah. I do." I blink at the road, my chest tightening. She's right.

There's a beat of silence before Rosa clears her throat. "Okay, I'll stop now before you get all weird and awkward. Love you."

"Love you too." I end the call and stare at the city skyline ahead.

I do miss my family. More than I let myself think about. Unfortunately, right now, there's no room for anything else. Not until this case is over.

By the time I step into my office, Ethan and Natalie are already seated in the leather chairs across from my desk, laptops open.

"Morning." I set my bag down and reach for the coffee I picked up on the way in.

"Big day," Ethan murmurs, flipping through a document. "You ready? Need anything?"

"Let's go through everything one last time." I perch on the edge of my desk, sipping my latte.

Natalie taps on her screen. "Caldwell's defense is clear—he's low-key throwing Seamus McGloughlin under the bus, painting him as an inexperienced, overeager resident who went beyond his role and caused the surgical error."

I nod, waiting.

"Caldwell's deposition seemed off," Ethan adds. "He wasn't as controlled as I expected him to be. He was dismissive. Arrogant. When we pushed, his answers didn't hold up."

"Which matches what we know about him," I say. "Two previous malpractice suits. Two other residents who found themselves blamed while Caldwell walked away unscathed."

Ethan nods. "Now McGloughlin is next in line."

"You think he'll go against Caldwell?" Natalie shuts her laptop.

I take a slow sip of coffee. "Not unless he has to."

"Ahhh." Ethan leans back. "Which is why we make him nervous."

I nod once. "He's a surgeon. He's prepared for medical questions, expecting us to hammer him on the procedure, on the science. If we shift gears and bring his personal life? Reputation? Then he'll have more to lose."

"You don't think he'll see it coming?" Natalie frowns.

"No." I shake my head. "His entire focus will be on justifying their actions in the OR. Not on defending himself."

Ethan closes his laptop and shoves it in his bag. "So, you'll shake him. Make him think twice about toeing the party line."

"He needs to see what Caldwell is doing to him." I stack my files and place them in my briefcase. "He needs to feel like he has something to lose if he stays quiet."

Natalie studies me carefully. "What if he doesn't crack?"

"We keep the pressure on." I lean back smugly.

Ethan grins. "This is so cool."

"We need to get to the hospital." I push off my desk and grab my coat.

The drive is mostly silent, filled only with the occasional rustle of paper and the click of Natalie's pen as she reviews notes. I keep my eyes on the road, navigating the car on autopilot. My mind is already in the deposition room. Already locking into strategy.

The possibility of Seamus McGloughlin turning from foe to ally if I play this right.

If I can keep my wits about me.

A flicker of something hot curls in my stomach. I know no matter how much I try, the second I see Seamus in person, my sex dreams are going to come rushing back. It's going to take all of my strength not to react.

I won't let it deter me, though.

To make my plan work, I'll need to ask questions to make him hate me. It will give me the best chance to make sure the Blacks are compensated for Caldwell's mistake. It also will endear me to my partners. Because the way Joe Finney championed Seamus's family and their deep ties to some of our firm's biggest clients, wasn't a directive—it was a suggestion.

Go easy on him.

Which I absolutely will *not* do. By the end of the day Sarah Mahoney will realize we'll need to combine forces and, with Seamus's help, take Caldwell all the way down.

God, I feel it—victory within reach.

We pull into the hospital parking garage and I kill the engine, glancing at my clock on the dashboard. Right on time.

Ethan lets out a low whistle. "So, this is it."

"This is it," I confirm, pushing open my door.

As we step into the hospital, the familiar scent of antiseptic and anxiety floods my senses. The halls are busy with doctors and nurses in scrubs. Patients being wheeled past. Conversations clipped and efficient.

The entire operation is a machine, its rhythm precise and controlled. It reminds me of a courtroom—everyone plays their role and the stakes are always high.

We take the elevator up to the administrative floor, the polished doors sliding open with a soft chime.

I take a deep, cleansing breath. It's time to work.

The conference room is at the end of the hall. As we approach, my pulse kicks up a notch, an unexpected rush of nerves threading through me.

I push the feeling down.

I am not nervous.

I reach for the door handle, open it, and step inside.

Then I see him.

Seamus McGloughlin.

Something inside me shifts. It's instant. A visceral jolt lands somewhere deep in my chest, spreading lower, sinking into my bones.

He's not merely attractive. He's undeniable.

Seated at the table with his hands clasped together, his wavy, light-brown hair is slightly tousled and his blue eyes are sharp and assessing. He carries himself like a man who knows exactly who he is—strong, commanding, capable. He seems completely unbothered with his shirt sleeves rolled to his elbows.

Though he's sitting, I can tell he's a big man. It seems like he takes up all the space in the room.

Good God, the charisma—he radiates something unshakable.

Fuck me, he is *young*.

Much younger than me. *Too* young for me.

Our age difference is forgotten when his eyes lock on mine with lethal precision.

Something flickers there—quick, sharp, dangerous.

Attraction. Appreciation.

Lust.

I freeze.

Suddenly, my dream doesn't feel so far from reality.

Every warning I've ever ignored lives in his eyes.

I came here to bury him.

Something tells me, I'm the one going under.

Ten

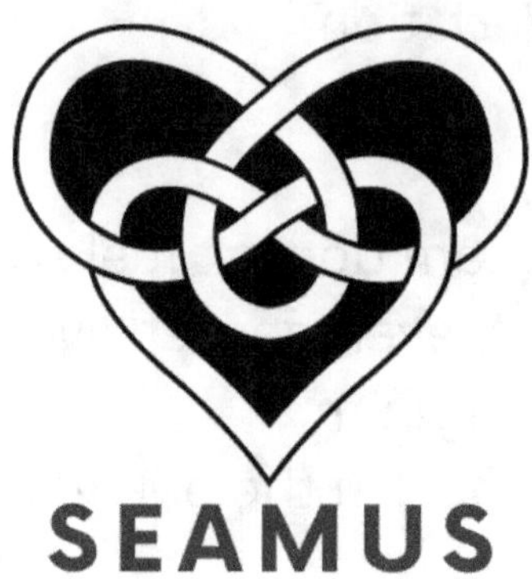

The Same Day

THIS CONFERENCE ROOM IS cold, sterile.

It reeks of over-brewed coffee and desperation.

Jesus. Of course it does.

The room is where careers end—quietly, efficiently.

Is this the end of mine?

Fuck me. If residency wasn't stressful enough, I've spent the past few months mired in a legal nightmare.

I never anticipated all my years of hard work, focus, and dedication could go down the tube in an instant.

Oh, it can. *Everything* rides on today.

I roll my shoulders back, unsuccessfully trying to shake the tension bearing down between my shoulder blades.

Marcella Delgado walks in, a picture of controlled power, with two other attorneys, probably junior. She wears an emerald-green blazer, cinched at the waist, paired with a black silk blouse skimming sinful curves. Her pencil skirt hugs her full hips, ending above the knee, and her heels—lethal, black, and at least four inches high—show off her shapely calves.

My mentor, Bryce Caldwell, lied. Told me she was a middle-aged ballbuster. A fat, ruthless bitch who would eat me alive if I let her.

The woman in front of me?

She's fucking *stunning*.

Not just beautiful. Luscious. Striking in a way I can't ignore. Her long, chestnut-brown hair is pulled into a sleek bun. Full lips are painted in some deep, red shade, making my mouth long to kiss them. She's impeccably dressed, poised, and wholly unimpressed with my existence.

With a calculated glance in my direction, I can already feel her pulling apart every molecule of my being. Dissecting me with nothing more than a sharp gaze and an air of ruthless determination.

Yet, I can't take my eyes off her, which is a huge fucking problem. The sharp pull of attraction is unexpected, so I immediately try to shove it down.

Get it together, Seamus. This woman is here to bury you alive, not join you in a fucking stairwell.

God, I'm pathetic.

Oh, I still feel it, though. Thrumming under my skin. A heat. A hunger. Instinctive. Desire, dark and inappropriate, curling low in my gut.

A reaction like I've never experienced in my life.

My dick is getting hard, for fuck's sake.

So *completely* untimely, it pisses me the fuck off.

I can't be thinking about her like this. Not when my career is hanging in the balance. Not for the one person who's bound and determined to make sure my future in neurosurgery ends before it even truly begins.

I exhale sharply, dragging my focus back to the task ahead. I'm on a razor's edge. Rattled beyond belief.

She hasn't even spoken yet.

Beside me, my attorney, Sarah Mahoney, clears her throat and leans in slightly, whispering, "Remember what we discussed. This is a deposition, Dr. McGloughlin. I can't interject or object to anything unless Ms. Delgado—" she gestures at my executioner, "asks you something blatantly illegal or improper."

I nod, barely listening, determined to pull my shit together.

"You need to answer everything and I strongly recommend keeping it brief. Stick to the facts. No embellishment, no unnecessary details. If she pauses, let her. Don't fill the silence. You're a doctor. You understand the power of controlled breathing," Sarah reminds me quietly, patting the top of my hand like a goddamn child.

Nevertheless, it's a good reminder to stay true to who I am. What I do. I know how to keep my hands steady under pressure. I'm cool as a cucumber when performing procedures requiring absolute precision.

Even if this isn't an operating room, I can rely on my usual instincts, can't I?

Sarah tilts her head slightly. "Seamus, did you hear me?"

"Yes," I answer simply, steeling my inner turmoil for the fight ahead.

She doesn't look convinced. "Good. One last thing—do not let her bait you."

"I think I can handle one lawyer." I try to sound confident, resisting the urge to let out the humorless laugh threatening to escape.

She juts her chin out. "I like your confidence—don't get cocky. You've never been in a room with Marcella Delgado."

I glance back across the table at Marcella, who's now seated in between her co-conspirators, arranging her papers into neat, methodical stacks. Clearly, she's done this a thousand times before.

Bryce's words echo in my head: *She'll eat you alive if you let her.*

Fuck me. I believe it.

I'm not going down without a fight.

When Marcella looks up from her papers, her hazel eyes—flecked with gold—lock on to mine, and for a split second, I forget how to breathe. How to think. How to do anything but fall into them.

Luckily she looks down at her notes and eases me into a false sense of security with a softball. "I'd like to begin. Could you please state your full name for the record?"

"Seamus Patrick McGloughlin." I lean back and clasp my hands on the table in front of me, hoping to convey my ease.

She doesn't even look up. "Your title?"

"Doctor. I'm nearly halfway into my fourth-year residency." I avoid Sarah's sharp glance when I ignore her instructions and say too much.

Marcella flicks her eyes to me. "You were present during Miranda Black's surgery?"

"Yes." I nod, resisting the urge to embellish.

There's a pause. Marcella scribbles something on her legal pad. When I say nothing, she strikes. "Let's talk about the day in question."

"Sure." I struggle not to clench my jaw. "I'm ready."

"*Dr*. McGloughlin," she points to her notepad with a dark-red-tipped nail, "I'd like to understand your particular role in Miranda's surgery."

I sit up straighter and work hard to keep my expression neutral. "I was assisting Dr. Caldwell."

"Okay." She nods like she expected my answer and scribbles something across the page. "What was the nature of her surgery?"

"We were removing six brain tumors using MRI-guided laser interstitial thermal therapy."

Her eyebrow lifts slightly. "Laser therapy? How are you qualified to assist in such a procedure?"

"I've been extensively trained in LITT and have assisted in over a dozen similar cases." I decide to look right at her, no matter what she asks.

She makes a note, her manicured fingers firm around the pen. Her pouty lips purse slightly as she writes. I shouldn't be noticing the way her mouth moves. Or the way her golden skin glows under the harsh lights.

Oh, I do.

I hate myself for it.

Sure, this isn't the first time I've been under pressure. It *is* the first time I've been this distracted in a life-or-death situation—mine.

I shift slightly in my chair.

Marcella leans in. "What was the risk of this procedure?"

"High," I admit, because it's true.

She arches an eyebrow. "Why?"

"The tumors were near critical structures—her brainstem and motor cortex. Inevitably, they would have spread to other parts of her brain or spinal cord, which would have tragic consequences." I sigh. "On the other hand, taking them out gave her a fighting chance, despite the risk of bleeding. Swelling. Neurological damage."

"You explained these risks to Miranda's family?" Marcella curls her lip in disgust for a millisecond before her professional composure takes back over.

"Yes," I say as evenly as possible. "Dr. Caldwell and I described these risks in great detail. Her parents understood and chose to proceed. They signed a standard waiver."

She's quiet for a moment, studying me like I'm an equation she's about to solve. Then she pounces. "During Miranda's surgery, did anything go wrong?"

I hesitate for only half a second because it was, possibly, the worst day of my career. "Yes. A blood vessel ruptured."

"What happened then?" She tilts her head.

It's an open-ended question. One designed to get me to talk. I manage to resist embellishing. "We tried to control the bleeding. The pressure in her brain spiked and we had to close the incision before all the tumors were removed."

"What was the outcome?" She stares into my soul because she knows *exactly* what happened.

I take a deep breath. "Miranda suffered severe complications including brain swelling. She's currently in a state of unresponsive wakefulness. We don't expect her to recover."

"So you failed." Marcella leans back. "Despite your so-called advanced techniques and training, the surgery cost her everything. Correct?"

I can't cover my annoyance. "As I said before. The surgery was high-risk. We did everything we could."

"It wasn't enough, was it?" She squints at me. Scrutinizing. Judging.

The words land like a blow, sharp and merciless.

My fist clenches tightly. "As I said before, the surgery was high-risk. We did everything we could."

"It wasn't enough, was it?" she repeats. Her gaze is unrelenting, picking me apart piece by piece.

I don't respond. Because there's nothing I can say.

No matter how many times I go over that day in my head—every move, every decision—I can't shake the feeling maybe there was something I could have done differently.

She's right. Despite my training, my skill, my best efforts, we failed her.

No, you failed her.

I swallow against the nausea rising in my throat.

I think about my brothers, successful in their fields—Connor, Liam, and Padraig, rockstars with Grammys to their names. Brennan, a tech mogul shaping the future of AI. Even Cillian, despite his struggles, has built something real.

Then there's me. The youngest. The perpetual student. The one who couldn't save a twelve-year-old girl.

Marcella leans forward, sensing the crack in my composure. "Dr. McGloughlin, let's talk more about your experience. As you mentioned, you were a third-year resident when you performed the operation, correct?"

"Assisted," I correct.

She continues her attack. "How many high-risk surgeries have you led?"

"As I mentioned, I've *assisted* in over a dozen." I exhale slowly, resisting the urge to raise my voice.

"*Assisted*," she repeats, letting the word hang between us. "So, you've never led one, have you?"

"No," I say evenly. "I didn't lead this one either."

Marcella stares me down. "A third-year resident is relatively inexperienced when it comes to high-risk cases, correct?"

Where the hell is she going with this?

"I've been trained by some of the best surgeons in the world." I sit up straighter. "I'm confident in my skills."

She lifts a single, perfectly arched brow. "Confidence is one thing, Dr. McGloughlin. Competence is another."

Something snaps. She can fuck right off.

"I followed protocol," I say, coldly. "I trusted Dr. Caldwell's judgment. I stand by the decisions we made."

She watches me, her expression unreadable. Then she shifts, flipping to a different page, her voice changing slightly. "Dr. McGloughlin, let's talk about your reputation with the women in the hospital."

I stiffen, shocked. A cold sweat prickles at the back of my neck when Marcella pivots—sharp, deliberate—straight into my personal life. *Fuck.* I never even *thought* to mention this to Sarah. Never imagined it would come up, and now I'm out on a limb with nothing to hold on to.

Sarah doesn't miss a beat. "Objection—irrelevant. You may answer."

Marcella barely glances at her. "Dr. McGloughlin, are you aware you have a reputation among the female hospital staff?"

"For what, exactly?" I try to appear unbothered by brushing the invisible lint from my shirt.

She lifts a brow, like she's daring me to play dumb. "For certain extracurricular activities..."

"Ms. Delgado, this has nothing to do with the case." Sarah shifts beside me, clearly irritated. Blindsided.

Marcella waves a hand. "May I remind you, this is a deposition. He must answer all my questions." She turns back to me. "Is it true, Dr. McGloughlin, you've had multiple sexual relationships with female staff members?"

"I wouldn't call them relationships." I hold her gaze, unblinking. She's not going to shame me.

Her lips twitch. "No. I suppose you wouldn't."

"I have never let my personal life interfere with my work." I shift in my seat, the heat in my chest now boiling anger rather than discomfort.

Marcella doesn't look convinced. "Yet, your name comes up a lot. In fact, some of your former—let's call them acquaintances—might say you have a pattern of getting what you want and then moving on."

I squint at her and stay silent. She's fishing.

Sarah crosses her arms. "Unless Ms. Delgado has evidence about how Dr. McGloughlin's personal life played a role in Miranda Black's surgery, we're moving on."

Marcella feigns disappointment. "Fine. Let's move on."

I don't miss the way her eyes flick over me, assessing, like she confirmed something she suspected all along. For some insane reason, I feel like I lost this battle.

For the next hour, she hammers me with questions—about my family. About my schooling. It's grueling. It takes everything I have not to let it show.

When it's finally over, Marcella gathers her notes with a little too much force, her lips pressing together in something like irritation.

I remain seated, unwilling to move. She's ripped me apart without remorse and I want to get out of here. I won't let her think she's thrown me for a loop.

Marcella's gaze flicks over at me—quick, assessing, not indifferent—for the briefest moment, before she schools her expression back to ice, but I catch it.

A spark of heat, quick and sharp. Like the flare of a match before the burn.

Wait, *what*?

Marcella fumbles a few papers and they scatter to the ground. When she leans forward to retrieve them the slightest gap in her blouse reveals the soft curve of her cleavage and a sheer, black-lace bra.

Her abundant tits nearly spill out of their dainty constraints. The glimpse alone is enough to make my pulse stutter and my attraction reignite.

Fuck.

For a brief, damning second, I can't look away.

My dick fills once again.

Marcella catches me gawking and her cheeks immediately flush crimson red. She narrows her eyes and her lips part like she's about to say something. Then thinks better of it.

If I'm not mistaken, for the first time since this deposition started, the woman looks almost shy. Embarrassed.

Quickly, she stands and straightens her jacket, breaking the spell. "Thank you for your time, Dr. McGloughlin."

"You're welcome," I rasp because my mouth is dry as a bone.

Our gazes lock. The air between us is thick, charged—an almost tangible energy. Crackling with a heat and tension so intense, if we don't look away we'll set the whole damn room on fire.

I jerk my head back and wrench my eyes to the table. I've never experienced something so potent in my life.

Suddenly, I've never wanted someone the way I want Marcella Delgado. It's a problem. A dangerous, fucking reckless problem.

I've made a lot of questionable choices when it comes to sex.

Her?
It's a line I can't cross.
Won't cross.
Marcella Delgado could ruin my life.
Why in the fuck do I want her anyway?

Eleven

One Week Later

Seamus McGloughlin is late.

I drum my fingers against my desk, inhaling slowly through my nose.

He's already dragging his feet, and we haven't even begun.

Across from me, Sarah Mahoney checks her watch. "He'll show. You know how this goes. People don't like facing reality, even when it's the only way forward."

I offer a single nod.

No emotion. No invitation.

This isn't about patience.

It's about control. Nothing more.

I already know what I'm going to say. How I'm going to get him to listen.

The reality is, my offer is his only option if he doesn't want to have a malpractice suit on his record. Whether he wants to admit it or not.

The door swings open, and Seamus steps inside. It's the first time I've seen him stand to his full height.

Jesus Christ. He's massive.

The Orgasm Whisperer is easily six foot five, broad as the damn doorframe and could throw me over his shoulder without breaking a sweat. He's all man—strong, solid, effortlessly powerful in a way having nothing to do with arrogance and everything to do with sheer biology.

No wonder every woman in the hospital threw themselves at him.

His dark jeans and button-down shirt only emphasize what's underneath—thick, muscular thighs, broad shoulders straining against the fabric and a trim waist. Like he doesn't lift weights—he destroys them.

Despite his strength, there's a tension in the way he carries himself. His neck is stiff. He looks exhausted, like he hasn't slept in days.

I know the feeling.

Seamus's blue eyes flick to Sarah and when they land on me, something ignites—deep and primal, like the slow burn of embers waiting to roar to life.

Desire. Unmistakable. Undeniable. Then—gone.

My breath catches and I blink, convinced I imagined it. I'm too old for him. He has no reason to look at me like he's interested. Yet—for one fleeting moment—he did.

Now it's gone, and his mask is back in place.

He drops into the chair beside Sarah and exhales sharply. "All right. I'm here. I have a lot on my plate. Why do you need me?"

I glance at Sarah and she nods, giving me the go-ahead.

Seamus looks me up and down and steels his gaze.

Without thinking, I tug at the fabric of my wrap dress, suddenly feeling foolish for choosing it this morning. It's a deep navy, cinched at the waist, and the soft jersey fabric clings to my curves more than I'm comfortable with. It's not my usual sharp, structured blazer and pencil skirt, and now, under his gaze, I regret the choice entirely.

Ah, well. I've got to forge ahead.

"You're here because we both know Caldwell is throwing you under the bus." I lean forward, folding my hands on the desk. "You seem to have been his star resident. It doesn't change the fact he was the lead surgeon and made the call leading to Miranda Black's catastrophic injuries. In my opinion, he's trying to shift blame to you."

Seamus doesn't react right away. Instead, his fingers drum restlessly against his knee. His eyes flick to the floor, his expression unreadable.

I see the way his breathing changes. The way his body stiffens at the mention of her name.

"Seamus." I lower my voice. "If you cared about Miranda…"

He exhales sharply, dragging a hand down the stubble on his handsome face. "Sarah, you told me anything I say here is protected, right?"

"Yes." Sarah nods. "This is a settlement discussion. Whatever you say in this room can't be used against you in court." She gives him a pointed look. "Marcella is a professional. This is a matter of legal ethics, so don't worry."

His gaze snaps to mine, and something fractures behind his eyes. This giant man's voice is barely above a whisper when he speaks, as if saying the words out loud makes them more unbearable.

"I stayed with her for hours after the surgery," he murmurs, almost like he's confessing something he's never said before. "I check in on her every night. When her parents go home to sleep, I sit by her bed. Adjust her ventilator. Watch the monitors. Not a day goes by where I'm not thinking, if I did one more thing…if I held my ground…maybe."

Seamus's throat bobs as though he's struggling not to cry. His fists clench on his thighs.

"She was twelve." His voice cracks, raw and jagged. "She loved horses. She wanted to be a vet. Her mom told me once she hated the smell of hospitals. Miranda never complained—not once. She was brave. Braver than anyone I've ever met. I—" He shakes his head, exhaling sharply, like he's trying to steady himself. "I didn't fail her. I know I didn't."

The pain in his voice betrays him.

He believes he *did* fail her. It's eating him alive.

Seamus swallows hard, staring down at his big hands, his voice thick with something broken. "I was there when it happened. I saw it. Now, I have to live with it."

He drags his fingers through his hair at the back of his neck, his breath uneven. "If I could tell her parents anything, it wouldn't be about the surgery. It wouldn't be some rehearsed explanation regarding risk or medical outcomes or statistics." He looks into my eyes and the devastation there wrecks me. "I would tell them I'm sorry. I'd tell them I whisper to her when no one else is around, even though I know she can't hear me. It sounds so trite—so stupid. I'd trade places with her. I really would."

Seeing the raw agony in his eyes, hearing the quiet, broken way he speaks of her—I believe him.

Completely. Unshakably. Like a truth so absolute, it settles in my bones.

Seamus's chest rises and falls, his breathing uneven, and for a long moment, none of us say a word. Because what could possibly be said in the face of grief so deep?

A few moments later, Sarah clears her throat. "Which is exactly why you need to protect yourself. You know the truth and if you don't speak up, Caldwell is going to let you take the hit."

"So, what? You want me to, what, testify against him?" Seamus exhales harshly, leaning forward and resting his elbows on his knees.

I rest my chin on my hand. "It's not about testifying against him. It's about telling the truth and allowing me to get the best settlement for Miranda's family."

"You say this like it's so easy." He shakes his head.

"Well, it is easy," I counter. "It's not comfortable. I get it. You looked up to Caldwell. You wanted to believe he was the kind of man who would own his mistakes."

Seamus lets out a bitter laugh. "Yeah. Well, so much for blind loyalty. Even though I always planned on telling my own truth, he made it clear—well before you contacted me—I needed to back him up."

I go still. "What do you mean well before I contacted you?"

"Caldwell pulled me aside for lunch at the hospital. He wanted to make sure we were 'aligned' before you deposed me." Seamus rubs his hand over his chin.

My stomach drops. Of course he did. "Did he threaten your job?"

"Not in so many words." Seamus hesitates, then shakes his head. "I know how this game is played. If I didn't back him up or if I made things difficult, my future in neurosurgery would be fucked. Utterly and totally fucked."

How incredibly infuriating. "I'm not going to sugar coat it. If this goes to trial, the hospital and Caldwell will not protect you. They'll do everything in their power to make sure you carry as much of the blame as possible."

Sarah nods. "They'll argue you were competent enough to know the risks and complicit in the decision-making process."

"Jesus." Seamus exhales.

"I'm offering you a settlement and release agreement," I continue. "It will protect you from liability—completely. Once you sign, you'll be out of this case. No financial risk. No career-ending consequences."

Seamus leans back, staring up at the ceiling, the weight of the moment pressing down on him.

"You don't have to decide right now," Sarah adds gently. "However, I think this is your best option."

Seamus shakes his head slowly. "Then what? I walk away?"

"No," I say firmly. "Then you work with me."

His brows pull together. "What?"

"Once you're out of the case, you help me build the one against Caldwell." I sit up straighter. "You make sure I have everything I need to go after him instead of allowing him—or the hospital—to turn it on you."

His gaze sharpens. "Wait, you want me to work with *you*?"

"Yes."

The word leaves my lips with more force than I intend, and my heart races—a deep, pounding awareness settling low in my stomach at the thought of spending more time with him. Of sitting across from him, watching his sharp mind at work, feeling the weight of his presence pressing into the space between us.

No!

I force myself to exhale slowly, to tamp down the ridiculous heat curling through my veins. I'm in a position of power here. I can't—won't—let this...

Not when I've already woken up to dreams of him too many times, my body flushed and aching. Dreams of his hands on me. His mouth wrecking me. His voice—a deep, knowing whisper—telling me exactly how he's going to make me fall apart for him.

Good God, my panties are instantly soaked. This is so inappropriate it's not even funny.

I shift in my seat, swallowing against the sudden dryness in my throat. Seamus McGloughlin is not a man I can want. Not a man I can even consider.

It doesn't matter how my body responds—like I've been asleep my whole damn life and only now, since I've become aware of him, am waking up.

Terrifying. I need to put him out of my mind. Immediately.

Seamus visibly scoffs. "You hate me."

I blink, caught off guard. When I open my mouth, the words get stuck in my throat. I don't hate him. I...resent how much I want him. How much I understand him, even when I don't want to.

Maybe it's better if Seamus thinks I hate him. If he only sees my sharp edges and ruthless determination—because anything is safer than letting him know the truth.

I clear my throat. "I want justice for Miranda. I think you do too."

He stares at me for a long moment. Looks at Sarah. Then, finally, he nods. "Fine. Let's do it."

Sarah exhales in relief. I feel something deep in my chest unclench.

Let him think I hate him.

Let him see only the blade, never the blood.

We don't trust each other.

We don't need to.

We're drawing the same line—and I know exactly where to strike.

Twelve

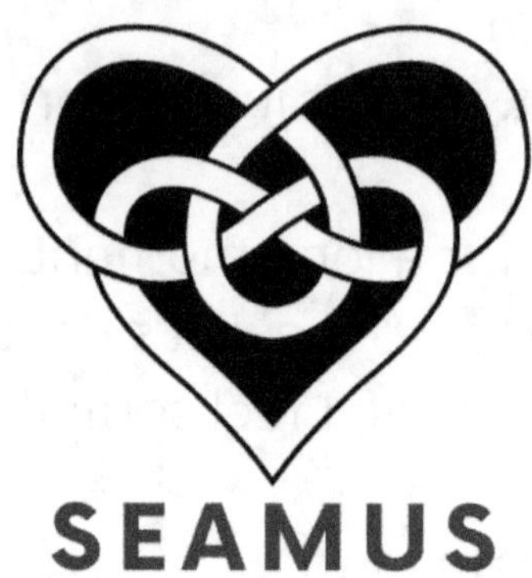

The Next Morning

I WAKE UP GRINDING into the mattress.

My cock hard and straining again, heat flooding every nerve.

No build-up. No lead-in.

My body moves like it knows what's coming.

Marcella.

Her mouth. Thighs. *Tits*. God, the way she fucking looked at me like she already knows her effect...

I haven't even touched myself yet.

Already too close.

My new morning ritual began the day after she eviscerated me. For the past week, I've been getting myself off to depraved fantasies of the woman who's determined to destroy my career one way or the other.

I'm a sick, sick man.

With no intention to stop. The end result is too fucking good.

I close my eyes and she materializes in my mind. *Marcella*. My new completely unexpected fucking obsession.

She's older than me, it's hard to know by how much. Doesn't matter, the woman is fucking beautiful. My fantasy woman come to life.

Poised and self-assured. Voluptuous with curves so sexy I'm practically salivating. Her gorgeous face could grace magazine covers...and I want to see it flushed and debauched with lust for me.

I see her on her knees, chestnut hair twisted in my fist, come streaking her face while she gasps for breath—messy, ruined, *mine*. Her eyes shine. Like she's proud of what she's done—made me lose all fucking control.

I'm getting ahead of myself, though.

My dick is diamond hard now, pre-come slicking the tip. Rewinding my fantasy, I've ripped open her blouse, revealing her incredible tits. They're soft and heavy in my hands, way more than a handful, with dark-brown nipples begging for my mouth. I can almost hear the needy sounds she makes as I suck and bite those sensitive buds.

I stroke up and down my shaft, hissing through my teeth at the electric pleasure of imagining Marcella before me, pouty lips strained around my cock as I fuck her hot, wet mouth. I want to see tears smeared in her mascara. Hear her gag when I hit the back of her throat.

My hips punch up, bucking into my tight fist. God, I want her. I want to manhandle those magnificent breasts, press them around my dick and thrust until I'm coming all over her pretty face.

With a final twist of my wrist, I erupt, ropes of come painting my chest and abs. I'm left panting and spent, shame quickly replacing ecstasy.

She's my goddamn nemesis. I have no business fantasizing about Marcella like this. I'm an idiot because no matter how wrong, I know I'll be jacking off to a new fantasy of her tomorrow.

Or later tonight.

With a frustrated exhale, I drag a hand down my face, forcing myself to push her from my mind. This is insanity. Grumbling at the mess I've made, I grab a tissue from the nightstand and wipe myself clean before tossing it into the trash. Ignoring the lingering tingling in my dick, I swing my legs over the side of the bed and stand, rolling my shoulders.

A cold shower. Coffee. Work. The trifecta of what I need.

Except I took the day off to regroup and decide what to do. I have the settlement paperwork in my in-box. Sarah signed off on it, told me it was an excellent deal—better than I could have hoped for under the circumstances.

Why, then, can't I shake the feeling putting my name on the dotted line will mean more than stepping out of the legal crosshairs I find myself in?

I know the answer. It'll mean I've got to accept Miranda Black will never wake up. Never have another birthday. Never get the life she should have had.

I'm not sure I can live with this reality.

I need to talk to someone. Who? None of my friends at the hospital, for obvious reasons. My brothers are all over the place.

I tried to meet up with Cillian for dinner last night after the meeting, it was a disaster. He was already four or five drinks deep when I walked in, blaming his problems on his break-up. Unfortunately, I know the truth. His reliance on alcohol started long before her. Despite Da's best efforts, he's still circling the drain, and I don't know how to pull him back out.

Brennan hasn't returned my last few calls or texts. He's buried in some corporate disaster at his company, Cognify AI, trying to keep it from imploding under the weight of whatever the hell's going on in Silicon Valley. It's always like this with us, he's either all in or completely absent.

Maybe I'll try Liam and Padraig. The twins have always forged their own path. They left home when I was a kid, chasing their music careers, and while they're closer to Connor than they are to me, they always have a good take on life.

I hit dial. It rings twice before Liam picks up. "What's up, everything okay?"

"You got a minute?" I rub my temple.

"Well, is it an emergency?" I can hear someone tuning a guitar in the background. "We're in London and it's time for sound check."

"Shit. Of course. It can wait, why don't you guys call when you have a minute." I sigh.

There's a pause, and for a second, I think he's going to tell me to spill anyway. Then Padraig's voice cuts in the background, calling Liam back to rehearsal, and Liam exhales. "I'm sorry, Seamus. It's bad timing."

"I get it. Talk to you soon." I end the call and dial Connor, whom I seem to be leaning on a lot lately.

He picks up immediately. "Hey, wee Seamus. Everything okay?"

I hesitate, then decide to spill. "Not really. You got time to talk?"

"Aye. Ronni's nursing Teagan and the boys are at nursery school. What's going on?" He always sounds so cool and confident, it's what I need.

"Well..." I run a hand through my hair. "I was offered a settlement agreement. It will fully exonerate me."

Connor is silent for a moment, then he exhales. "And?"

"Sarah says it's solid. It clears me completely. Signing it means I have to work with Marcella Delgado against

Caldwell." I try to keep my tone neutral and hide the buzz I feel at the thought of being close to her.

He whistles. "Good deal. You should sign the feckin' thing."

"You don't think it's weird? Working with the woman who's been trying to take my mentor down?" Part of me hopes he agrees, the other part wants permission. Go figure.

"Jaysus, lad. Caldwell's a snake. You don't have a choice. From the sound of things, he's been trying to blame it on you. Don't youse forget it." Connor sounds spitting mad. "*You* didn't fuck up her surgery, Seamus. *He* did. If you truly believe he's been setting you up to take the fall, sign the agreement. Make sure he never does it to anyone else."

I close my eyes, nodding, even though he can't see me. "Yeah. You're right."

"If you're worried about the lawyer, do you want me to ask Zoey to give you a heads up on Marcella?"

I frown. Why would his bandmate's wife be involved. "Zoey?"

"Remember, she worked at Finney Cooper when she got out of law school," he reminds me. "She might have useful insight."

I consider it. "Maybe. If it gets weird. Right now, I'm trying to wrap my head around all this. It's surreal."

"I get it." His voice softens because he's been through the wringer as a famous person. "Take it step by step.

My suggestion is to get yourself out of this situation and move on."

He's right.

Yet, even after getting solid advice from Connor, I can't bring myself to sign the damn papers.

The gym seems like a good place to work off the restless energy clawing at my insides. I push myself hard—sprints, heavy lifts, anything to exhaust my body so my brain will shut the hell up and resist the urge to masturbate.

It doesn't work.

Even after the second cold shower of the day, fantasies of her naked body beckoning me make my dick stir. Once I'm back in my car, I pull up the Finney Cooper website and stare at her polished headshot. She's so professional. Composed. Did she feel the heat crackling between us, dangerous and undeniable?

Am I losing my mind?

Goddammit. My cock is hard as a rock again.

Insanity.

With a muttered curse, I throw my phone on the passenger seat and start the car. I'm having a late lunch with my ma. I can't go to her like this—sex-starved and restless. I concentrate on the one thing that'll get my dick under control.

Wrinkly grannies. Wrinkly grannies. Wrinkly grannies.

Jesus.

When things calm down, I head to my parents' house. Da is on the jobsite covering for Cillian, which doesn't surprise me in the least considering the state of him last night. It'll give me time alone with my ma.

The second I step inside, the rich, familiar scent of her famous Irish stew wraps around me. Lamb, slow-cooked until it falls apart, thick with potatoes, carrots, and onions, simmered in a rich broth perfected over generations. A fresh loaf of bread is wrapped in a dish towel.

My stomach growls despite the knot of anxiety sitting heavy in my gut.

She turns from the stove, eyes warming when she sees me. "Seamus, love, perfect timing. Sit, I'll fix you a bowl."

"Ma, I need some advice." I sink into one of the kitchen chairs. "I'm conflicted."

She ladles the stew into a bowl and sets it in front of me with a thick slice of brown bread slathered with grass-fed butter. Only when she sits across from me with her own lunch does she speak. "What's troubling you?"

"Yesterday, I was offered a settlement to help bring Bryce down." I stab my spoon into the stew and swirl it around. "My gut tells me to save myself. My head tells me to remain loyal and hope things work out."

Her spoon hovers mid-air. "You know Bryce threw your name out there. So, what's the conflict?"

"I'll be working with the lawyer who deposed me and tore me to shreds." I dunk a piece of bread in the broth and nearly groan with pleasure when I shove it in my mouth.

She studies me carefully. "Do you trust her?"

"I don't know." I try to get the vision of her beautiful eyes out of my brain.

Ma tilts her head skeptically. "You want to."

I don't answer.

She puffs out a breath. "Seamus, love, you've carried the weight of this surgery on your shoulders for months. It's not your burden to bear."

"I'm not so sure." I clench my fist. "I can't stop thinking about Miranda."

She reaches across the table, resting her hand over mine. "Maybe helping this attorney will give you some peace when it comes to the wee girl."

"I'll have to spend a lot of time with her." I stare at our hands, at the delicate lines of her fingers against my rougher skin.

Ma lifts an eyebrow. "Miranda? Ach, no, you mean the lawyer?"

"Yeah." I swallow. "I... I don't know what I think."

A knowing glint sparkles in her eyes. "*Huh.*"

"Don't even. Marcella is going to ruin my career," I fire back.

Her smile widens. "No, she's your advocate. I think she likes you."

I open my mouth, then close it.

Ma pats my hand. "You remind me so much of your da when he was your age."

"I'm nothing like Da." I tense.

"You are." Her gaze softens. "You have his heart."

I shake my head. "No, I wouldn't ever put my own family through what he put us through. I don't understand why you stayed."

She winces like I've slapped her. "Love isn't about perfection. It's about standing by your person, even in their worst moments. It's about seeing past their mistakes to the person they're trying to be."

"He hurt you." I look away. "He hurt all of us."

"He did," she admits. "He fought to be better. I believed in the man he could be and now we have him back."

I swallow hard. "I've never wanted to fall in love. I don't think I have it in me."

"You have more love in you than you know, Seamus. I'm sorry for not getting you boys help. It never occurred to me, it's not the old-school Irish way." She reaches over, cupping my face.

I shake my head. "I don't want love. I don't need it."

"Ah, my sweet boy. You do and you'll fall hard and give yourself to the right woman." She gives me a sad smile.

Give myself? Does she know my secret?

No. there's no possible way.

I finish the last bite of my stew and shove back my chair. "Fine. I'm going to sign the settlement."

"Good man, yerself." She nods, as if she already knew.

After I help her with the dishes and head back home, her words stay with me. Wrapping around me like a warm hug. Making me believe I don't have to be alone anymore.

Somehow, I feel at peace for the first time since we failed Miranda.

Ma's words follow me into the quiet.

They don't haunt—they settle.

Maybe I don't have to carry this alone.

Thirteen

Ten Days Later

Ten days since the settlement.

I told myself I'd let it go—walk away clean, finish what I came here to do.

Instead, I'm checking the time again.

Seamus is late again.

Not by much. Enough to make me wonder if this was a mistake.

I was so relieved when he finally signed, it brought me one step closer to bringing Caldwell down and giving the

Blacks the peace they deserve. Getting him here tonight hasn't been easy, though.

After he executed the paperwork, I pushed to meet before Caldwell could get to him at the hospital. His lawyer reminded me—more patiently than I probably deserved—Seamus was already drowning in work because of the lawsuit and as an R4, he was mostly in the lab not the OR.

He's working hard to make sure he doesn't fall behind before his winter break.

It was a reality check. As much as I need Seamus for this case, he has a whole life and career to worry about.

Of course now, as Ethan, Natalie, and I wait for him in the conference room, my patience and understanding is wearing thin. He was supposed to be here half hour ago.

Meanwhile, we're going over our notes, prepping questions, and reviewing Caldwell's deposition. The more I dig into the man, the more I know we're on the right path. Seamus has firsthand experience to finally pin Caldwell down. Getting him to talk freely might take some finesse.

I check my phone again. No message.

"He better not bail," Ethan mutters, drumming his fingers on the table.

Natalie glances at me. "You think Caldwell got to him?"

No. I don't want to believe it. Seamus seems too damned principled to go back on his word. Then again, what if he is having second thoughts?

As the minutes drag on, frustration creeps in.
A text from Seamus finally pops up.

Seamus: Running late. My car battery died. Had to get a jump. Be there in 10.

I exhale sharply and set my phone down. "Seamus is on his way."

"I really thought he might've chickened out." Ethan leans back in his chair, smirking.

Natalie grins, twirling her pen between her fingers. "It's nice when a man keeps his word. I like him."

Something akin to resentfulness gnaws at me. Natalie is only a couple years younger than Seamus, far more age appropriate.

Shut up, Marcella. There's no competition, you're not even in the running and you know it.

Exactly ten minutes later, the door opens, and he strides in. Seamus McGloughlin is a lot of things—frustrating, broody, intelligent, entirely too attractive—and, thankfully, a man of his word.

Tonight, he's in dark jeans and a charcoal hoodie stretched perfectly across the breadth of his shoulders, every inch of him looking like a man built to ruin me in the best possible way. His hair is slightly tousled, as always, and the shadow of exhaustion under his sharp blue eyes seems more pronounced than it was ten days ago.

There's something else, though. Something quieter, more subdued. He's here, not because he wants to be.

It's resignation. He has no choice.

I didn't give him one.

"Sorry I'm late." He plops into the chair across from me. "It's been a day."

Natalie flashes him a dazzling smile, leaning forward a little too much. "No worries, we were just getting started."

I fight the urge to roll my eyes. Seamus doesn't even glance at her. He leans back and exhales heavily like he'd rather be anywhere else.

"Let's get to it." I decide to cut to the chase so we can let him go home as soon as possible. "We want to go deeper into your time working under Caldwell, particularly what you saw in the OR. How he operates, his decision-making, and how he treats his patients from start to finish, especially during high-risk procedures."

Seamus's expression shifts into something more guarded. "Right."

He shifts in his chair, the fabric of his fitted hoodie pulling across his broad chest as he crosses his arms. He looks down for a second, like he's seeing something only he can.

"Caldwell is—" He stops, searching for the right words. "Brilliant. Uncompromising. The kind of surgeon people write about in textbooks. He knows it too. Walks into every OR like there isn't a single person in the world more capable than him. For a long time, I believed it."

His fingers flex against his biceps, tension radiating through his frame. "He has this way of making you feel like you're chosen. Like if he sees something in you, it means you have 'it'—raw talent, instinct separating the good from the great. He said he saw it in me," he snarks, shaking his head.

"The thing regarding Caldwell? He never second-guesses himself. Ever. Not in surgery. Not in teaching. Not in anything." Seamus leans forward, elbows resting on the table, voice quieter now. "When you're in his orbit, his kind of confidence is intoxicating. You start to believe if he doesn't question himself, you shouldn't either. Hesitation is weakness."

Something dark flickers across his face. "It's a problem. Because I saw it. The mistake." His fingers curl into fists on the table. "I saw the vessel on the monitor before he did. I told him to stop. I didn't push hard enough. No, fast enough. He was determined to keep going, and in my head, I thought—who am I to question him?"

"One split second. My hesitation. The next thing I knew, Miranda was gone." His throat bobs, and when he looks at me, there's something raw in his expression.

He scrubs a hand down his face, then drops it to the table with a quiet thud. "I used to think being the best meant never questioning the choices you made. Confidence was the most important thing." He shakes his head, near tears. "Now? I know better."

I watch him carefully as he speaks, taking in the way his fingers flex against the table, the way his throat works when he swallows between thoughts. He's guarded. Tormented. His emotion bleeds through—I can see how much Miranda's case weighs on him.

Damn it, his reaction affects me more than I'd like.

Natalie reaches out, resting a hand on Seamus's forearm in what she clearly thinks is comforting. "That must have been so hard for you," she murmurs softy, her tone filled with sympathy.

My teeth clench with irritation. I tell myself her gesture is unnecessary. Unprofessional. Whatever the case, it sets something off inside me I don't have the time—or the patience—to analyze.

And Seamus? He looks like he'd rather be anywhere else.

I clear my throat, forcing a calm I don't quite feel. "Let's take a quick break." I push back from the table, needing a moment to gather myself. "Five minutes." My voice is steady. My pulse isn't—especially when I glance at Seamus, who still looks utterly wrecked.

Ethan shows Seamus to the restroom, allowing me to pull Natalie aside. "A word?"

"Sure." She glances up from the tea she's making.

"Knock it off," I admonish.

Her eyes widen. "Excuse me?"

"The flirting." I cross my arms. "He's not interested. Even if he was, this isn't the time."

Natalie stares at me for a minute, shocked. Then she presses her lips together before walking back to the conference room. "Noted."

Shit.

I feel a flicker of guilt. She's young, ambitious, and she has eyes—Seamus is handsome. I know my irritation isn't entirely about her behavior.

It's about me.

I'm fucking jealous.

The way I keep dreaming of Seamus, waking up breathless and satiated. Aching in ways I shouldn't be.

I've tried to tell myself it's because he happens to be in my orbit and it's been a long time. It isn't true, though. He's compelling in a way I can't quite reconcile. When I go back to the conference room and catch the way his tired eyes flick to me, something shifts in my chest.

I push it down and force myself to focus. Do my job. Be professional.

By the time we wrap up, we have more than enough to work with for the time being. Ethan and Natalie gather their things. There's a new stiffness in Natalie's posture. She adjusts the strap of her bag with a little too much precision, her expression unreadable as she leaves without saying goodbye.

There's no outright defiance, no snide remark—just a deliberate coolness toward me.

Does she suspect I'm attracted to Seamus?

"I'm out." Ethan salutes before dashing toward the elevator to join Natalie.

Leaving me alone with Seamus. He sighs, checking his phone as we walk to the elevator. "Shit. My Uber is still five minutes out."

"Your car really died today?" I sling on my crossbody bag.

"Yeah," Seamus mutters. "Perfect ending to a long-ass day."

Something about the sight of him, tired and worn down, tugs at me in a way I can't comprehend.

"The Metropolitan Grill is a block away," I blurt out before I can second-guess myself. "If you're hungry, we could grab a bite."

Seamus's brows lift slightly, like he wasn't expecting me to invite him to dinner.

I wasn't expecting it either and I feel like a schoolgirl waiting to see if he'll accept.

I'm a goddamn hypocrite. I chastised Natalie for her undisguised interest because I wanted be the one to comfort him.

Fuck. Well, it's too late now to revoke the invitation.

"You're right about it being a long day." I feign nonchalance. "We've gotta eat, right?"

He nods, easy and unbothered, like I didn't just cross a line I swore I'd never touch. "Yeah. Okay."

I tell myself it's only dinner.

My pulse calls me a liar.

Fourteen

Same Night

THIS DOESN'T FEEL REAL.

Marcella walks beside me in a coat worth more than my car.

I'm tired. Starving. Running on fumes, wired from everything and nothing.

The night air is cool, carrying the crisp scent of autumn as Marcella and I walk the short block to the Metropolitan Grill.

I want her so badly my chest aches.

With the way my cock is reacting to her presence, the distance might as well be a mile.

She's close enough so her perfume—rose layered over leather, delicate with an edge sharp enough to bleed —curls around me, embedding itself in my senses. I shouldn't be thinking about how good she smells. Or how good she looks. The dress she's wearing hugs every curve just right and the neckline dips enough to make me swallow hard.

She's sin. Pure fucking sin.

Her suggestion to get dinner came out of the blue. My day in the lab sucked ass capped off by being forced to bare my soul in her conference room. I'm wrung out. Broken. Have been for months. The way she looked at me as if I were a kicked puppy makes me think she feels sorry for me.

I should be offended. Hell, let's be honest, I'm happy to share a meal if it means another hour in her company.

Hunger aside, I'd prefer to spend the time burying myself balls deep inside of her.

She's who you've been waiting for.

We reach the entrance of the restaurant. I hold the door open and she gives me a polite nod as she steps inside. There's something uncertain in her expression, almost wary. Maybe she feels it too—the tension thrumming between us like an electric current. Or, she senses how attracted I am to her and is trying to be polite to let me down easy.

The hostess leads us to a booth in the back, dimly lit and tucked away from the rest of the restaurant. Probably a good thing, considering the way my body is betraying me around her. I'm pretty sure every diner saw the telltale bulge in my crotch as we made our way here.

Sitting across from her, it's all I can do not to let my gaze linger on the way the soft lighting casts a golden hue over her skin. Or the way her full lips press together as she scans the menu.

Silence expands between us, thick and awkward. We're not enemies anymore. We're not friends either. She needs me to help her take down my mentor. It's the only reason we're in each other's orbit. I sincerely doubt she'd be too impressed if she knew how many hours I've spent with my hand wrapped around my cock imagining fucking her tits...

Or how her ass would jiggle if I rammed into her from behind...

Watching my cum spill out of her pussy...

Christ. I need help.

The waiter brings us two glasses of wine Marcella requested from the hostess while I was lost in my own goddamn thoughts. I won't touch it—I don't drink, but I don't have the energy to get into that particular conversation.

Instead, I order a porterhouse steak medium rare, a baked potato, a salad and a side of fries. I haven't eaten since breakfast and let's be real—I'm not a small guy.

Marcella only orders a dinner salad, and my brow furrows. "You're not hungry?"

"Not really. I'm glad we're here because it looks like you are." She lifts a shoulder in an offhand gesture.

"No judgment—I'm not sure how you come to Seattle's most famous steak restaurant and not indulge." I tilt my head, studying her. "Your willpower is insane."

Her lips press together, then she exhales and sets her menu down. "My family owns a Spanish restaurant in Tacoma, I grew up around food. It's part of who I am. I've also spent my whole life being aware of my weight. When you grow up as a bigger girl, it's…something you learn to manage."

"Manage? How?" I frown, thinking about Caldwell's inappropriate jabs at her.

"Ahh." Her lips curve into a wry smile with no humor to it. "Control your food intake. Make sure it doesn't get out of hand. People like to remind you if you don't."

Something sharp twists in my chest. "Bullshit."

She blinks, like she wasn't expecting my reaction and isn't sure whether I believe her or empathize with her.

"People should mind their goddamn business. You're beautiful," I word vomit against my better judgment. Hell, it's the truth. "If you want a steak, you should damn well eat a steak."

Her mouth opens slightly, and for a second, she looks at me. Like she's trying to figure me out. Then she shakes her head. "You don't hold back, do you?"

"Not usually." I look her directly in the eye.

Marcella exhales softly, tracing the rim of her wine glass with one manicured finger. "My dad has been slowly turning things over to my sister, Rosa. She went to culinary school, trained in Spain, and came back ready to take the restaurant to the next level." A small, wistful smile tugs at her lips. "She's implemented updated menus, wine pairings, a whole rebranding thing. My parents pretend to fight her on it, but they're proud. You can see it every time she talks about some new dish she wants to introduce."

I watch as she pauses, like she's lost in a memory. "They all work together. My dad's the face, my mom keeps everything running behind the scenes. My brother Lucas—" She shakes her head with a soft laugh. "He's in real estate but helps with the books. The restaurant is his favorite place to bring clients. Says it helps close deals."

I'm fascinated. She's so much different when she talks about her family. All the rough edges smooth out.

"I should see them more," she admits. There's something heavy in her expression now, a weight that wasn't there a moment ago. "I want to. Work always gets in the way."

I know the feeling. Too well.

"You should make time," I encourage. "Before you look up and realize you missed more than you meant to."

She lifts her gaze to mine. Something unreadable flickers in her mesmerizing hazel eyes. Maybe it's the atmosphere of the dimly lit restaurant. For a moment, it feels like we aren't adversaries, or even uneasy allies. We're two people, trying to navigate the choices defining their lives.

"Yeah." She exhales, a slow, measured breath. "I should."

The tension between us shifts, softening into something else—something more comfortable. Making her next question feel even more direct.

"So tell me, Doctor McGloughlin." She swirls her wine like she's a bit uncomfortable. "What's with the extracurricular activities in the stairwell?"

I nearly choke on my drink. "Excuse me?"

"The women. The rumors. The, uh...apparent exceptional level of anatomical knowledge." She flicks her gaze to mine.

I drag a hand down my face. "*Jesus.*"

"What? You've got to realize everyone is talking about it." She tilts her head. "The lawyer in me worries you're setting yourself up for a different kind of lawsuit."

I push the wine glass away as I weigh my words. The truth feels too raw—too personal to lay out in a casual conversation over dinner with a woman I barely know. Marcella watches me with sharp, assessing eyes, and for some reason, I don't want her to assume the worst about me.

"I've never analyzed it too deeply," I admit, rubbing the back of my neck.

She quirks an eyebrow, clearly waiting for more.

I exhale and lean forward, lowering my voice. "Look, I'm not an idiot. I know what people say. Hell, you brought it up in my deposition. I won't lie—there's a reason I've had my fair share of...experiences. Not *exclusively* in stairwells, for fuck's sake, though they're awfully convenient when you fucking live at the hospital. Definitely not in the way you're thinking."

"What do you mean?" Her brow furrows slightly.

I glance around the restaurant, feeling an unfamiliar wave of nerves tense in my chest. I don't usually get anxious. Not in surgery and sure as hell not when talking to women. With her?

This is uncharted territory.

"It means," I say carefully, "if you did your homework you'd know I never actually fucked anyone in said stairwells. Let me blow your mind. Technically, I'm still a virgin."

Marcella's lips part with shock. She says nothing. Stares at me like I've grown a second head.

"You can pick your jaw up off the floor." I fight the urge to smirk.

She blinks, shaking her head slightly. "I'm sorry. I find it difficult to believe with your reputation—"

"A reputation I've never bothered to correct because my sex life is no one's business unless I choose to share it." I narrow my eyes.

She studies me and there's a palpable shift in her demeanor—curiosity laced with desire? "Why do you do it then?"

"I got into medicine because my family has a history of alcoholism." I gesture to my untouched wine. "I wanted to understand why some brains are wired toward addiction."

Marcella moves the glass away. "I'm sorry for being presumptuous about the wine. Let's order something else."

"It's fine. I'm good with water." I hold up my glass and take a sip.

She nods. We look at each other for a beat.

She purses her lips and smiles. "Continue…"

"Ah, right. You're not letting me off the hook." I lean back and give her the rundown on how it all started. "At the end of the day, understanding how to give a woman pleasure became a challenge. I wanted to be the best." I tilt my head. "What started out as an experiment with two friends in medical school expanded. No two women are the same and this fascinated me. Things got a bit out of control, apparently. Hence, the reputation I never asked for, but can't deny."

Marcella's throat bobs when she swallows, her gaze flickers down my body for a brief second before snapping back to my eyes.

"I see," she murmurs as her cheeks flush red.

I watch her carefully and notice something I didn't expect—interest. *Genuine* interest. It's subtle. Unmistakable.

Holy hell, this is getting dangerous.

I shift in my seat. "You wouldn't understand."

"Why?" A flash of hurt crosses her face.

I shift, extending my legs under the table. This woman knows more about me than my own brothers, why not leave it all out there? "Look, I come from a family of men who are larger than life. Three rockstars. A tech mogul. A man who's taken over the family's construction empire. I was the sensitive, quiet one. The one who always followed the rules. When you grow up watching your brothers get all the attention, you start to wonder what you're missing."

Marcella giggles nervously. "Jesus. That's…"

"Ridiculous?" I supply.

She stabs at her salad. "Not the word I was going to use."

"Look, it stopped being fun years ago and I stopped. It wasn't fulfilling for me. After Miranda…" I trail off, running a hand through my hair thinking of my encounter with Cecily and how empty I felt. "Pointless."

Her brows draw together. "Why wouldn't you think I'd understand? Do I come across as uptight? I was twenty-nine once, you know."

I roll my shoulders, feeling the weight of the admission before I even say it. "Because you're probably used to being worshipped. You don't seem like a woman who'd ever stoop so low to let some creep get you off in a stairwell and not remember your name."

Marcella exhales sharply, like I've struck a nerve she wasn't prepared for. Her fingers clamp around the stem of her wine glass, and for a second, I think she's going to brush it off, give me some cool, unaffected lawyerly response.

Instead, she lets out a bitter laugh. "Guys don't worship fat girls like me, Seamus. They fuck them in secret. Or they don't bother at all." She looks off into the distance, not before I catch the flicker of something in her eyes—raw and unguarded.

Beneath all her armor, she's as lost as me.

"*Christ*. That's the dumbest fucking thing I've ever heard." I can't help myself.

Her head jerks toward me in surprise.

I lean forward, elbows on the table. "You're not fat. You're the most stunning goddamn woman I've ever seen." The words come out rough, guttural. "I can't get you out of my head. I can't sleep. Or concentrate. It fucking kills me you think I'm some misogynistic asshole who'd treat you that way. If circumstances were different, would you even give me the time of day?"

Her lips part slightly. No words come out. A flicker of shock—like I've caught her completely off guard.

She doesn't speak. Doesn't blink.

Whatever walls she built, have I somehow slipped through the cracks?

Her silence dares me to make the next move.

It's all I can do to hold the line—for now.

Fifteen

MARCELLA

Same Night

My heart seizes.

Not from fear—from recognition.

Seamus McGloughlin stands in front of me, wrecked and brazen, saying out loud every impossible thing he's whispered to me in my dreams.

Time to shut this down. Protect myself.

I open my mouth to tell Seamus to stop. He doesn't give me the chance.

"I can't get you out of my head," he grits out, his voice lower, rougher. "I can't sleep. Or concentrate. It fucking kills me you think I'm some misogynistic asshole who'd treat you that way." His gaze drops to my lips before flicking back up. "If circumstances were different, would you even give me the time of day?"

I can't breathe.

I've spent weeks having vivid, explicit, orgasmic fantasies about this man. The way his hands and mouth worshipped me has felt so real, I wake up aching and desperate for something I never thought was possible.

This gorgeous, younger, hotshot surgeon who, apparently, has every woman in the hospital clamoring for him thinks I'd never give *him* the time of day?

What alternative universe am I living in?

My lips part. Still, no words come out. I've got nothing but shock, disbelief, and something dangerously close to hope clawing at my chest.

Until reality douses me with ice.

Or, maybe, insecurity.

Who the *fuck* does this little shit think he is? He's suckered me into feeling sorry for him with his stories of virginity and complicated family dynamics. Now he's pretending to be attracted to me.

I can see why the women of the hospital fell for his charm. He's *good*. A player. Earnest. Bold. Self-assured.

Insincere.

Right. Because, if he says he's attracted to you, there's no way he could be sincere.

My inner voice spears me like a sword. I'll never believe him. Age difference or not, Seamus McGloughlin reminds me of men who—time and time again—have made me feel like I'm not enough.

I'll never be enough.

I need to leave—reestablish the boundary I blurred the moment I asked him to dinner. What the hell was I thinking? I've let this veer too far. My judgment slipped when personal curiosity outweighed my professionalism.

This isn't friendly conversation; it's now something—dangerous. On all levels.

Focus, Marcella.

I need this guy for one reason—to take down Caldwell. Time to shove this personal shit back into the box and lock it tight before I make a mistake I can't take back.

I curl my lip and a layer of armor slips into place. "If circumstances were different, I wouldn't even be in your orbit, Dr. McGloughlin."

"You're wrong." A muscle ticks in his cheek. His gaze stays steady on mine.

"No?" I arch a brow, willing my voice to stay steady. "You can have any woman you want. You *do* have any woman you want and don't give any of *them* any part of yourself." I tilt my head, giving him a once-over. "Do you really think I'd have such a low opinion of myself I'd fall for your BS? So what if I've never been with a man who takes the time to get me off. I'm not your experiment. Or problem to fix. I want more in my life than getting rubbed off by some fuckboy in a stairwell. Have a little respect."

Oh. Holy. Fuck. What in the hell did I say?

I can feel my face redden.

His face crumbles for a second. He shifts in his seat like he's incredibly uncomfortable. Seamus McGloughlin—the golden boy of neurosurgery, the too-good-to-be-true man who women practically climb over each other to get to—is at a loss.

I didn't mean to slice him open, though. I just wanted space. Control.

God, I certainly didn't want to see this hollowed-out look in his eyes. I should've taken the high road—held the line without making it personal.

We sit across from each other, both of us stunned—by what's been said, what hasn't, and wherever this places us now.

Then he doubles down.

"*Whoa*. You're not talking about respect, Marcella," he finally says, low and rough. "You're talking about a fucking *tragedy*."

Good God. The air between us shifts, heavier. Even more charged, if possible.

Nope. No. *Nada*. This ends now.

"It seems to me, you've lived your entire life doing what you want with little regard to the people around you." I dig back in. "You've built a reputation around being a man who always takes, never stays."

His expression shifts—subtly. Enough to make me wonder if I went too far again.

Almost.

"You think those encounters define who I am as a person? You don't know me. Not at all." There's definitely something wounded in the way his voice cracks.

I swirl the last of the deep-red liquid in my glass, thinking.

He needs to hear this. Someone needs to say it to him.

"Seamus." I soften my tone. "Have you ever considered...the women? Did you ever think those stairwell rendezvous weren't casual to *them*? It might've started out a certain way for them—for you. I'm guessing many of them agreed to your conditions to get a turn with the great *Orgasm Whisperer*. So, you give them more pleasure than they've ever experienced in their life...only to toss them aside? Do you not understand how confusing emotions about experiencing sexual pleasure are to most women?

He flinches slightly, like my words land somewhere deep in his psyche. Somewhere he's never accessed before.

"I never..." he croaks. "I wasn't trying to hurt anyone. I figured if I was honest about what it was—no strings, no expectations—we'd be on the same page. It works for my brothers—"

"Let me lay it out for you," I interrupt. "Your friends Tara and Priya were right. Most men don't care about what their partner feels in bed. They focus on themselves, on their own release, and leave the rest up to chance. You seem to know *exactly* what you're doing. You studied to be 'the best,' for God's sake. I don't get it. Why put so much effort into making sure your women see stars and rainbows and fairy dust only to throw them away? For someone who prides himself on his bedside manner with patients, I'm shocked at how cavalier you are when it comes to sex." I take a breath. "If I had to guess, most of them didn't even know what an orgasm felt like before you got involved. So yeah, they probably caught actual feelings. While you maintain a clinical distance and walk away, oblivious."

His nostrils flare, and for a second, I think he's going to argue.

He doesn't. His palms rest on the edge of the table like he's bracing for impact.

"I didn't ever consider...I didn't know," he says sadly.

"I'm not surprised. I don't think you ever thought past the moment." I signal the waiter for the check. "From how you've described it, for you, it was research. A little release. For them? It was something else entirely. Something they probably didn't even expect to feel until it was already too late."

Neither of us speaks for a second, the quiet settling in like a storm about to break.

His throat bobs. "Fuck." He looks tortured. "I *hurt* them?"

"Yes. You're a fool to think otherwise." I exhale with exasperation.

He stares at some invisible spot on the table.

Seamus McGloughlin is completely, utterly shaken.

Needing a moment to steady myself and give him a break, I focus on paying the bill. This conversation has veered into dangerous, deeply personal territory, and the way he looks now? Like I've stripped him down to nothing?

It's rattling something in my chest I don't want to examine too closely.

The waiter hands me the receipt and I reach for my purse so I can get the hell home.

"Who made you feel this way?" He peers from under his unruly hair as we put on our coats.

I blink. "What?"

"Which guy hurt *you*?" He gestures at me. "Made you feel like you weren't good enough. Made you believe you didn't deserve to feel good?"

I nearly choke. I'd hoped he missed that particular revelation. "None of your business. We're *not* talking about me."

"You opened the can of worms so we are now." His gaze sharpens when we step outside and begin walking toward the office.

Seamus's hands are shoved into the pockets of his jacket. He doesn't rush me. He waits.

The weight of everything I've kept buried for too long presses against my ribs. Seamus is watching me in anticipation—his blue eyes locked on to mine, intense and unyielding.

Well...he wants to know. He asked.

So I decide to give it to him. All of it.

I let out a sharp breath and break eye contact because there's no fucking way I can do this if I'm looking at him. "It wasn't one guy. It was *all* the guys."

Seamus makes a low, irritated sound in his throat. To his credit, he doesn't interrupt.

Apparently, I've lost all sense of self-preservation tonight, and I begin to spill my deep-seated insecurities to a guy who has no business knowing any of them.

"I was a late bloomer. The quiet girl. Smart. Not the type who got asked to dances. In high school, the boys called me Marshmella behind my back. *Hilarious*." I laugh spitefully. "In college, I decided to get thin. I lost forty pounds. Nearly passed out every time I stood up. But, hell. I fit into a size six, so—hey—I must have been *winning*, right?"

Seamus low-level growls beside me.

"The first time I had sex, I was drunk. It wasn't some tragic after-school special, I wanted it. Thought I was making some grand feminist statement." I dig my fingernails in my palm. "He lasted about ninety seconds, rolled off, and a week later, I overheard him telling his friend he didn't 'date girls over 125 pounds.' Wash. Rinse. Repeat. Over and over."

"By law school, my self-esteem was in the gutter. Then I met a guy who was like me. We were both bigger, so I figured, hey, common ground. Turned out he also had a limit. Didn't mind fucking me for thirty seconds every night. Didn't want to be part of a 'fat couple.'"

We arrive at my building. "So yeah, after dozens of similar experiences on dating apps over the past decade...I'm over it."

"Jesus fucking Christ." Seamus takes my elbow.

I look at my shoes and shake my head. "It's fine."

"It's not." He squeezes lightly.

Tears threaten to spill, which cannot happen. "It is what it is."

"I have a confession to make." He tips my chin up to look at him. "Clearly you're not interested so I'm not trying to make this situation weirder. I'm going to tell you because somehow you believe you aren't fucking desirable. You need to know it's the biggest load of horseshit I've ever heard."

I freeze.

"The truth is, I've been jerking off to various fantasies about you for weeks, Marcella." He doesn't smirk. Doesn't tease. Says it like a fucking fact. Like he's telling me what time of day it is.

The breath catches in my throat.

I stare at him, my pulse hammering in my ears.

Naturally, I default to self-degradation. "Seamus. *Stop*. I'm supposed to believe I'm the fantasy of a devastatingly handsome neurosurgeon-to-be who's essentially a decade younger than me—and a virgin to boot?"

"Yes. You *should* believe. It's true." He doesn't flinch.

I roll my eyes way back into my head. *"Seamus—"*

"Are we so different? You bury yourself in your work. So do I. You're lonely. So am I. You come from a big, chaotic family. Same. You're close with your parents. Same." His eyes flick over my face, searching. "Neither of are fulfilled in our sex lives because we want to be with someone who matters, which I realize makes me sound like a fucking hypocrite. Everything you said about me tonight is true. It's why, except for one time after Miranda, I put an end to the stairwell encounters two years ago. I want to be with someone who matters. I want to *be* someone who matters."

My heart trips over itself.

His voice dips lower, like he's saying something dangerous. Something true. "Every part of me wants to prove to you how fucking beautiful and desirable you are. Right. Fucking. Now."

I swallow. Hard.

"I won't though, because I respect you. We need boundaries. I won't do anything to make you question your professionalism or mine." He threads his fingers through his hair. "We have a job to do. Miranda deserves justice. Caldwell needs to be held responsible." His lips quirk up, barely. "For now, maybe we can take the walls down and be friends."

I stare at him, trying to piece together what the fuck is happening here.

Then he takes a step back, hands still in his pockets, like he hasn't ripped apart everything I've ever believed about myself. "All bets are off once you get the settlement for Miranda, though."

My stomach plummets.

I've been the dirty secret. The side piece. The one you fuck, not the one you keep.

I've never been the woman men fight for.

Seamus doesn't look at me with shame.

He looks at me like I'm wanted—fully, publicly, dangerously.

My brain tells me to stay sharp.

My heart and soul want to believe him.

Sixteen

Three Weeks Later

THREE WEEKS SINCE DINNER.

Three weeks replaying every word we said. Every word we didn't.

I dumped more honesty than I've ever let anyone know.

She offered truths buried deep enough to permanently scar—and eviscerated me in the process.

We haven't spoken since.

Aside from a handful of emails about the case, of course. Certainly not about our confessions. Or what it all means.

Which is a problem. A huge, gut-twisting, life-altering problem.

Whatever's brewing between us—it's not small. It's not casual. It's a goddamn tectonic shift. I'm not going to let it pass me by.

I'm also not ready for it.

Clearly, given the lawsuit, the timing couldn't be worse. Plus, my most brutal years of residency are ahead of me and once I'm through school, I'll be building my practice from the ground up. If I work my ass off, maybe I'll be half as successful as Marcella by the time I'm pushing forty.

For now, I've been arriving in the lab before dawn and I'm the last to leave at night. Making up for the weeks lost to the lawsuit. I'm grateful for the distraction—the routine. The past seven months have been a whirlwind. Finding out my mentor was a snake. Signing the settlement. Wondering if my career will suffer. *Marcella*—there's too much noise in my head.

I'm trying to quiet it by keeping busy.

It's the only thing I know how to do. Throw myself into work like my life depends on it.

In some ways, it does.

Until this nightmare is over with Caldwell, my entire life is in limbo. The last I heard, his lawyer was making scheduling impossible. I could ask Marcella for an update. I want to. I'm trying to respect the boundaries I set the night we had dinner.

For now, the less I know the better. If the case goes to trial, I'll likely be the star witness.

Grabbing my coat from the closet, I flex my shoulders and decide I need caffeine if I'm going to make it through the afternoon. Lab-coffee sludge won't do, I need the good stuff. There's a cafe across the street from the hospital with the strongest espresso I've ever had. I plan to inject it straight into my bloodstream and take some with me for later.

On my way back, with both coffees in hand, I nod to a few colleagues, trying to force my mind to focus. Hoping for an update from Marcella, I decide to swing by the lounge to check my emails before I head to the lab.

Then, I see him.

Caldwell.

Coming straight for me.

I barely register what's happening before he's storming across the corridor, face flushed red with anger. *Murderous.* Livid, beyond anything I've ever seen.

"*McGloughlin,*" he thunders. "My office. *Now.*"

A few staff glance our way. Sensing a scene in the making, I nod once and follow him down the hallway.

Pressure builds though I keep my stride steady.

I knew this was coming. I didn't know when. Or how.

Here we fucking go.

Caldwell shoves the office door open so hard it bangs against the wall. He doesn't bother closing it behind us—he wants people to hear this.

Wants them to know I'm being dragged in like a schoolboy caught with his hand in the fucking cookie jar.

I hold my ground as he rounds the desk, fists clenched at his sides.

"You ungrateful little asshole," he spits. "After *everything* I've done for you."

I don't say a word. Cross my arms and wait.

"I was in mediation all day yesterday." He narrows his eyes. "Do you know what I learned?"

Yes. Yes, I do.

My lips stay sealed.

"You're working with *her*." He sneers the word like it's poison in his mouth. "The fat, desperate ambulance chaser?"

Something inside me snaps at the crass way he speaks of Marcella. I try like hell not to let it show.

Caldwell keeps going, pacing behind his desk. "*You*—of all people—siding with her. Letting her spin her bullshit case while I'm fighting for my reputation. For the program. For this *hospital*." His eyes flash with something cold. "You've sold your fucking soul."

"No, I signed a settlement and release to avoid culpability. I'm out of the case." I lean against the wall by the door.

Caldwell's laugh is jagged, feral. "You arrogant little *fuck*. That fat bitch has been sharpening her knives for months and you've dropped your pants and let her castrate us both. You pissed on your own future for a woman who'd slit your throat in a heartbeat."

"I'm doing what's best for Miranda." I calmly look at my phone. "Are we done? I need to get back to the lab."

He steps closer, lowering his voice. "Why bother. You still think you'll be a neurosurgeon? Have a future in this field? You may have avoided a lawsuit where insurance would have saved us both. Instead, you fucked yourself out of a career, McGloughlin."

A wave of nausea flickers in my gut—he's confirmed my biggest fear. I know how the system works. I know how whispers can ruin careers before they even begin.

I also know the truth.

I saw it with my own eyes.

"Do you know what's funny?" I manage to stay calm. "I thought you had my back and would have had yours until the end. I trusted you implicitly and thought you gave a damn about not only my career, but me as a person."

"I did—*do*," Caldwell snarls.

"No." I tilt my head. "You only care about yourself. About saving face. About throwing people under the bus when it suits you." I step forward, close enough he has to tilt his chin to meet my gaze. "You disappoint me on such a deep level it's astounding. Miranda Black's life is over because you didn't listen to me and then you tried to throw me under the bus leaving me no choice but to try and save myself. You're the one who's going to tank your legacy if you don't pull your head out of your sanctimonious, egotistical ass."

Caldwell stares at me confounded, his hands clenching at his sides. For a second, I think he's going to hit me. Instead, he turns on his heel and storms out of the office, slamming the door behind him.

Only then am I able to let out a breath I've been holding.

Holy shit. Threats aside, it's almost over.

Once Marcella settles and Miranda's parents are compensated, this nightmare will be behind me.

My heart's pounding. Shockingly, I don't feel rattled—I feel fucking alive. Furious, but clear. Like something's snapped into place.

Caldwell showed me exactly who he is.

There's no more doubt now. No more misplaced loyalty. The man I once admired and helped shape me into the surgeon I'm becoming—he's gone. Or maybe he was never real. I likely saw what I wanted to see.

On my way back to the lab, I walk with purpose, ducking my head as I pass a group of interns huddled around the nurses' station. My body is running hot, buzzing with adrenaline and residual anger. My mind's already shifting. I've got a full protocol to run tonight and I'd rather be elbows-deep in analytics than replaying Caldwell's bullshit on loop in my head.

I'm halfway there when my phone buzzes in my pocket. I almost ignore it until I glance down and see the name.

Marcella.

My pulse jumps for a completely different reason.

I swipe to answer. "Hey."

"I hope this isn't a bad time." Her throaty voice feels like a warm blanket.

Never.

Ducking into one of the unoccupied procedure rooms—dim, quiet, sterile, I lean against the counter and take a deep breath. "It's a perfect time. I wrapped up a hellish confrontation with Caldwell. What's going on?"

She's silent for a moment. Then, carefully, "Did he threaten your residency?"

"Yeah. I got the message loud and clear." I pick at a piece of tape stuck to the counter. I'm not going to ever tell her what he said about her. I feel guilty for not coming to her defense.

"I'm sorry."

I nod, even though she can't see me. "It's fine. I figured some sort of confrontation was coming."

Another pause. This one is heavier. Tighter.

She clears her throat, shifting gears. "Well...the reason I'm calling is Caldwell's attorney wants me to jump through a few more hoops."

"Yeah?" I freeze, waiting for the other shoe to drop.

She continues, "He wants to depose you, Kendrick Lyon, and the two nurses on duty before making any final decisions on the settlement."

I fist my hand in my pocket. "Why?"

"You were in the room," she explains. "The only people who can speak to what actually happened in the OR, moment by moment."

I pinch my nose. "So this is their way of figuring out if we're a threat."

"Exactly. They're gauging risk," she confirms. "Trying to decide if you're credible, whether you could hurt them if we go to trial. If you're too much of a liability—if you back up what we've already gathered—then they'll have no choice but to settle big. If you come across unsure, or leave any room for doubt, they'll seize on it."

"Shit. They'll lowball the Blacks. Or drag them through court." I shake my head at the audacity.

Marcella sounds tired. "Yes. It could mean years of litigation, expert witnesses, more trauma, and less payout at the end. *Not* what we want. *Not* what they deserve."

The silence—dense, suffocating, loaded—between us is full of implications neither of us wants to say out loud. I shift my weight and glance out the window without really looking.

"What do you need me to do?" I'll do anything to spare the Blacks from facing Caldwell.

"Be yourself," she says, almost too quickly. "I need you to be as clear and factual as you were with me a few weeks ago. You don't need to dramatize anything. You need to be honest. Direct."

"Okay." I don't hesitate.

She pauses, and when she speaks again, her voice softens. "Thank you, Seamus. I'm fighting so hard to keep you out of the crosshairs. This is still high-stakes. I need you to be ready."

"I am. I want this over. Tell me when you need me." I nod, even though she can't see me.

"It'll probably be within the next few days."

"The sooner the better." I practically beg. I want this over.

A beat of hesitation. "You're sure?"

"I've been carrying this around long enough." I slap the counter. "Let's finish it."

"Okay. I'll text you some options as soon as I know them." There's another pause.

She's ready to hang up, I can feel it. Back to business. Keeping things on script.

Hell, I'm not done. I can't resist.

"*Marcella*."

A beat. "Yes?"

"I can't stop thinking about you," I admit.

Silence.

I lean against the counter, my pulse kicking up. "I know I'm not supposed to say this to you. I know we're supposed to keep this professional. The thing is, I haven't been able to stop—imagining."

"Seamus...don't." She sighs softly—frustrated, conflicted.

"You don't feel it?"

"Not the point." She's firmer now. "This case is important. You're a witness."

I nod, swallowing the lump forming in my throat. "Right."

"I need to get back to work." She dismisses me. "I'll follow up when I have a date from opposing counsel."

She's about to end the call.

"*Wait.*"

Another beat.

I let the words come out before I can talk myself out of it. "Do you think about me?"

The silence on the line expands, taut.

Then, barely audible—

"*Yes.*"

One word slices through me.

"*Marcella...*"

The line dies in my ear.

I stay there, phone to my chest, breath stuck somewhere between wanting and regret.

This is what it feels like to almost have a chance...

And lose it.

Seventeen

MARCELLA

Three Weeks Later

THREE WEEKS LATER, THE storm outside matches the one I've kept buried.

Rain lashes the glass walls of the conference room we've occupied all day.

Gray light dulls everything but the tension in the room.

I have everything I need for a record-breaking settlement.

Relief should feel like a win.

Instead, I watch Seamus from the corner of my eye, trying to pretend today is routine. Standard. Nothing to make my pulse jump.

Ethan leans back in his chair, arms behind his head, a satisfied smile tugging at his mouth. "I'm telling you," he points at Seamus with his thumb, "if I ever get sued, I want this guy to sit for my deposition."

Seamus rolls his eyes, his expression casual in a way I haven't seen since I met him.

"Glad I could impress the audience," he says dryly.

I sip the last of my coffee—lukewarm now. Doesn't matter. I need something to occupy my hands, I'm too keyed up.

I should be celebrating too. He nailed it. Steady, precise, and careful with every word. Not too rehearsed. Not too defensive. Enough righteous frustration when he talked about what happened to Miranda.

He didn't even need to throw Caldwell under the bus outright. Anyone with a brain could ascertain who made the final decisions in the OR.

Best of all? Caldwell didn't show up.

The egomaniac couldn't be bothered. Instead, he let his attorney, Luther Young—with his smug, clinical questions—handle everything.

Seamus held his own and then some.

Ordinarily, after a deposition, I'd be gone right after. This afternoon I stayed to get more time with him by pretending to need a post-depo debrief.

Ignoring the fact I've spent the last few weeks picturing the way his hands would look as they skimmed my body. The way his blue eyes bored into mine when we kissed.

Hearing the desperate tone of his voice when he told me he masturbated thinking about me.

How I nearly cracked right open when he promised to prove I was beautiful.

Seamus hasn't brought any of it up since.

Does he still feel the same way?

It's hard to know. We've exchanged a few emails. Strictly professional. No innuendo. No flirting. Not even a winking emoji. I told myself it's what I wanted. What I needed. We're working together. He's not my client, but I'm relying on him. On his memory. His insight. His testimony.

I wore my hair down today. Paired a new black wrap dress with a crisp, hot-pink blazer and heels an inch taller than I normally wear. I want to tell myself I dressed like this to intimidate Luther.

I know better.

Seamus shifts in his chair. My eyes immediately flick to him without permission. Fitted gray sweater. Black jeans. Silent confidence pours off him in waves. He still looks tired—yet significantly less stressed than he did a few weeks ago.

When he catches me eyeballing him, he smiles and I swear something lodges in my throat.

Stop it, I tell myself. *Focus.*

Ethan glances at his watch. "Alright. I've got to head out. Cy got us tickets to a concert at Neumos and we're going to dinner first..."

He turns and leaves the room with a wave.

I shout after him. "Tell him thanks a million for stealing you away in the middle of a victory lap."

Ethan looks over his shoulder. "You've got this without me."

Silence settles again. Seamus's eyes track me as I pretend to collect papers, to organize notes that are already neatly filed. Anything to keep from meeting his gaze.

My phone buzzes against the table, saving me.

Until I glance down at the screen. *Mama.*

My heart drops. She never calls me at work. I swipe to answer. "Hey, everything okay?"

"Marcella, it's your father," she blurts out, high and tight.

I freeze.

I see in my periphery concern instantly darkens Seamus's expression.

"What about him?" I'm already grabbing my bag.

"He's okay. He's home. I guess he had one of those—what do they call it? A TIA? The doctor said it wasn't a stroke, but it could've been. They said it was a warning. He needs to rest. See a specialist—"

"I'm on my way." I jump up. "Are you with him?"

"It's fine, *mija*—" she starts to protest. I don't let her, reiterating my intention and hang up, heart hammering.

Seamus stands too. "I'll drive you."

"What?" Shocked, I shake my head. "No, you don't have to—"

"I know I don't have to." He steps closer. "You're upset. The road is going to be slick. Let me make sure you get there safely."

Something breaks in me at the steadiness in his voice. At the idea of someone other than my immediate family looking out for me. I nod once. "Fine. We're taking my car."

I glance out the window. Outside, the rain comes down in sheets. Seattle at its most biblical.

We take the elevator to the garage and my Audi hums to life as Seamus settles into the driver's seat, folding his large frame into the space with surprising ease. I clutch my purse tightly in my hand, envisioning the worst and mentally chastising myself for blowing family time off for so many months.

We don't speak as the car crawls through down I-5 rush hour traffic toward Tacoma. I stare as the rain streaks down the passenger window in steady, hypnotic rivulets. The wipers swoosh sheets of water from the windshield and I'm grateful to have Seamus focusing on the road while my mind jumps all over the place.

"She said it wasn't a full stroke," I murmur, mostly to myself. "She said he was up and talking."

Seamus nods, glancing at me briefly. "Sounds about right. If it was a TIA, those usually resolve quickly. The biggest concern is what it means for his risk going forward."

"You're not helping me feel better," I sigh.

"Sorry," he says soothingly. "Let me see if I can ease your mind. We just went through this in my family with my da. The good news is, if caught early and treated, it can prevent a real stroke. Medications. Diet. Maybe surgery depending on what they find. Try not to worry. This kind of event is a warning not a death sentence. Far from it."

I exhale through my nose, eyes scanning for the exit I know too well.

"Thanks for coming with me," I acknowledge after a beat. "You didn't have to."

He shifts in his seat. "I wanted to make sure you got here safely so you could be with your family."

"It's...sudden. He's not old. He's active. Last week he was losing his mind about shrimp prices." I manage a laugh, barely.

Traffic slows to a near halt. Brake lights stretch ahead in a glittering red snake. The sky's pitch black though it's barely five. Typical November.

Then, Seamus's right hand pats my knee and rests there. "He's gonna be okay."

His simple touch—steady, warm, grounding—cracks something open inside me I've been holding together with stubborn pride and metaphorical paperclips for years.

Seamus's hand on my knee isn't sexual. It's not overt. It's comfort. It's presence. It's the unspoken understanding of a man who doesn't expect me to be strong every second of the damn day.

For someone like me, who's built an entire life pretending I don't need this type of support... It's devastating.

Heat spirals up my spine. Not desire—at least, not only desire. It's something more dangerous. Terrifying.

I lean back and close my eyes. For a breath. For a moment.

Because right now, I need a small break.

The air between us is thick. Heavy. The kind of quiet making me hyperaware of everything—his presence, the way he smells faintly of cedar and spice. I feel him looking at me every so often, but stay exactly as I am. Afraid to break the spell.

"You haven't said anything about the deposition." His voice is soft. Curious.

I don't move a muscle. State the truth. "You were perfect."

"Seriously?" His eyes widen.

"Seriously." I allow myself to steal a glance at him, and something clenches in my chest. "You were clear, confident. You didn't take the bait. You kept the focus on Caldwell. I think Luther was caught off guard by what an excellent witness you were."

He exhales and slouches slightly and doesn't break contact with my knee. "So...what happens now?"

"I think they'll make an offer," I eke out. "A real one."

"If they don't?"

I grit my teeth. "Then we go to war."

"Wow." He chuckles under his breath. "Remind me not to get on your bad side."

"You already did. You're lucky I'm forgiving." My lips curl into a smile.

The moment lands between us—soft, teasing. Underneath it, something heavier simmers.

It's been five weeks since the night I confessed embarrassing truths I've never told anyone and heard things from him I still don't know how to process.

He told me I was beautiful. That he couldn't stop thinking about me. That he fantasized about me and jerked off to me every night, after I told him I'd never been loved. Not really. Not in the way I've always wanted. Hell, he knows my deepest secret—I've spent most of my life feeling like a loser at love.

Since then...radio silence. Emails, brief and businesslike. Dry. Because it had to be.

Didn't stop the dreams, though. If anything, they've become more vivid.

We reach the exit and I direct him all the way to the driveway of my parents' house. He barely manages to throw the car into park before I'm out the door and running up the walkway. He's not far behind.

When I burst into the house, familiar smells envelop me. Garlic. Wood polish. A hint of my mom's perfume—orange blossom and vanilla.

"Chellie!" My mother's voice rings out when she peeps out at us from the kitchen. "He's resting. He says he's fine. I made him tea and chicken soup. He's so *grumpy*."

Her eyes flick to Seamus behind me.

"Oh." She wipes her hands on a dish towel. "You brought a handsome young man."

"This is Seamus," I say. "He's a...colleague helping me with my case. I was upset and he offered to drive me here."

Seamus smiles and steps forward, extending a hand. "Nice to meet you, Mrs. Delgado."

"Call me Ana." She assesses him. "You're very tall."

He laughs. "So I've been told."

"He's a doctor—in his residency," I add, and her eyebrows shoot up.

She blatantly looks him up and down. "No wonder we haven't seen you in a while."

"Mama!" I'm mortified.

Seamus stifles a grin.

My father's voice cuts from the living room. "Ana, who's here?"

I rush to him before he can get up from the couch, crouching at his side. His face is pale, drawn. His eyes are as sharp as a knife.

"Hi, Papa." A tear leaks from the corner of my eye.

He brushes his fingers over my hair. "You didn't have to come all the way out here."

"Don't be ridiculous." I lean my head on his chest.

He kisses my head. "I'm fine."

"You need to take care of yourself. I won't survive if you're not around. What did they tell you?" I love my dad so much, this is such a wake-up call to spend more time with the people who are most important to me.

He sighs. "Give me my bourbon and let me die in peace."

"Luis," my mother scolds.

Seamus steps forward, hands in his pockets. "If it's okay, I can take a look at your discharge papers. I'm happy to answer any questions you might have."

"And you are?" My father lifts a brow then looks to me.

"Chellie's boyfriend. He's a doctor." My mother's voice further humiliates me.

I'm about to correct her when Seamus sits on the ottoman across from him. "Yes, sir."

"You look like you should still be in school." He scrunches his lips together.

"Papa." I squeeze my eyes shut, mortified.

"Technically, I am. Fourth year neurosurgery resident." Seamus chuckles. "Fair enough on the age thing. I get it a lot."

My mother hands Seamus a manila envelope, and he scans the pages quickly. "Your blood pressure was high. They'll want to monitor you for a while. They probably started you on aspirin?"

"Yep," my dad confirms.

"Did they talk to you about follow-ups? Maybe a carotid ultrasound?" Seamus glances up from the paperwork.

Papa nods. "I'm scheduled for the Monday after Thanksgiving."

Seamus explains the risks, how his father has recovered from a stroke, the signs to watch for, and the urgency of follow-up care in a way so thorough and calming, my parents actually listen.

He seems to walk on water.

We stay and visit for about an hour before my dad nods off. On the way out the door, my mom hugs both of us goodbye and shoves two Tupperware containers of flan into his hands.

"Take it," she insists. "Thank you."

As we walk back out into the dark, wet night, Seamus nudges me with his elbow. "See? I win over moms."

"You're impossible." I try to keep stoic, but my heart is swooning.

When we settle back in the car, with him at the wheel, he turns to me. "How are you doing?"

"Tired. It could've been worse. Thank you." I breathe out a sigh of relief.

He stares out the windshield for a beat. "I meant what I said, by the way. About how I feel about you. It's only gotten stronger."

Gravity shifts.

"I haven't been able to stop thinking about you. I know we set boundaries and—"

"*Seamus*," I interrupt before he can finish. "Let's get through the settlement."

He doesn't say anything for a long moment. Then leans back in his seat and whispers, almost to himself. "Okay. No promises when…"

He doesn't finish the sentence.

He doesn't need to.

Once this thing with Caldwell is done, I don't think anything will hold us back.

I'm terrified of what happens next.

Eighteen

Present Day

THE ROOM IS TOO quiet.

It shouldn't be. Not with the soft wheeze of machines still rhythmically pushing air into Miranda's lungs. Not with the low murmur of hospital sounds drifting in from the hallway.

Inside this room, with drawn blinds and dimmed lights, silence wins.

Marcella stands beside me, her arms crossed tightly over her chest like she's trying to hold herself together.

Surrounded by their family, Daniel and Myra Black hold Miranda's hands and each other, every breath they take ragged and fragile.

This is it. The end.

I can't save her.

I tried. Jesus, I tried.

Marcella's hand brushes mine, accidental, maybe. I take it as a sign and thread her fingers with mine. She grips me tightly and we stand there. Two ghosts in a room already haunted by what could've been.

Should've been.

The priest's voice breaks the silence. "Before we begin the final prayers, Miranda's parents wanted to share something with all of you."

Myra steps forward, a sheet of notebook paper clutched between her shaking fingers. Her voice quivers. "She wrote this last spring right before her operation. It was an assignment for her Language Arts class. We didn't think much of it at the time...now, it feels like she might have known."

She clears her throat. "It's called *If I Were a Whisper*.'"

If I were a whisper, I'd sneak
into hearts

To leave little glimmers

Of light in the dark.

I'd ride on the wind

When the thunder is loud,

And curl into corners

When no one's around.

I'd never be seen,

But I'd always be near—

A whisper of hope

To chase away fear.

My chest caves in. Tears flow freely down my face.

Daniel, who's been pretty stoic this afternoon, can't hold it together either. He lets out a harsh, guttural sob, pressing his face into his wife's shoulder. Myra shakes in his arms.

My throat burns. I have to look away.

The priest steps forward again, calm. Steady. "We now commend Miranda's spirit."

Several colleagues take charge and then the machines stop. Miranda slips away quickly.

Though I knew exactly what would happen, it's like a punch to the chest. The absence of sound. Of breath. Of everything.

Marcella clutches my hand, silently sobbing.

Daniel turns to us, eyes bloodshot and red-rimmed. "Thank you both. For being here. For everything."

Marcella nods, her voice gone.

"She mattered to me," I barely manage to utter.

Marcella and I leave the room so her family can have a few final moments of privacy before they transport Miranda away. I head toward the east wing—one of the older parts of the hospital currently closed for renovation.

It's instinct, not strategy. I need to be somewhere quiet and away from anyone I know. Somewhere away from the grief clinging to my skin.

Marcella follows, silent.

We step into a vacant room, air tinged with a faint scent of antiseptic. The equipment's been cleared out. The bed and furniture remains.

"This okay?" I turn toward her.

"Yeah." Marcella sits on the edge of the bed and buries her face in her hands.

Her shoulders start to shake. I kneel in front of her.

"Hey," I repeat gently. "You okay?"

Stupid question.

She chokes out, "I've never watched someone die. She didn't deserve it."

"I know and you fought hard for her." I stand and then sit next to her.

Marcella sobs. "Forty million dollars means nothing if it won't bring her back."

"It does mean something." I smooth the hair back from her face. "Maybe it keeps this from happening again. I know it's changed me forever."

She stares at me for a long moment. "You really believe that?"

"I have to." I bite my lip as a tear escapes.

She reaches for me and we cling to each other in sorrow.

Her guttural cries wreck me though I can't stop either. Marcella's embrace is the only thing keeping me sane. Her head fits perfectly in the crook of my neck and I close my eyes, breathing her in. She smells like vanilla and heartbreak.

We stay cuddled together until we cry ourselves out.

When she finally pulls back, her face is blotchy, mascara smudged. Utterly the most beautiful woman I've ever seen.

I can't bring myself to regret we're together like this, even if grief is what cracked us open. I reach for her hand and squeeze. "She would have changed the world."

"She already did," Marcella murmurs. "She changed ours."

We stay quiet for a bit.

She turns toward me, her eyes unreadable. "I keep thinking about the look in her mother's eyes when the monitors flatlined. Like something in her own soul had been unplugged."

"Brutal." I nod slowly, remembering the moment vividly. The priest finishing the blessing. Miranda's mother, unable to move. Her father rubbing his hands over his face like he could physically push the pain away. "I wanted to do something. Say something. There aren't any words to make it better."

Marcella exhales. "It's the worst thing I've ever been through. I'm also glad we were there. We needed to be."

She looks up at me and I see the weight she's been carrying—the long hours, the pressure of this case, her own loss. Something about her vulnerability hits me so hard I feel like the air's been knocked out of my lungs.

"How's your dad?" I stop myself. "Sorry. I know now isn't the time..."

"He's better," she says softly. "Getting checked again next week. You coming to Tacoma with me meant a lot."

"I was glad to." I wonder if she's missed me as much as I've missed her. We haven't really spoken other than to coordinate today.

Her eyes search mine. "You didn't have to."

"You didn't have to let me." I meet her gaze, questioning. Hoping.

The moment shifts.

Marcella tilts her head slightly and my eyes follow the curve of her cheek. The way her mouth trembles before she tries to steel herself again. Always so composed. So in control.

Except now.

Now she looks at me as though she's unraveling from the inside out—and I get it. I am too.

I lean toward her an inch. Close enough to feel her breath when it stutters out. My hand lifts slowly, cupping her jaw. I brush my thumb against the soft skin below her cheekbone. Her eyes flicker shut for half a second, like the touch undoes her.

When they open again, there's a question in them. A warning.

She doesn't pull away.

I don't say anything because I can't drag my eyes from her beautiful face. I'm trying not to give in to how much I want her. Not only her body. Her mind. Her voice. The parts she tries to hide.

"I haven't let anyone in like this in a long time," she admits. Her tone is raw. Honest. "Not since I didn't think it was worth it."

"You're worth it."

"Seamus." She swallows.

My name on her lips is my undoing. "I meant everything I said. About how I see you. I still can't stop thinking about you."

"This doesn't make any sense." Her breath hitches as she gestures between us.

"Maybe not," I whisper. "And yet, it does make sense."

I reach up, brush her hair back, and she closes her eyes.

"I can't think," she whispers. "When you're this close."

"Then don't think." I lean in, slow and deliberate, until her lips are right there—soft, trembling. Inches from mine.

When our mouths finally meet, it's not rushed or frantic. It's not needy or wild.

It's reverent.

A slow slide of her pillowy lips against mine. Warm. Careful. Unbelievably tender.

I feel her breath hitch when I angle my head and brush my mouth against hers like I've been dreaming about for months. This kiss has been building since the second I saw her—since the second she shattered every expectation I had and rebuilt it into something I never saw coming.

Her hand curls into the fabric of my shirt. Not pushing me away—holding on. Christ, I feel it everywhere. The heat. The ache. The impossible rightness of this.

When her lips part and I taste more of her, I swear it almost drops me to my knees. It's a promise. One I feel in the center of my chest—steady and deep and terrifying as hell.

When our kiss deepens and becomes more urgent, my hands find her waist. Hers thread through my hair. When we finally pull apart, both of us are breathing like we've run a marathon.

Marcella's eyes are wide and glassy. Her breathing is shaky. "We shouldn't."

"Tell me to stop." I call her bluff.

She hesitates. Then she doesn't, kissing me again. Harder this time.

My hands skim her back and I pull her closer. She gasps when I lift her into my lap. Her skirt rides up and she doesn't seem to care. I'm drowning in her. In *us*.

As fast as it starts, she breaks the kiss, pulling back, her hands on my chest.

"No. We can't." Her voice cracks. "Not like this. Not tonight."

I breathe hard, nodding, even as I try to slow my pulse. "Okay. Okay."

She scrambles off my lap and starts to pace, her arms crossed over her chest.

"I'm sorry," she says. "I shouldn't have."

I stand too, closing the distance between us. "We didn't do anything wrong."

"I'm afraid of what it means." She looks at me, conflicted.

"Why are you afraid?"

Her shoulders fall. "What if it means *everything*? Only for it to end?"

"We won't let it. End." I reach for her hand.

She squeezes my fingers. Then let's go.

We stand there in silence for a moment longer until she crushes me. "No. We can't. Not now. Not *ever*."

"Marcella…"

"It's not right." She smooths her skirt.

"I don't agree, maybe…"

"No maybes. It's wrong." She steps away, flustered.

This pisses me off immensely. Not because I'm mad at her. I hate she feels like I'll let her down. "Why doesn't it feel wrong? For me, being with you feels inevitable."

She whirls around. "No, being with you is a *problem*."

Then she's marching toward the exit.

"Marcella."

She doesn't turn around. Instead, pushes through the door and I hear her heels clicking down the hallway toward the elevator.

I grab my phone and text her.

Me: Come back.

I wait. Every second feels like an hour. I'm convinced Marcella hasn't seen my text or worse, she's seen and ignored it.

Then I hear something.

Heels. Echoing down the hall. Getting closer.

The door swings open and she's back—eyes wild, breath shallow, fire in every step.

She doesn't speak. Neither do I. Her mouth finds mine and nothing else exists.

No courtroom. No hospital. No rules.

Only this.

The inevitability we've been circling finally breaks.

I know with gut-deep certainty—

Marcella was *always* mine.

Nineteen

MARCELLA

Present Day

I SHOULD HATE HIM.

After what happened. After what I'm about to do.

The hallway seems endlessly long.

Fluorescent lights above flicker faintly, casting long shadows on the sterile walls.

My heels click against the polished floor, the sound sharp and echoing in the emptiness. This has been the worst day of my life. Unbelievable grief. Confusing emotions.

The air is thick, charged, like the calm before a storm.

I see a sliver of light seeping out of the room. My feet move on their own, drawn to it like a moth to a flame. The door is slightly ajar. I push it open, my breath catching in my throat.

The stark room is bathed in warm, golden light, a stark contrast to the cold, clinical hallway. A hospital bed sits in the center, and perched on the edge is Seamus. Right where I left him.

His longish, wavy hair falls into his face, the brown strands catch the light as his piercing blue eyes lock on to mine. He wears blue scrubs, the fabric clings to his muscular frame making my stomach flip.

A slow, knowing smile spreads across his face, and my heart skips a beat.

"*Marcella*." His deep tone is like velvet.

I should turn around and leave again. This is wrong. My feet won't move. Instead, I step inside and the door clicks shut behind me. I can't tear my eyes away from him.

"I shouldn't be here," I whisper and swallow hard.

I *want* to be here. My nipples pebble under his heated stare. Arousal soaks my panties.

Seamus stands, slow and deliberate and takes a step toward me. "You should." He takes my hand without breaking eye contact. "You want this as much as I do."

I open my mouth to deny it. The words won't come. He's absolutely right. I *have* been thinking about him nonstop. For too long. Now, we're close enough for me to smell the faint scent of his cologne—warm and woodsy, with a hint of spice.

His free hand cups my cheek tenderly. I shiver at the contact.

"You're so beautiful," he murmurs, his gaze roaming over my face. "So sexy in your power suit. Your warrior princess armor."

"I don't know what you're talking about." I try to step back, never comfortable being assessed this way.

"Yes, you do." He rakes his eyes up and down my body appreciatively. "You hide behind the wall you've built. Afraid to let anyone see the real you. I do, Marcella. I see you and tonight, I want *all* of you."

His words cut through me, stripping away the layers of defense I've built over the years. I'm exposed, vulnerable, and yet...I know I won't run anymore. I've been fantasizing about this moment for too long. I *want* to be here with Seamus.

He steps closer, his body inches from mine. Heat radiates off him. My breath hitches as his hand slides down to my hip, his touch firm but gentle.

"You don't have to be afraid," he whispers, his lips brushing against my ear. "I'm gonna take care of you."

I close my eyes, my mind spinning. This is inappropriate. Morally. Ethically. Except, my body responds to him instinctively, leaning into his touch, craving more. He tilts my chin up, forcing me to meet his gaze.

"Tell me you want this," he drawls like liquid sex. "Tell me you want *me*."

I should say no. I should push him away. The words coming out of my mouth are the opposite.

"Yes," I whisper. "I want you more than anything."

"Thank Christ. I can't resist you." His lips crash down on mine, and the world tilts.

The kiss is fierce, hungry. It steals the breath from my lungs and sends sparks through me like I've never known. When his hands move to my hips to pull me to him, I instinctively flinch and he leans back, concerned.

Goddammit. My insecurities always fuck things up. Why am I so self-conscious? Aware of every extra pound. My arms cross over my stomach as I shift uncomfortably under his intense gaze.

"Please don't hide. Let me worship you." He nuzzles my ear and yanks me flush against the hard plane of his body. "You deserve pleasure. Your curves are *exquisite*."

I melt into him, hands tangling in his hair. Seamus's lips press against mine with slow, deliberate intensity. His tongue traces the seam of my mouth before he deepens the kiss, exploring every curve and contour with a hunger leaving me breathless and trembling.

When he finally breaks the kiss and looks down at me with dark, smoldering eyes, his hands slide to the front of my blazer and he unbuttons it. "You're perfect. Every inch of you."

I glance around the empty hospital room, the sterile scent of antiseptic lingering in the air, mixing with the heat radiating off him. The silence is unnerving, amplifying the sound of my own unsteady breathing.

"Are you sure about this?" I whisper, my fingers curling into his shirt as I look up at him. "Won't someone come in?"

Seamus's lips twitch, yet there's something serious in his gaze. "This floor is being renovated next week. It's been cleared of all patients and staff." He drags a slow hand down my back, grounding me. "The bed's clean. Sterile." He leans in, his breath warm against my ear. "No one's coming. No one will hear us. No one will ever know we've been here."

Then his lips are on my neck, trailing hot, open-mouthed kisses down to my collarbone until I can't think anymore. My blazer falls to the floor, followed by my blouse, and his hands are everywhere, exploring, claiming. Deft fingers unclasp my bra, peeling the cups away, exposing my puckered nipples.

He drinks in the sight of me, causing a flush to rise from my chest.

"You have most luscious breasts I've ever seen," he breathes.

Seamus cups them in his palms, swiping his thumbs across my peaks. I gasp because I've visualized him doing this to me so many times. Now it's happening and the actual sensation arrows straight to my core.

He lowers his head, taking one nipple deep into the wet heat of his mouth. I cry out, pleasure spiking as he sucks me, nibbling then laving it with his tongue before switching to the other. He takes his time, worshiping them until I'm writhing and flushed, shamelessly moaning with pleasure.

When he finally lifts his head, my nipples are swollen and glistening.

"I need to taste the rest of you," he rasps.

His strong hands smooth down my sides, tracing the dip of my waist and flare of my hips with appreciation. He unzips my skirt and lets it drop to the ground before plunging his fingers down the front of my panties.

"God. You're so wet for me," Seamus growls, gaze locked on his fingers dragging through my glistening folds.

He places one hand low on my belly, making me acutely aware of every soft curve. There's no judgment in his eyes, only hot, avid hunger. He lifts me effortlessly onto the crisp, white hospital bed and lays me down gently.

His eyes never leave mine as he removes his scrubs, revealing a body even more breathtaking than I imagined. His muscles are defined. Skin golden, smooth and warm. Good Lord, his thick, gorgeous cock juts out proudly.

Much bigger than I ever comprehended.

I want to touch him. He catches my hand and intertwines our fingers, leaning down to kiss me again. This time, it's slower, more tender, and it makes my chest ache with something I can't name. His free hand trails down my side, leaving a trail of fire in its wake, and I arch into his touch, craving more.

Seamus moves to the base of the bed and seizes my ankles. "I'm gonna worship your pussy for a while. I've never wanted anything so badly."

His words send a shiver down my spine, and I feel tears prick at the corners of my eyes. No man has ever looked at me like this. Like I'm something precious. Something to be cherished.

For the first time in my thirty-seven years, I let myself believe it to be true.

Seamus presses my thighs up, exposing my soaking folds with his thumbs. The first wet stroke of his tongue against my clit wrests a strangled cry from my throat. He moans into my heat, like I'm the tastiest treat he's ever eaten.

"So responsive," he rumbles against my slick flesh. "Fucking delicious."

He takes his time, exploring every inch of my pussy, lapping up my juices and swirling his tongue around my swollen bud again and again, winding me tighter. Two long fingers slide into my channel, pumping slowly, curling against a spot deep inside I've never been able to locate.

In seconds, I'm mindless with pleasure, bucking into his mouth wantonly, chasing the ecstasy he's stoking. I'm out of control. My hips rock in time with his clever fingers and sinful tongue. When he sucks hard on my clit, I fly apart, screaming his name as my walls clamp around him greedily.

He continues to explore every inch of my pussy with his hands and mouth, until I'm mindless and floating from coming over and over again. I'm writhing, so overstimulated I can't take one more minute yet Seamus manages to wring one more shudder from me before withdrawing his fingers.

The Orgasm Whisperer. I get it now. His reputation is well earned.

Soothingly, he presses kisses to my inner thighs before rising up and wiping his glistening mouth.

This time when I reach for him, he guides my hand to grasp his thick cock. "Yeah. Touch me."

I feel clumsy and hesitant. Seamus is patient, coaxing. He shows me exactly how he likes it, his deft fingers covering mine. Together we stroke his impressive length, from root to tip. His velvety skin burns against my palm, pulsing with his rapid heartbeat. His eyes are heavy-lidded. Mouth slack. He grunts in short, throaty bursts to my rhythm.

Seeing him lost to pleasure, muscles taut, head thrown back as he rocks into my fist—it's the most erotic sight I've ever witnessed. I feel powerful, bringing this sexy man to the brink.

Seamus stops me before he hits his peak. "I don't want to come like this. I'd like to be inside you."

Wait, what? Is he really choosing me? Why?

"Do you want a condom? I'm on the pill. I'm clean..." I hear myself saying. "Are you sure?"

"I *am* sure. I've never been more sure of anything in my life." He notches his cock at my entrance, watching in awe as he slowly sinks into my body, stretching me exquisitely. A helpless whimper escapes both of us simultaneously.

He fills me completely. Like I'm meant for him.

Seamus sets a sensual pace, each deep thrust winding me tighter. I moan encouragement, lost to the unbelievable sensations of fucking the man I've wanted more than anything. Somehow he manages to hit the same perfect spot inside me over and over with every roll of his hips.

"Oh, yeah. Clench around me, baby," he gasps. "God. I never imagined...ah *yeah*."

My walls instinctively squeeze his driving cock. We move together in perfect sync, panting and moaning. The room is filled with the erotic slap of flesh on flesh, the musky scent of our sex.

"Look at me," Seamus demands. Our eyes lock as the tension crests. I shatter completely, waves of intense release crashing over me. Seeing me come undone triggers his own climax. He shouts my name, spilling deep inside me.

Spent, he collapses on top of me, sweat-slicked and sated. We stay joined for a while until he softens and slips out. He shifts to curve his body around me protectively and wind me tightly in his embrace, my back to his front. Presses a tender kiss to my shoulder as our breathing slows.

He's heat and hunger and every mistake I swore I'd never make.

I have no regrets.

For once—

Being ruined feels right.

Twenty

Same Day

She hasn't moved.

Neither have I.

Her skin is still warm against mine, flushed from release, glowing in the dim light. Her breathing's quiet. Controlled. Like she's trying not to give something away.

My fingers trace a slow path along the curve of her hip.

It's the only place I let myself touch her now—gentle, steady, safe. The last thing I want is to make her feel exposed. I already sense she's pulling herself tight, wrapping up whatever we just shared in armor before I even get a chance to speak.

She's probably convincing herself this was a mistake.

It wasn't.

I've thought about this moment longer than I should probably admit. Fantasized about it. About her. The power in her voice. The way her mouth moves when she argues. The confidence in her stride. The way she looks at me when she doesn't think I notice.

I once imagined how she'd sound. How she'd taste. How it would feel to be inside her—tight, wet, velvet heat wrapped around my cock like she was made to fit me.

The fantasy didn't come close.

Nothing in my imagination prepared me for the way her body clutched at mine, the way she gave in without losing herself, the way she made me feel like I was finally home.

I waited for her.

Not because I had to. Because I *knew*.

Knew if I ever gave myself away, it would be like this—devastating in the best way. No—

Sacred.

Marcella Delgado didn't steal my virginity. I gave it to her. Deliberately. Without hesitation. Like a vow I never needed to say out loud.

I don't regret a thing.

She shifts slightly, but she doesn't roll away. Doesn't speak.

I keep my hand steady, gearing myself up for...

Ahhh. If she tries to say this meant nothing, I won't fight her. Not yet.

I'll prove it. Every day if I have to.

She's it for me.

Even if she runs—

I'm not letting her go.

Twenty-One

MARCELLA

WHAT THE HELL AM I doing?

Lying against Seamus in an abandoned hospital room, his fingers tracing slow patterns over my hip.

This isn't what I came here for.

This isn't what people like me get to experience.

Right now, I don't want to move. Everything's quiet, save for the hum of overhead lights and the occasional creak of aging pipes. The sterile scent of disinfectant clings to the air—a jarring contrast to the raw, intimate thing we've done.

We had sex. Real, actual sex.

Not *just* sex—it was Seamus's first time.

He could have chosen anyone and he gave his virginity to me—a nearly forty-year-old, body-negative, jaded professional who's been convinced men like him didn't exist outside of her dreams.

I don't know what to do with this kind of devotion—if it's for real—so, for now, I lie here tensely, trying to breathe around it.

Seamus shifts slightly to his side and his hand cups the soft curve of my belly—my most guarded, resented part. With quiet confidence he caresses me there. Stroking. Touching. He's not repulsed. The knowledge of which nearly undoes me.

Unlike other lovers, there's no hesitation. Or avoidance. Flinch of disgust. His elegant, precise surgeon's fingers, which manipulated my body into multiple orgasms, exploring the abundant curves I've spent years trying to shrink, flatten, and make disappear.

I tense, instinctively.

He doesn't move. Or let go. His thumb drags a slow, reverent line over my skin, like he's mapping a place he has no intention of forgetting.

It's too much. Too intimate. I'm trying to be comfortable in his arms on the thin mattress. *Impossible*. I'm naked. He's naked. We're in a damn abandoned hospital room like some ill-conceived fantasy. Is this even hygienic? Won't there be security guards?

My brain is spiraling and Seamus seems entirely at peace, his mouth-watering body long and sprawled out like he owns the place.

"Are you always this comfortable being naked in public places?" I mutter, trying to pull the sheet up to cover my chest as discreetly as I can.

He glances at me with a lazy, satisfied grin. "Not always. I'm feeling pretty good right now, though. What happened was incredible. *You're* incredible."

"Like you'd know. I'm your only frame of reference." I snort, trying to pretend like the compliment doesn't make my insides flutter.

"Well," his hand glides over my thigh, "as far as I'm concerned, it was perfect. I'm ready for round two."

My smile doesn't quite reach my eyes. The truth is, I'm not some wildly experienced femme fatale who's had dozens of lovers and years of practiced confidence.

Not even close.

If we're being technical, Seamus has more hands-on experience than I ever have. More bodies. More skin. More ways of making someone feel good.

What guts me a little—catches me right in the center of my chest—is why he chose *me*. With all the women who've thrown themselves at him over the years, he could have had anyone. Clearly, he thought of his virginity as something sacred. He picked *me* for his final step.

I'll always have that honor.

I'm not sure how to feel. I never thought I'd be in this position. I've spent my life trying to be smart and capable and good, I don't allow myself to want. Or believe I could be wanted like *this*.

There's no way I'll make this moment about me, though, so I smack his chest playfully. "You're incorrigible."

He catches my wrist and kisses the inside of it, and I swear my heart skips a beat. Then props himself up on one elbow and the sheet shifts off us.

Lying bare beside him, I'm painfully aware of how my body settles. My breasts—heavy and full—spread slightly to the sides, the weight of them unmistakable against my ribcage. They've always felt like too much. Under his gaze, my nipples pucker, making me more aware of every inch of myself.

I breathe slowly, trying to keep still. The rise and fall of my chest gives me away. I feel exposed in every possible way—yet I don't move to cover myself. For once, I resist the urge to hide.

"Marcella," his thumb traces the edge of my jaw, "are you okay?"

I blink, taken off guard. "Yeah. I...someone could walk in."

He chuckles. "I told you. No one's using this floor. You saw the signs—'Renovation Begins January 1st.' We have, what? Three weeks? Think of the damage we could do to this bed."

"Stop." I laugh, then bite my lip. "Seriously, though. We should go."

Seamus brushes a lock of hair from my face. "Come to my place. I'll make dinner. Or order dinner. Whatever you want. I'm not ready for this to be over."

I open my mouth, then close it again.

Come to his place? The idea sends a bolt of panic and excitement through me. I don't know what I expected to happen. It certainly wasn't him wanting more.

If anything, I figured he'd already be gone.

"I'm sweaty and my hair's a mess," I stall.

"You're perfect," he says without hesitation. "If you're more comfortable at your place, I'll come with you."

My eyebrows lift. "You want to come over?"

"I want more. I want to give you more." He kisses me sweetly. "Anywhere you are is where I want to be."

I blink, thrown. I've heard a lot of lines in my life—some sweet, some gross, some downright manipulative. Seamus? He's not laying it on thick. He's being honest.

"I don't know what to do with you," I whisper, almost to myself.

He smiles. "Oh, I have some ideas. Let me show you."

God help me.

We get dressed slowly. Well, I do. Seamus slips his scrub pants back on with zero urgency, like we didn't shatter every professional boundary known to man. He moves with this lazy confidence, like he's got nowhere to be but here, bare-chested and entirely too at ease.

Meanwhile, I'm wrestling with my bra and trying to slide into my suit skirt without flashing him. My blouse is wrinkled, buttons all out of order, and I'm painfully aware of the way my hair's probably a mess and my lipstick's long gone. I'm used to commanding courtrooms in this outfit. Now I'm hoping I don't trip over my heels on the way out.

He watches me with a lazy kind of amusement, his gaze fond and hot all at once.

"You're staring," I mumble, fumbling with the zipper on my skirt.

"I like what I see." He waggles his eyebrows. "I'm curious why you're trying to hide yourself when I was inside your body twenty minutes ago."

"I'm *not* hiding," I lie.

He raises a brow.

"I'm not used to parading around naked in abandoned buildings." I pout.

Seamus laughs and pulls on his scrub top like he's got all the time in the world. The picture of unbothered. Meanwhile, I'm adjusting my blazer and trying not to freak out in the wake of what we did.

It's not the sex causing me to spiral—it's everything around it. The uncertainty.

His eyes flick over to me with a lazy, post-orgasm grin. It's infuriating how damn good he looks for someone who had his first time in an abandoned hospital room.

"So...I've got some time off," he says casually, like we're colleagues making small talk. "Have to burn it before the year ends."

I glance at him skeptically. "Didn't you take time off for the settlement?"

"Yeah, I didn't realize how little PTO I've used over the past few years. I still have more than two weeks I haven't touched. They won't roll over to next year. This lawsuit shit aside, residency is chaos." He shrugs. "So, I'm off until January."

"Must be nice," I murmur, trying to smooth my hair into place.

He watches me for a beat. "Do you ever take time off?"

"Sure. I've been leaving early every Friday to drive to Tacoma before rush hour," I say. "After Dad's health scare, I realized how important it is to prioritize my family a bit more."

He nods slowly. "Yeah, Sunday nights are McGloughlin family dinner nights. Whoever's in town shows up. It's the one good meal I eat each week. Ma's a great cook."

I'm caught off guard by the softness in his voice. "It's been good," I admit. "Needed, really."

He fixes me with the quiet, steady look he's so good at. His confidence makes me feel like I'm standing too close to the sun.

"I was thinking." He helps me on with my coat. "Maybe we could spend some time together."

I pause, surprised by how easily the words land. He's not asking for a weekend hookup. There's something intentional about the way he puts it. Like he's not trying to impress me—he's trying to *be* with me.

"It's the holidays. Don't you have plans?" I ask, hedging.

"As I said. Sunday dinner at my folks." He smirks. "A little Christmas shopping for the kids."

His casualness makes me laugh, and he smiles wider, like he's been waiting to hear it.

"You're serious?" I ask. "You want to spend time on your break with me?"

He raises an eyebrow. "Marcella, I had the most meaningful moment of my life with you. I'm not exactly rushing to fill my calendar with other things. Not if we can get to know each other better. Fuck like rabbits, of course."

I look away, pulse fluttering. I'm not used to this—being wanted without a catch.

"I mean," he adds, gentler now, "unless you're a one-and-done kinda girl."

"Not even close," I murmur.

He leans in and tugs one of the buttons on my blazer. "Good. 'Cause I'm not sure I'll ever be done with you."

The air shifts a little as we gather our things. I glance at the spot on the bed where we went at it and my fear about what happened gives way to a strange mix of vulnerability and awe.

He chose me.

Despite everything—our age difference, my plump body, the roadblocks I've thrown at him, and this lawsuit, we're here. Together.

He opens the door and holds it for me. As we step into the quiet hallway he takes my hand and our fingers lace together like it's natural.

"I'll drive." I glance up at him. "So, yes. You can come over."

I wait for the distance—the exit, the cold change I've come to expect.

It doesn't come.

A grin spreads across his face so bright it makes my heart skedaddle all over the place. He looks at me like I'm *everything*.

Like this isn't the time when it ends.

Like maybe this is how we begin.

Twenty-Two

Two Mornings Later

Jesus. God.

I'm so glad I waited for her.

Nothing could've prepared me for this. Not books. Not theories. Not every stairwell encounter I thought would protect me from experiencing something real.

We're sprawled across Marcella's bed, limbs tangled and sheets rumpled around us. The only light in the room comes from her bedside lamp, dim and golden, casting flickering shadows every time one of us moves.

Her head rests on my chest and her hand absently trails over my ribs. I've lost track of how many times we've done the deed this weekend. It doesn't matter. It's never enough and never the same. We've fucked. Made love. Screwed. Melded. Banged. Tangled. Humped. Railed. Merged.

Every time with her feels like a new discovery, like my body has been waiting my whole life to learn hers.

She shifts slightly, brushing her lips against my shoulder, then turns her face up to look at me. Her hair is a mess, cheeks flushed, eyes heavy-lidded and bright with mischief.

"You know," she murmurs, "you really need to illuminate how you're this good."

I grin. "Good at what? Cuddling?"

"You know exactly what I mean." She arches a brow, and I can see she's fighting a smile. "No matter how much you explained it to me, there's no way to comprehend your skill until...I mean, I can't fathom how you were a virgin before this weekend."

I kiss her temple. "Maybe it's less about the clinical stuff and more about wanting to give pleasure. Or, it's instinct. Who knows."

Her laugh is soft and low. "It's *not* instinct, Seamus. It's practice. Technique. Clinical-level knowledge. You know what you're doing and you know exactly how to do it." Her fingers press lightly into my side. "Tell me."

I trace a lazy circle on her bare hip, thinking.

"It's not magic," I say eventually. "I studied."

Marcella lifts herself onto her elbow, fully interested. "I know, I know. I've heard the cliff notes. Give me the deep dive. Studied how?"

"I've never taken much time to analyze my motives until this lawsuit. By med school, I ended up becoming obsessed with how little people knew about women's sexuality." I try to articulate my inner thoughts. "I still am, in a way." I take a second to think. "I guess it really originated with my classmates...men always come. Always *expect* to come."

She watches me, silent now, the teasing gone from her expression.

"I hadn't really paid much attention before then. Then it became so fucking obvious. Guys walk around like they're God's gift to women in bed and they don't even care where the damn clitoris is," I fume. "It's so stupid. Selfish. I didn't want to be one of them."

Marcella presses her lips together. "Go on."

"So, I started reading more. Research. Clinical studies. Old theories, new theories. Stuff Freud said got women labeled as frigid because they didn't orgasm from intercourse alone." I snort. "Don't get me started."

"I mean..." She tilts her head, lips twitching. "He was kind of a dick."

"Right? Then I came across this theory from a French princess—Marie Bonaparte. She believed some women couldn't orgasm during intercourse because their clit was too far from the vaginal opening."

Marcella's brow furrows. "Wait, *what*?"

"Yeah. She actually had surgery. Multiple times. Tried to reposition it so she could experience orgasm from penetration alone." I wince at the idea, surgery back then was a little barbaric.

"Jesus." She's fully upright now, sitting with one leg folded beneath her. The sheet falls away from her chest revealing a dark nipple, and I try to stay focused on the conversation.

"She wasn't the only one. Researchers tracked what they called the CUMD—the clitoris-to-urethra distance," I continue. "They found women with shorter distances had a higher chance of reaching orgasm during intercourse. Even then, it was never a guarantee."

She stares at me for a beat, wide-eyed. "You're telling me you read clinical studies to figure out how to get women off."

"Anatomy is kind of my thing." I let my hand trail up her spine. "If I wasn't set on neurosurgery, I'd probably be an OBGYN."

Her cheeks flush pink. "You're insane. In a good way."

"From what I've heard, most guys treat sex like a formula—insert my cock into her pussy, pound until I come. It's no wonder so many women fake orgasms when their pleasure is so much more nuanced. It's not only about mechanics—it's trust, attention, attunement. You have to listen."

"You really are the Orgasm Whisperer." She bats her eyelashes at me.

"Yeah…well, it's not so complicated. I don't know why men aren't more curious about their partner's pleasure." I pause.

Marcella looks at me like I've told her I'm from another planet.

Ah. It's time for the million-dollar question. One I need to get answered before she and I take this much further. "Does it bother you? I've…experimented with a lot of women."

"I don't think so," she says slowly. "I mean, numbers are numbers. We both have them. It explains a lot, actually. The way you touch me, I feel like my body isn't even mine—it's yours, in the best possible way."

A flush creeps up my neck. Her honesty always hits me like a punch in the chest.

She runs a hand through her hair. "You know what's wild?"

"What?"

"At dinner I confided something to you I've never told anyone. I spent years assuming there was something wrong with me. Convinced other women knew something I didn't. I thought I was too hard to please. My mind was too complicated to let go." She swallows. "Of course, mainly I struggle with a deep-seated belief: if I were thinner or more conventionally desirable, my past lovers would have taken the time to learn me. I would have been worth it. I've carried insecurities around my sexuality for years—you've opened my eyes a bit. I thought they took what they wanted and I let them. Maybe it wasn't so personal."

"Of course it's personal." This angers me. I sit up, legs crossed, facing her. "You're not complicated. You're not hard to please. They were lazy." Her eyes glisten, and I reach forward, brushing my fingers down her jaw. "You're not some puzzle to solve, Marcella. You're a woman who deserves to be worshipped. Touched with care. Looked at like you're fucking art."

She looks away. I don't let her retreat. I tuck a strand of hair behind her ear.

"I wish I knew...before," she murmurs.

"Well," I say softly. "I'm telling you now."

We sit in the quiet for a beat until she exhales. "I don't get it, Seamus. You're not a callous asshole. It's hard to reconcile. You studied all of this. Applied it. Perfected it. For what? Random stairwell hook-ups?"

Wow. Her words sting. I deserve it.

"I thought I could separate it," I admit. "Use what I learned without getting attached. Give someone pleasure and then walk away, no strings."

She raises an eyebrow.

"Obviously, I was completely wrong, as you pointed out. The truth is—I was lonely. Medical school is a long road. Neurosurgery is even longer. Things are different with you, Marcella. I want more with you."

The air shifts. Something deeper settles between us. Marcella reaches out and wraps an arm around my neck, her forehead rests against mine as she takes hold of my cock. "You're a goddamn unicorn, Seamus."

"I've been called worse." I suck in a breath.

She presses her lips to mine, slow and lingering. When she pulls back, she says, "For the record, I'm honored you chose me to be your first."

"Let's go for twenty, no fifty more times tonight." I buck into her hand.

She rolls her eyes. "God, you're obnoxious."

"You love it."

"I really might."

Marcella lies back on the bed, hair fanned out like a halo, curves soft and plush and goddamn perfect. Her lips are swollen from kissing. Her nipples tight.

I've made her come so many times I've lost count. Now, I want to go deeper. Show her what I've learned—not from a textbook, not from some article—from intuition. Dedication to loving her body. Show her the pleasure it gives me to tease out every gasp, every twitch, every moan. Make her *believe* in the satisfaction I feel every time her thighs tremble and she breathes my name like it's the only word she remembers.

I drag my palm slowly down her belly, letting it rest above the soft patch of hair between her thighs. She shivers. It's not cold. It's anticipation.

"Right. Let's consider this extra credit." I slide two fingers between her folds and find her already slick. "I've been taking really good notes."

Her breath catches when I press my thumb to her clit—barely. Not rubbing, not circling. Just holding. Applying the right amount of pressure. Enough to keep her poised in a delicious limbo between tension and need.

"I figured out something about you," I murmur, dipping my head to kiss the inside of her thigh. "You like a slow build. You think you don't. Your body tells me otherwise."

She exhales shakily. "I can't believe you're analyzing me like I'm your research project."

"No, I'm learning the woman who means the world to me. It helps you're my favorite study." I grin against her skin.

Her hips jerk when I finally press my tongue to her clit, not softly—intentionally. Slow, firm laps, interspersed with the occasional flick, the occasional pull with my lips.

She moans, her hands flying to my hair. I gently pin her hips down, holding her in place so I can truly see what her body wants. Her thighs fight to close around my head, but I growl and press them apart.

"Stay open for me, baby," I murmur, breath hot against her.

She nods, eyes wide, lips parted.

Then I switch it up—two fingers slip inside her, curling forward while my tongue strokes in rhythm. Her whole body arches. Her special spot. I've mapped it for hours.

Every time I feel it and witness how she comes undone? Nothing compares.

"There," I whisper, watching her. "I've found it, haven't I?"

"Yes," she chokes out. "Seamus, Jesus—don't stop."

"I wouldn't dream of it." I resume my favorite task.

She grabs for me, not to push away—to ground herself. Her fingers curl into my forearm as I keep the pace steady—unrelenting, patient, exacting.

She comes with a strangled cry, clenching around my fingers. Thighs quivering as her whole body locks and shakes as wave after wave crashes through her. I don't stop. Not until I've wrested six orgasms in succession. Then, finally, I allow her tremors to subside and she collapses, boneless and panting, on the sheets.

When I finally slide up beside her, her eyes are still glassy. Her lips curve into something disbelieving and wild.

"You were right," she whispers. "You really have been paying attention."

I pull her into me, press a kiss to her temple. "From this point forward, only to you."

She nuzzles into my chest, one leg sliding over mine, like she can't get close enough. Fuck if it doesn't do something to me all over again.

I spent years learning a woman's body—nerve, rhythm, response.

None of it prepared me for Marcella.

Sex with her isn't technique.

It's everything I never knew I was missing.

Twenty-Three

A Few Days Later

WE HAVEN'T COME UP for air.

Every moment blurring into the next—bodies, mouths, hands, heat.

It's been days and Seamus has only left my place once. Monday, when I was on a conference call I took from home, he popped out to grab some clothes and groceries.

He's been here ever since—like he belongs with me.

We've fucked so much, I'm half-convinced my body's permanently shaped to fit him.

As incredible as the sex is, my favorite thing is what happens after. He caresses me like I'm something sacred. Always pulling me into his chest when we sleep, like he can't stand being apart.

He's so different than I imagined. When I first heard about the stairwell thing, I figured it was some cocky med-school flex. Now I realize it's never been about skill, it's about care.

Seamus McGloughlin was trying to prove he's worth loving by showing exactly how to give it.

So, why am I so I'm scared?

I know the answer. This thing between us is too easy. Too good. Too *fast*.

He's saying all the right things. Doing all the right things. I'm head over heels for the man.

I'm not ordinarily one for woo-woo manifestation bullshit. Sometimes—like right now, with Seamus half-asleep beside me and his hand resting protectively on my hip—I start to wonder if the universe was holding out. Like maybe my bad luck with men was because Seamus had to age into the man he is today.

It's wild, really—how easily he touches me, holds me and treats me like I'm the most beautiful woman he's ever seen. If I'm honest, I've been bracing for the shoe to drop. With Seamus, however, there's no catch. He's as straight a shooter as I've ever known.

Which is why the idea of meeting each other's families hasn't sent me into a full-blown panic.

Today, we're heading to Tacoma to have dinner with my parents, brother, and sister at the restaurant. I'm nervous. Excited. Sunday I've agreed to attend his family dinner with him. No big deal, me meeting a good portion of the McGloughlin clan including all his older rockstar brothers.

It's not lost on me what it means. I'm bringing a younger man home to meet my family. Tomorrow, the youngest McGloughlin is bringing home an older woman to meet his.

I'd like to talk about it. It's too soon so I'm trying to go with the flow. How are we going to introduce each other to our families? To the world? Caldwell is still Seamus's boss. While the settlement's wrapped, their dynamic hasn't exactly untangled itself.

At the very least, the rest of his residency is going to be awkward no matter what.

Then there's Joe Finney and the rest of my partners at the firm. I know how people get into everyone else's business. It's human nature. Yet, I've built my whole career on being unshakeable. Controlled. When this gets out? It'll be gossip fodder for sure and I don't like it.

The problem is, the sex is so good there's not a lot of time for talking. He's now trailing kisses across my bare shoulder and his monster erection burrows into the cleft of my ass.

"Fuck, Marcella. Your tits are incredible." His hand snakes up to cup my breast. "So full and soft. I could spend hours worshiping them."

How am I supposed to resist? I can't. Don't want to.

Seamus rolls me on my back and sucks a nipple into his hot mouth, flicking the tip with his tongue until I'm writhing and whimpering. He laves each of my breasts thoroughly, biting gently on the full curves before moving down my rounded belly, dipping his tongue into my navel.

He runs a finger through my slick folds and curses under his breath. "Your pussy is so goddamn pretty," he growls, parting me with his thumbs. "Look at you, dripping for me. I need to taste your honey."

Seamus doesn't seem to care it's morning, we're barely awake, and I'm—funky. We've been at it all night without showering. Yet, he buries his face between my thighs, lapping at me with enthusiasm. The first swipe of his tongue through my center has us both moaning. He explores every inch of my dripping heat, swirling his tongue on my clit every now and then.

He slides two fingers inside, pumping them deep and slow, curling to rub my G-spot, matching his gentle sucks to his thrusting fingers, quickly pushing me toward the edge. Pleasure crashes over me in a blinding rush. I cry out his name and Seamus laps at me through the tremors, like he can't get enough of my—our—taste.

When he's had his fill, Seamus pushes himself up to kneeling. I take in his ripped body—broad pecs, tight abs, thick thighs—and his cock flushed dark with arousal.

I slide my hands up his thighs as I glance up at him, heat curling low in my belly. "Come here."

His eyes flare and without hesitation, he shifts forward, straddling my shoulders as if he's wanted this as badly. The sheer trust in his eyes as he looks down at me steals the breath from my lungs. Wrapping my fist around his impressive girth, I pump up and down his length. He thrusts into my hand, groaning. Leaning in, I suck on his crown, probing the slit with the tip of my tongue.

"*Yessss*, Marcella." He tangles his fingers in my hair. "Suck me. Hard. Let me fuck your mouth a little."

God, yes. I widen my lips around his thick cock, taking him deep. He's velvet-soft on my tongue. Searing hot. I slide up and down his length, relishing the silky skin stretched over stiff flesh. Hollowing my cheeks, I suck him with filthy abandon.

"Ah *fuck*," he grunts, thrusting shallowly into my mouth. "I love seeing those pretty lips around my dick. You have no idea."

I moan around his girth and allow him to push against the back of my throat.

"Ohhhhh, shit. Marcella—baby, I'm gonna come," he warns, trying to pull back. I clamp my hands on his ass, holding him deep. I want to taste him. With a harsh groan, he erupts, shooting thick, salty cream into my mouth. I swallow him down greedily, coaxing every last drop.

He shudders through the aftershocks, stroking my hair. "Incredible." He pulls me up for a searing kiss.

We collapse back onto the bed, breathless and slick with sweat. I barely have time to relax before I feel him hardening against my thigh again. The thing about being with someone in their late twenties—or maybe it's just Seamus—recovery time seems to be more of a suggestion than a requirement.

"Baby." He caresses my cheek. "Can we try something? I want to watch you ride me in front of your full-length mirror. See your tits sway and your curves jiggle when I'm inside of you. Let me show you how goddamn sexy you are."

I bite my lip, heat rushing to my cheeks before I can stop the words. "It will turn you on?"

"Feel my cock drilling into your thigh? How hard you make me?" His cups my chin, thumb brushing over my flushed cheek. "I've never wanted to see anything more."

Without waiting for my answer, Seamus sits up and scoots against the headboard with his legs extended out in front of him and helps me straddle his hips, my back to his front. He shifts slightly beneath me, his hands prying my thighs apart. He spreads them wide until his cock rests between my pussy lips—thick and pulsing.

In the mirror across from the bed, we both watch as he slides one hand up my rounded belly, the other down between my legs. He encircles the base of his cock with his hand and taps my clit with his fat crown. We both gasp at the exquisite sight when he feeds his length into me.

"Ride me," he encourages, latching his palms around my hips. "Work yourself up and down on my cock. I want you to watch yourself too."

I shiver at his instruction, doing as he says. I position my knees on each side of his powerful thighs and lift up then sink back down cautiously, feeling the blunt head catch on my entrance. He's so big this way, the stretch intense as I impale myself on his rigid length.

Leaning forward slightly, I brace my hands on his thighs, rocking slowly. This feels incredible. He knows exactly what my body needs.

"Fuck," Seamus breathes, kneading my ass cheeks. "Your pussy is so tight, Marcella. It feels so goddamn incredible."

Encouraged, I gain confidence and watch myself slide up and down his shaft, raising myself almost all the way off before sinking back down. I watch in the mirror when his cock appears, glistening with my arousal and then vanishes into my puffy folds. I'm mesmerized. Every nerve is alive with the most intense pleasure I've ever experienced.

We've spent days fucking each other in every position possible. This is different. Now, I can see the way he watches me. His expression isn't merely hunger or lust. It's something quieter. Deeper.

Love.

He hasn't said the word, and neither have I.

Yet, I feel it settling into the spaces between our bodies. Anchoring itself in the way he fucks me like I'm some kind of miracle. The way his hands worship my full hips, plush thighs, and pillowy belly like they're his most-cherished prizes. A week of fucking him has brought me to the point where I don't flinch or suck in my stomach or try to cover myself anymore.

This impossibly beautiful, brilliant man isn't just inside my body, he's carved himself into my soul.

I know we're new. The timing's all wrong. I'm too old for him. None of it matters to me anymore.

Not when I feel like this.

Time doesn't exist.

Age is just math.

He's mine.

So, I let go.

Of the fear. Of the doubt. Of the skepticism.

"Ah fuck, *yesssss.*" He winces when I circle my hips and squeeze. "Use me, baby. Get yourself off."

His words inflame me. I'm liberated. Uninhibited. I slam myself down on his pumping hips, impaling myself over and over, chasing the delicious friction. The room fills with the obscene wet sounds of me fucking myself on his cock like a woman who's gone mad.

"You look so hot riding me like this." Seamus pants. "Keep it up, baby—milk every drop from me. Your tight pussy's got me ready to blow."

Seamus winds an arm around my waist, yanking me down as he bucks up to meet me. He ruts into me with hard, short digs, precisely targeting my G-spot with every thrust.

I reach back, threading my fingers into his hair as I grind on him in wild circles. "Oh fuck," I whine. "You're like magic the way you fuck my pussy. Harder, Seamus. So hard I squeeze every ounce of your come into my body."

His eyes meet mine in the mirror, wide for just a second. My unfiltered commentary has caught him—and me—off guard. A slow, wicked grin spreads across his face, and the heat in his gaze triples. I actually feel his cock thicken.

He likes it. Me, talking dirty. I feel powerful. Wanted. Wild.

"I'm close," he pants. "You're gonna make me come so hard. I'm gonna flood your tight pussy."

His fingers slip between my thighs, circling my clit with deliberate pressure. I can't look away from the way his hand moves. The way his pupils are nearly black with desire as he watches me fall apart under his touch.

My breasts bounce and sway with every grind and thrust—full and flushed, nipples drawn tight and needy—so obscenely perfect I'm almost able to see myself the way he sees me. It's hypnotic. Raw. For the first time in my life, I don't look away from my naked reflection—I revel in it.

"God. Seamus!" I wail, bucking desperately when I feel the telltale flutter low in my belly.

"Yes. Come for me." His fingers dig into my hips. "Squeeze me. Take it all…"

Visceral pleasure erupts and my pussy clamps his shaft. With a harsh curse, Seamus yanks me down, seating himself to the hilt. His cock twitches and swells before he spurts inside me.

I'm utterly debauched. Thoroughly fucked. Trembling. Gasping. Unable to do anything but slump back against him. Seamus wraps his arms around me, dropping kisses on my neck and shoulders. We watch his release leak out of me and pool on the sheets underneath us.

Filthy, erotic evidence of our passion.

When he slips out, we roll to the dry side of the bed, cuddling and caressing, basking in the afterglow.

Worshipping each other with gentle touches and more words of endearment.

I think dreamily…

If I'm a late bloomer…

Damn.

Blossoming was well worth the wait.

Twenty-Four

Later That Day

A GLOOM SEEMS TO cling to everything.

Winter in the Pacific Northwest never pretends to be anything else.

It's late afternoon and the rain's been coming down steady since morning. It's more mist now than anything—a constant silver veil draped across the windshield of Marcella's sleek black Audi as we wind down I-5 toward Tacoma.

As the city gives way to trees and highway blur, inside the car it's quiet. Not quite peaceful, though. Marcella grips the steering wheel like she's bracing for brutal cross-examination. Her stormy, hazel eyes are focused straight ahead and her face is frozen in deep concentration. I doubt she even notices me watching her.

She hasn't said much since we left her condo. A few offhand comments about traffic and weather. The silence wouldn't bug me if we hadn't spent so many days and nights talking and laughing nonstop in between fucking each other raw.

I mean—my cock has practically taken up residence inside her. I've watched her fall apart with my name on her lips more times than I can count. Every night I've fallen asleep with her magnificent tits pressed against my chest and her arm banded around my waist like she can't bear not to touch me.

I'm not sure why she's suddenly acting like we're strangers carpooling to a dentist appointment. Then again, I'm not an expert at this boyfriend thing, so...

I'm half-waiting for the moment she tells me this has all been a mistake.

Fuck it. The vibe is driving me batshit. I shift in my seat, drumming my fingers on my thigh. "Are you okay?"

"Yep. Fine." She glances over at me quickly before fixing her eyes on the road again.

Immediately I realize the trap I've fallen into. A classic one-syllable female landmine. I may not be relationship guy, but I've worked with many women colleagues. Walked down too many metaphorical hallways with warning signs painted on the walls.

I know better. Still. I clear my throat and try harder. "You've been unusually quiet."

"I'm thinking about something I hadn't considered." Marcella exhales, long and slow.

Oh, holy hell. Talk about vague. "I have zero clue what you're going to say next. I'll bite. What haven't you considered?"

"Um..." Another pause. Then, without looking at me, she asks, "You mentioned we don't need to have labels, but things have...um, changed since the last time you saw my parents. You've not met my brother and sister before. So... how do you want me to introduce you?"

Nope. Wouldn't have guessed. In fact, it's pretty much the last thing I thought she'd say. "*What*?"

"When we go in." She stares straight ahead. "How should I introduce you?"

I try not to laugh. "Um...Seamus McGloughlin, your *boyfriend*?"

"I truly wasn't fishing." She glances over at me nervously, then back at the road. "I mean, no. God. I don't know. I mean—I didn't want to assume."

Okay. There it is.

I stare at her profile—sharp cheekbones, soft lips, hair pulled back in a low twist, somehow both severe and sexy. She's beautiful, brilliant, and utterly maddening. I fight the urge to say something flippant because she's not mad...she's worried.

"Why wouldn't you fish? It's worth talking about unless you're worried about how your family will react." I place my hand on her knee. "To the nine-years-younger boy-toy situation..."

"Eight," she corrects automatically. "Well...yeah. Although, I'm getting the better end of the deal."

"Okay, then what's the problem?" It's time to nip all of this in the bud. We're together. If people don't like it, fuck 'em. "I'm sorry if I made you feel like I wasn't sure about labels. Mainly I didn't want to spook you with the intensity of where my head's at. I never thought we wouldn't tell our families, Marcella. We're together. I don't want us to be a secret."

She pulls into the lot behind the restaurant and parks. Her hands rest on the wheel, knuckles white.

"I don't want to hide you either, Seamus," she says quietly. "I'm not bringing this topic up to diminish what we're becoming to each other...it's fast. Complicated. The truth is, I'm older and people are going to gossip. Also, you're in the middle of your residency. Caldwell's still your boss. You've just been through hell with the case. I'm trying to be practical."

"If practical doesn't mean honest, it's not worth it to me," I counter. "I want you. I want *this*. I've never been more sure of anything."

She finally turns to face me fully, her expression softening. "I know. I do too. I'm scared, though. We've been in our bubble. When we're out in the world, I'm gonna worry what people think."

"Baby, stop." I lean my head back against the headrest and stare out at the back of the restaurant. "It's funny, given my history. I never thought I'd be the one pushing for labels when I've deliberately stayed away from them my entire adult life."

Marcella laughs. "Yeah, well...you're full of surprises."

"Not really." I reach over and thread my fingers through hers. "I'm glad you decided not to shut me out, okay? Say what's on your mind. We don't have to be perfect. We don't have to have it all figured out. If we're going to do this for real, we need to be real with each other."

"I'm trying, which is why I had to let you know how I was feeling," she assures me.

I believe her even though it took nearly an hour for her to open up. Still, I lift her hand to my mouth and kiss the back of it. "Boyfriend, by the way."

"Good." She bites her lip. "Although, you calling me your 'girlfriend' seems a little twisted. Maybe 'cougar mama' or 'seasoned cradle-robbing vixen.'"

I adore sarcastic Marcella. I'm grinning like an idiot as we step out of the car into the cool, wet air.

The moment we walk into the restaurant, I'm hit with warmth. Not only from the heat—though the place is cozy and smells like heaven—it's the laughter. Wine corks popping. The low hum of voices. The Spanish guitar playing faintly in the background. Soul is baked into the walls.

Marcella's mom greets us near the hostess stand with sharp eyes and a radiant smile. She pulls Marcella into a hug bordering on a squeeze.

"Chellie." She kisses both of Marcella's cheeks then turns to me with an appraising look. "Doctor. You've been dominating my daughter's time, I hear?"

I offer a sheepish smile. "Hi, Mrs. Delgado. Yes, I can't lie."

"Hmmm." She tilts her head. "Well, because you're so handsome, we'll let it pass. Come. Sit. Lucas's already at the table."

We follow her to a corner booth where Marcella's brother, Lucas, is nursing a beer and scrolling through something on his phone. He looks up as we approach and offers me a nod before standing to give Marcella a one-armed hug. "You brought the baby doctor," he says to her. Then to me, "Nice to meet you."

Ah, we're starting by busting my chops. As the youngest of six brothers, I've learned reacting negatively to a harmless dig will make a guy double and triple down, so I pretend not to understand.. "You too. And, I'm actually a neurosurgeon."

Lucas opens his mouth to correct me just as Marcella's dad materializes, kissing her forehead and shaking my hand like we're old friends. Immediately, the meal unfolds in a blur of sizzling platters and overlapping voices. Eventually, Marcella's mom and brother ease into questions about the hospital—subtle. Not aimless. Mainly, wondering if the dust is finally starting to settle after the lawsuit.

"More or less," I lie. Tonight isn't the time to get into hospital dynamics.

Her mom tilts her head, thoughtful. "Does it help to know your family's been through these kind of storms before?"

She's not being judgmental, just curious—like someone who's either heard some things from Marcella or read all the headlines and knows better than to ask outright. I don't blame her. Between the band scandals, corporate fires, defamation lawsuits and deep-fake identity challenges, navigating public messes has become practically a McGloughlin family tradition.

I nod, keeping it light. "They've taught me a few things."

Marcella doesn't say anything. Her fingers brush mine under the table. A quiet gesture. Grounding. Protective, even. This is her world—and she's making space for me in it. Her family is protective of her, though. I can feel every pair of eyes at the table trying to figure out whether or not I'm worthy of her.

"I must tell you." I change the subject and address her father who's setting another platter of some delicious meat dish in front of us. "The food you're serving should be illegal."

"Thank you," he raises a glass of Rioja as a toast, "Rosa's reinvented the whole damn menu. You'll never eat better Spanish food in this country."

"I believe you." I try not to moan as I take a bite of braised short ribs over saffron risotto.

Halfway through the meal, Marcella excuses herself to the bathroom. The minute she disappears, her mother wastes no time. "She looks happy."

"I hope so, I want to keep a smile on her face," I reply honestly.

Lucas raises an eyebrow. "How old are you again?"

"Twenty-nine." I meet his eyes.

There's a beat. He's a year older than me, I already know this.

"You're young," he says, like an accusation.

He's not going to scare me off. "I am young-er."

"She can be tough. Stubborn." Her mom squints.

"She's strong," I counter. "Knows what she wants."

Rosa appears, hair tied up, apron smeared with some sort of sauce, and a look of surprise on her face when she sees me. She blinks, then turns to her mother. "This is him?"

"I am him." I look up at her, not letting anyone answer for me.

Rosa steps over to me and sticks out her hand. "Nice to finally meet you. I've heard...things."

"I've heard...things about you too." I grin, taking her hand.

She leans closer. "She's much older than you."

"I'm aware." I release her sister's hand.

"She's got a hard shell. And a soft heart." Her eyebrow quirks.

"I know."

"She's been burned."

I nod.

"Don't be the guy who doesn't measure up," she warns.

I glance back toward the bathroom, where Marcella's stepping back into view. Her eyes land on the table and widen slightly when she sees the four of us mid-interrogation.

"I won't be," I promise. "You've got my word."

Marcella slides into the booth beside me and gives her sister a wary look. "Were you grilling him?"

"Of course." Rosa shrugs like it's a foregone conclusion.

I can't resist saying, "And?"

"I approve." Rosa turns with a little flair then disappears back into the kitchen.

Marcella exhales. "Sorry."

"It's fine." I nudge her knee under the table and whisper into her ear, "I can handle it. Better to get it over with so we can move on."

Dinner settles into something more relaxed after the stand-off—at least on the surface. Marcella's mom keeps the conversation moving, throwing in stories about when Marcella was little and refused to eat anything green. Lucas talks about work. Her father talks about opening the restaurant and how far it's come from a ten-seat dining room in the front of their house.

There's something grounding about being here. Her family and mine are similar. Loud. Boisterous. Passionate. I've been invited into her inner world, allowing me to access a fuller picture of Marcella. This isn't the courtroom version or the woman I've been naked with for the past week. This is her with her people.

The real her.

When dessert arrives—a creamy, golden-brown Basque cheesecake with a drizzle of sherry reduction—Marcella hums softly in approval. "This is new." She glances at her mom.

"Not my recipe." Her mom beams. "Rosa's been working on it for weeks. Which brings me to a bone I have to pick with you, my darling." She clears her throat. "Having you—and Seamus—here makes me happy. Please. Can we keep our Friday dinners on the calendar?"

"I wish I could commit…" Marcella catches herself. "You know what? Yes. We can. I'm prioritizing our family time. The McGloughlins have a family dinner every Sunday. It's an important tradition."

Her mom's face softens, and she reaches over to squeeze Marcella's hand. "Thank you. I missed you when we went so long without seeing each other."

"I missed you too." Marcella's eyes glisten.

The table goes quiet for a beat, the only sound the clink of forks against plates. I reach under the table and brush my fingers against hers. She doesn't pull away.

We stay another hour, sipping coffee and helping clear plates when things slow down. On our way out, her mom gives me a to-go box "in case the doctor needs snacks later."

When Marcella ducks into the back to say goodbye to Rosa, her mom pulls me aside for more insight. "She doesn't bring boyfriends here," she whispers, folding her arms. "Not since college."

I nod. "She told me."

"She works too hard. Holds everything too tight." Her mom takes both of my hands in hers.

"I know."

Her gaze softens, just slightly. "She'll pretend like she doesn't need you. That's her way. But she does."

"I'm not going anywhere," I assure her.

She presses a warm hand to my cheek in a gesture so motherly and unexpected, I blink.

Then Marcella's back, putting on her coat. "Ready?"

We drive in silence for the first few minutes, this time it's comforting, not disquieting. It's late and the rain is still coming down in a steady rhythm against the windshield. Marcella's hand rests on the center console, and I cover it with mine.

"Thanks for bringing me to dinner." I squeeze gently. "It was nothing short of amazing. Our families are so similar."

The corner of her mouth tugs upward. "They liked you."

"I liked them too," I say honestly.

Marcella shoots me a look. "Even Rosa?"

"Especially Rosa. She has your back and wasn't afraid to let me know."

Marcella laughs. "Sorry…"

"Don't be. If I had a sister like you, I'd be protective." I lean over and kiss her temple. "My brothers are the same with me."

She smiles and turns back toward the road. "It meant a lot you came."

"Eventually you'll get it through your thick head I'm going to follow you anywhere." I stroke her cheek with my thumb.

She doesn't answer. The way her hand slips over to rest on my thigh tells me all I need to know.

Half hour later as we near our exit, Marcella says quietly, without fanfare, "I'll follow you anywhere too."

No conditions. No defense.

Not a promise.

A true beginning.

Twenty-Five

A Couple Days Later

THE DRIVE TO THE McGloughlin house takes less than twenty minutes, though my pulse seems to think I'm heading into a courtroom with no prep.

I've made corporations fold with a single citation. Stripped arrogant surgeons down to raw nerve in front of a jury. Walked into boardrooms packed with men twice my age and walked out with settlements they never saw coming.

Visiting Seamus's family home and being introduced to his mother as his girlfriend feels infinitely more dangerous.

For once, the outcome might matter more than I want to admit.

He's driving my car, one hand on the wheel, the other resting over the center console, fingers lightly brushing mine. It's casual. Effortless. Like we've done this a hundred times. Every tiny graze of his skin against mine ratchets my heart up another beat.

I don't want him to see me nervous. Not tonight.

"You okay?" He glances at me as we pull onto a quiet, tree-lined street in Capitol Hill.

I nod, loosening my grip on the armrest and attempt humor. "Yep. Totally fine. Why wouldn't I be? Oh. Right. I'm meeting the entire McGloughlin clan for the first time. No big deal."

"It's Sunday dinner." His lips twitch into a grin. "Ma will cook enough to feed a rugby team and Da will yammer on about construction and the Troubles."

The house appears like a warm, golden beacon. A classic Craftsman—broad front porch, gabled roof, and enough charm to feel like something out of a Nancy Meyers movie..

I smooth my jeans and glance down at my oversized sweater. I've gone casual, per Seamus's suggestion. I feel like I'm walking into the lion's den in sneakers instead of my ordinary power suit.

"You're not nervous." He parks in front of the house. "Right?"

I arch a brow. "I'm a nearly forty-year-old woman who's never been introduced to a boyfriend's family before. So, you know, totally chill."

"You're thirty-eight." He kills the engine and leans across the console, brushing his lips over mine. "They're going to love you."

"You say it like a foregone conclusion." I swat at him playfully.

He pecks my cheek. "It is."

As we approach the front door, it swings open before we can knock. Connor, tall with a mane of curly auburn hair and amber eyes grins at us. He's so much bigger in person than he appears in music videos and on stage. He's like a Celtic god—his shoulders fill the doorway and even though his menacing face breaks into a wide grin, I can tell he's every inch the older rockstar brother who once ran this entire family like a battlefield medic.

"You must be Marcella." He offers a hand.

I manage to keep my composure. "I am. Nice to meet you."

"Likewise." He motions to the living room. "Come in. Everyone's been dying to meet the first woman Seamus has ever introduced to any of us."

Seamus snorts. "No one knew I was bringing her until a few days ago."

"Ach." Connor shakes his head. "Go with it, wee Seamus."

Inside, the house is chaos—in the best possible way. The scent of something delicious wraps around me the second I cross the threshold. It reminds me of my dad's restaurant. There's also laughter echoing down the hallway. The sound of shrieks and thud of little feet racing from room to room.

We barely set foot in the house before Seamus is mobbed by two tiny whirlwinds—Torin and Tristan. Nearly five years old and full of unrelenting energy. Seamus drops to his knees like it's instinct, wrestling them both into giggles, one tucked under each arm as they shriek and pretend to fight back.

My heart trips. Watching him with his nephews—playful, joyful, completely present—wakes something in me I thought I'd buried. A whisper of want. The ache of a dream I'd already let go and need to keep at bay because by the time Seamus is established as a neurosurgeon, I'll be too far past possible.

Of course, assuming he and I will still be together.

I don't have an opportunity to dwell. A woman with perfect glossy hair and effortless confidence only born of fame steps into the foyer. I recognize her instantly. My favorite actress, Ronni Miller. Connor's wife. The star of a teen show I was obsessed with, *Hawaiian High*. Also the lead of a long-running sitcom, *She's All That*. Now she produces and guest stars on my current favorite show, *The Boyfriend Experiment*.

To say I'm a fan is an understatement.

"Hi, I'm Ronni," she introduces herself like she's not a cultural icon. "You must be the badass attorney who got justice for Miranda."

I blink. "I—yes. Marcella."

She steps forward and hugs me with no pretense. "Thank you for standing up for her. Seamus told us you were a force."

I glance over at him. He's still tangled with the boys, laughing like it's his version of heaven.

"Thank you. I need to let you know, I'm kinda obsessed with *The Boyfriend Experiment*," I admit like it's a confession.

Ronni shoots me a grin. "Really?"

"I watch it because of Clover," I gush a little. "She's smart, complicated, gorgeous—and not a size two. I grew up trying to emulate perfect, thin women and it messed my body image up immensely. Your show is one of the first to make women like me fell...uh, *seen*."

Ronni's smile softens. "So cool. Thank you. I get a lot of similar comments, which is exactly why I fought so hard to cast her."

Seamus's mom, Maureen, emerges from the kitchen. She's fit and wiry, with thick auburn hair pulled into a braid. Here mere presence makes you straighten your spine. She wipes her hands on a linen towel as we enter.

"You must be Marcella. I'm Maureen." Her Irish lilt is amazing.

"Lovely to meet you." I try not to curtsy, though I want to a little.

She pulls me into a hug instead. "We've all been so excited for you to get here. He's never brought someone home before."

"Well...I hope I live up to expectations." I glance over my shoulder at Seamus. He's tossing one of the twins over his shoulder like a sack of potatoes.

Maureen laughs. "You're grand, love. Sit. Dinner's almost ready. No, you may not help."

"Wouldn't dream of it." I lift my hands in surrender.

We gather around the dining table—long, dark wood worn smooth by years of use. Seamus sits beside me. Connor and Ronni with the kids on one end. Liam and Padraig opposite each other. Cillian, quiet and tired-eyed, tucks into a spot near their father. Rory carves the pork roast with ceremony, while Maureen brings out tray after tray of food—roasted potatoes, buttered cabbage, parsnips with thyme, a thick, onion gravy, soda bread still warm from the oven.

I can't get over how similar the McGloughlins are to the Delgados. I feel right at home.

The conversation is nonstop—loud, overlapping, full of in-jokes and references I don't catch. No one ignores me. If anything, they go out of their way to loop me in.

"Is it true you're working on a case against the caregiver in the nursing home who overmedicated a bunch of the patients?" Padraig asks, pouring himself a splash of juice.

"I do represent three of the victims and can't really talk about it, for ethical reasons," I answer honestly.

Rory claps. "Aye, a woman with integrity and teeth. I like youse."

I catch Seamus watching me, a slow smile tugging at his mouth like he's proud. It's been this way all day—his eyes always finding me, like he can't help himself. There's something else I've noticed. A quietness I hadn't expected. Around his family, he fades a little—still warm, still engaged, decidedly less...open.

Less *Seamus*.

It makes me wonder. Is it the weight of being the youngest? The pressure of living up to the McGloughlin name? Or maybe it's hard to be loud when everyone else already takes up so much space.

With me, he fills every inch of the room. With them, he pulls back.

I don't think they notice.

I do.

As the evening unfolds, Seamus's twin brothers fall into a low-grade argument about the band. Fireball is, apparently, riding an unprecedented wave of success. Liam nurses a soda water, the heat of his frustration barely contained.

"We finally get *SNL*," he mutters. "We've been clawing for this for a decade. *Now* you want to breathe?"

Padraig doesn't even flinch. "Yeah. Maybe I do." He pours himself even more juice from the bottle on the table. "We've been pushing. For years. Maybe now's the time to slow down before we burn out. Or our private lives get us dragged through the mud."

Hmmmm. Interesting. Seamus looks at me and casts his eyes down and back again. He'll fill me in later, I surmise.

Connor, with his arms crossed, leans forward—he's calm but his tone is lined with something earned. "It's not just about now, lads. LTZ hit our peak and we ran ourselves into the ground chasing every next big thing. You remember how it ended for us."

The room goes quiet for a beat. Even the fire seems to hush.

"Took years to recover and we're finally doing it right," Connor continues. "Touring on a schedule we're all comfortable with. Prioritizing our families. On our terms. Fame's not worth shit if you lose everything else in the process."

Ronni rests her hand over his bicep, her expression soft and knowing. "He's not wrong."

Padraig lifts his glass slightly in acknowledgment. Liam looks like he wants to argue. He doesn't.

Seamus, watches quietly—I can tell he's listening. Maybe more than anyone.

Later, I find myself alone in the kitchen, stacking plates into the dishwasher despite Maureen's insistence I shouldn't.

She joins me and grabs a tub of whipped cream from the fridge and begins dolloping it on individual servings of homemade brownies. "So. You like my son."

It's not a question.

"I really do." I nod, unsure what my face is doing.

To my surprise, she doesn't bring up our age difference. "He's different since Miranda. More careful. More focused. He hasn't admitted it but I think he's questioning it all."

"Because of the lawsuit?" This information is news to me.

"Yes. He chose neurosurgery for a reason." She puts the leftover cream back in the cooler. "He's been singularly focused for years and now his future is a bit uncertain."

I grip the edge of the counter, the ceramic edge cool and solid under my palm. "He hasn't mentioned any of this to me."

Maureen exhales gently as she wipes her hands on a towel. "He probably wouldn't. Not until he's sorted it through himself. Seamus is consistent. Always has been. He digs in deep. Commits like it's a sacred vow—even when the ground shifts under him."

A chill moves down my spine. Suddenly I feel a flicker of panic. What if Seamus wakes up someday and realizes this—me—isn't what he truly wants? I don't want to be something he stays in out of duty. I want to be chosen. Willingly. Fully.

God, I'm selfish. What if he's struggling with something else?

Maureen doesn't notice the internal war I'm fighting. Or maybe she does and she's too gracious to call it out. She turns back to the tray of dessert and speaks quietly, more to the memory than the moment. "This Miranda situation. It shook him to the core. Not because he's lost his love for medicine, it's because he saw what happens when his mentor's ego trumped empathy. It's not who my Seamus is."

I nod because I'm unable to speak.

"He's always wanted to help people," she continues. "I think maybe *how* he wants to help might be shifting."

For a second, I wonder how much of this he's confided in her. Or, how much she's intuited from watching him. Knowing him.

It occurs to me how wrong I was earlier.

It's clear his mother sees him. *Really* sees him. Regardless of how quiet he is around his boisterous family. How easily he fades into the background and lets them shine.

"I know it's early days with the two of you." She gently touches my hand. "I'd never try to put pressure on your relationship. If he means anything to you—please let him be who he is, Marcella. Not who he thinks he's supposed to be. Or who he thinks *you* want him to be. He doesn't need a mother. He needs a partner."

Ah. There it is. She's addressed our age gap in the most thoughtful way.

What Maureen wants for Seamus is all I've ever wanted, too. I don't want to hold my years of experience over his head. He's smart. Strong. Capable. I value his insights tremendously.

We're already on the way to being partners.

Somehow, without fanfare or grand gestures, Seamus has shown this level of respect to me. With words. Behavior. Sweet gestures. How he makes love to me. It's the first time I've ever felt seen. Desired.

Enough.

Not for what I do or what I've achieved—but for who I am.

I've taken his gift—greedily and gratefully.

Now, I want to give it back to him. Seamus shouldn't always have to be the steady one. The sure one. He deserves reassurance too. A place to land. Someone who sees him as the wonderful man he is.

I realize in this moment—our age difference means *nothing*.

When I return to the living room, Seamus is cuddling Teagan. Her tiny head is nestled against his shoulder as his palm cradles her back. He's bouncing slightly, soothing her without even thinking about it.

He holds her like he was born knowing how.

Our eyes meet. Something inside me aches. Literally aches.

I love him. I know how I feel without a shadow of doubt.

He smiles. I smile back.

I realize the right person may not show up early or in the package you anticipated. The universe sends him once you've done the work, survived the battles and built a life you can invite them into.

In Seamus, I see the man, not the age, not the risk.

He's *mine*.
It's time to stop bracing for the fall.
For him, I want to leap off the cliff.

Twenty-Six

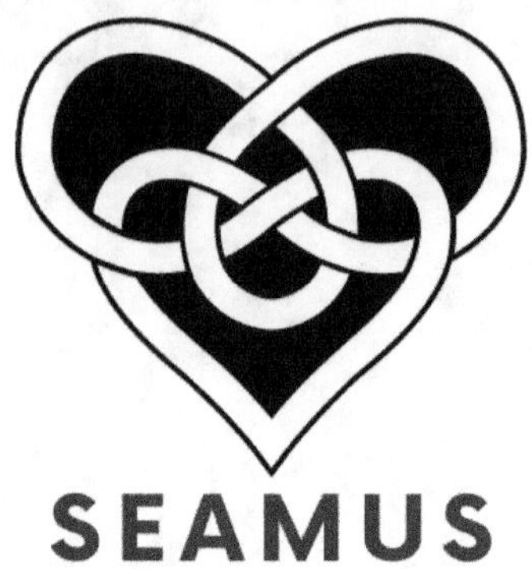

New Year's Day

IT'S BARELY 8 A.M. on New Year's Day.

My body's wrecked, my mind wide awake. I can't stop watching her.

Marcella sleeps curled against me, her breathing soft and rhythmic, her cheek resting on my chest. Every so often she lets out a sleepy hum, like she's exhaling whatever stress she carried into this new year. Her hair spills over my arm and her thigh is slung over my leg like she owns the space between us.

She does. She *absolutely* does.

The sky outside her window is a soft, wet gray as expected. Seattle in winter rarely delivers anything other than misty rain and today's no different. Drops sploosh steadily against the pane, making the light diffused and low, like the world hasn't quite decided to wake up yet.

I don't mind.

Not this year.

Not with her.

I'm completely obsessed with Marcella Delgado, the woman who has bulldozed every obstacle in her life with stilettos and sarcasm. She trusts me. Sleeps against me like I'm home.

I never knew I needed this. I can't live without her.

We didn't go out last night. No crowded parties or loud music. It was just the two of us, curled up on her couch watching the ball drop on TV. Our champagne flutes were untouched because we were too busy kissing when the clock struck midnight. Then we fucked until dawn.

It was perfect.

We didn't spend Christmas together—our first major holiday as a couple felt too soon to crash into each other's long-held family traditions. We more than made up for it this past week—a blur of slow mornings, hard laughter, another dinner at her parents' restaurant and Sunday at mine. Stolen glances across the room and hours of mind-blowing sex.

Truth be told, I've barely been home since the first night I slept here. My townhouse smells like Pine-Sol and neglect and I only know this because I stopped by a few days ago for more clothes and my toiletries.

Marcella stirs beside me and shifts onto her back, blinking sleepily. Her eyes meet mine, and her mouth curves into the softest smile. "Happy New Year," she whispers, her voice still husky.

"Best one I've ever had." I smile down at her.

She yawns and extends her arms over her head, causing the sheet to fall down, exposing her glorious breasts. My gaze drops and I'm not even subtle. My eyes drift over her luscious curves, taking in her dark, puckered nipples, the dip of her waist, the flare of her hips. I've explored every inch of her silky skin and I'm thoroughly addicted. I trail my fingers lightly down her spine, savoring the way she shivers under my touch.

A blush creeps across her chest. "Don't start," she warns. "You're insatiable and I can never resist."

I cup her breast, brushing my thumb over her tight nipple until she squirms under my touch. "Why would you resist?"

Her breath catches. She tries to act unaffected. It won't work, I know her body like the back of my hand now. Her tells. We've been here a lot lately.

It never gets old

I've never been happier.

My cock thickens against her plush thigh in spite of the countless times I've spent myself inside her over the last few days. She's right. I am insatiable. So is she. I pull her closer, peppering her face with soft kisses. "Want you so much, beautiful girl."

"Mmm, I want you too," she admits happily, snuggling into my chest. "My amazing man."

I never knew it could be like this, so perfect and right. The way she touches me, worships me, I feel like a king. "I'm so lucky I found you."

"I feel like the lucky one." She smiles and slides her thigh over mine, opening herself to me.

In one motion, I gently roll her under me. I kiss my way down her chest, worshipping every inch of her smooth, caramel skin before palming her heavy breasts, squeezing gently, and sucking a dark nipple into my mouth. I swirl my tongue around the pebbled peak until she's writhing beneath me, her hips rocking restlessly.

Slipping my hand between her legs, I'm not surprised to find her slick with arousal. "*Mmm*, always wet for me," I rasp, parting her slippery folds.

I circle her swollen clit with the pad of my finger, nice and slow, to tease her. She whines low in her throat, spreading her thighs wider.

"Seamus, *please*." She cants her hips, desperate for more. "Need you deep in my pussy."

God, I love it when she tells me exactly what she wants using words she probably never uttered before me.

I settle into the cradle of her hips. My cock nudges against her entrance and I moan brokenly. Fuck, she's scorching. Drenched for me. I push in slowly, savoring the feel of her body accepting me, inch by incredible inch. She's snug, even after the countless times we've fucked this month. I have to grit my teeth against the urge to thrust wildly. She's bound to be sore after how hard we went at it last night.

"Yes. Go slow," she whimpers, her nails digging into my shoulders. "You're back where you belong. Fill me up."

Jesus. This woman. I bottom out, my hips flush against hers, and groan at the exquisite sensation. She's made for me. I'm made for her. This is exactly where I belong at all times.

I start to move, slowly rolling my hips, gliding in and out of her in long, smooth strokes. Deep and slow. I want it to be so good for her she'll come apart for me, soreness be damned.

Our mouths move together in a rhythm mirroring the deliberate roll of our bodies. Every kiss is hungry. Slick lips and searching tongues, like we're trying to memorize each other from the inside out. Her little whimpers hit me like lightning, soft and desperate, and I swallow them down greedily, wanting to hoard every sound she makes.

Her hands fist in my hair as her hips lift to meet me on every thrust, and I can feel her getting close—constricting around me, her breath catching on every gasp.

"Seamus," she pants. "God, I'm—so close—don't stop."

"I won't," I promise raggedly. "I've got you."

Then it slips out, not planned, not rehearsed—just real.

"I love you, Marcella."

Her eyes snap to mine, wide and stunned. Not afraid. Not for a second.

Something shifts in her face—softens, deepens—and she pulls me closer, nails digging into my back.

"I love you, too" she whispers. *So much.*"

The words punch through me like a heartbeat and I kiss her harder, deeper, like I can fuse us together with my mouth and cock working in tandem. She gasps, her body tensing, shaking apart beneath me.

"Come for me," I pant against her lips. "Let go, baby. I've got you."

I reach between us and rub tight circles around her slippery clit, just the way she likes. She comes with a keening cry, her pussy rippling around me, massaging my cock. I follow her over the edge with a guttural cry, spilling deep inside her.

We lay tangled together, my cock still buried, basking in the afterglow. I pepper her face with soft, reverent kisses, overwhelmed with love for this woman in my arms. "You're incredible," I whisper against her kiss-swollen lips. "So beautiful. So sexy. So mine."

"Yours," she agrees, her hands caressing the side of my face. "Yes."

We stay this way for a while—our bodies still joined, breath mingling in the quiet aftermath. Her fingers trace lazy patterns across my shoulder, and mine roam slowly over her curves. Almost like I'm trying to memorize her in this exact moment.

Because I am.

Eventually, she shifts with a soft sigh and I slip out.

She kisses my nose. "I need a shower."

"Don't be long," I murmur.

I watch her pad naked across the room, unhurried and unbothered, the curve of her ass swaying like a silent victory. She's not covering herself. Not glancing back to see if I'm looking. She's bare. Beautiful.

She's stopped trying to hide her naked body from me. Jesus, her newfound confidence does something to my heart.

Steam starts curling beneath the bathroom door within seconds. I lay there for a beat longer, letting the warmth of her body fade slowly from the sheets.

Then I follow.

Marcella doesn't look surprised when I step in behind her, just smiles softly and lifts her face to let the water run down her cheeks. I wrap my arms around her from behind, pressing a kiss to the back of her neck, and she leans into me without a word.

We don't do much talking. Or washing. Mostly touching. Kissing. Letting ourselves linger in the quiet before the world starts moving again.

Eventually, we emerge clean and flushed, wrapped in towels and sleepy grins. Marcella tugs on a hoodie and leggings, her hair piled into a loose, wet knot. I pull on the same scrubs I've been rotating through for the past few days, too content to care I look like a med school dropout.

She moves toward the kitchen, and I trail after her lazily. The room smells like rain—wet pavement and winter air drifting in through the cracked-open window. Light slants in, watery and gray. A winter morning begging for coffee and slow starts.

Marcella busies herself at the counter, pulling mugs from the shelf, starting the French press. I settle at the kitchen table, watching her move.

For the first time in days, my breath hitches uncomfortably. Not from love. Not from lust. From the low, creeping ache of dread.

Real life is coming. Fast.

Three days from now, I'll be back at the hospital, under Caldwell's watch. I have no idea what the hell's going to happen. What version of him I'll be facing. The fallout waiting for me.

I've spent the last few weeks in a beautiful, fantastical bubble with Marcella. This morning, I can feel it thinning. Expanding. Ready to pop.

Marcella turns and catches me staring, her expression softening immediately. "Okay," she walks over with the mugs, "you're officially stressed. What's going on in that brain of yours?"

"It's January." I take the mug from her and try to smile. "Caldwell's back next week."

Her brow furrows. "Do you think he'll retaliate?"

"No idea," I say honestly. "He hasn't reached out. I haven't spoken to him since the day he confronted me."

Marcella's quiet as she sips her coffee. Watching me. Not pushing. It's one of the things I love most about her. She lets me work through things without jumping in to fix or soften. When I speak, she really listens.

"I'm not scared of him," I say finally. "I don't trust him. I'm not on board with pretending like nothing happened."

Marcella sets down her mug and reaches across the table, curling her fingers around mine. "You don't have to pretend, not with me. Not with yourself. You'll figure it out as you go."

I stare at our hands, the way her thumb brushes over my knuckles, and something in my chest loosens. "Thanks, baby."

"You still love it, don't you? Neurosurgery?" She tilts her head.

I nod. "I do. What happened with Miranda changed something. Not my love for the work, my tolerance for people who treat it like a god complex. I just want to do it right. Help people. Not become some asshole surgeon who thinks he's above accountability."

"You won't. I know you won't." Her eyes soften.

The trust again. Marcella seems to see the best parts of me even when I'm second-guessing myself.

I don't know what it is about this woman. Her steady fire. Her insight. Her wit. Her body, for fuck's sake. She makes me want to be better. Want to fight harder for the life I actually want. My thumb skims the back of her hand. "Can I say something ridiculous?"

"Is it about how hard you are? Again?" She raises a brow.

I laugh. "No. Though, thank you for the segue."

She rolls her eyes, grinning.

I lean in, heart thudding. "I love you. I'm going to marry you."

Her smile slips. Not in fear—more like awe.

"I know it's early and it may not happen for a while," I add quickly. "I also don't expect you to be ready yet. I just want you to know where my head is at. This isn't about sex, though it certainly sweetens the deal—you're the woman I want to wake up to. Every. Fucking. Day."

Marcella stares at me like she's trying to process my confession. Then she stands, walks around the table and straddles my lap.

I look up at her, breath stuck in my throat.

"I love you so much," she whispers. "I'd marry you tomorrow."

I'm gone.

My hands slide under her hoodie, up her thighs, until I'm palming her ass and kissing her like I'll never stop. She moans into my mouth, grinding against me, and I feel myself harden beneath her.

"Are you sure?" I murmur.

She grins against my lips. "We haven't had kitchen table sex."

I don't argue.

We knock over a salt shaker. She tears off my shirt as I hike up her hoodie and slide her leggings down just enough to give me access. Her fingers are yanking down my waistband when I turn her and ease her over the edge of the table, spread her legs and slide in. She's slick and ready, as always.

Her hands slide down the table, anchoring her as I start to move. Intense, reverent thrusts sending sparks flying up my spine. She meets me stroke for stroke, her neck craned and eyes locked on mine.

This isn't just sex.

It's communion.

Her lips part in a whimper and I watch her come undone for me, again, and again—until I follow and fall against her, completely wrecked.

A few minutes later, as we clean up—laughing, breathless—she wraps her arms around my waist and rests her cheek against my back. "I'm not looking forward to work either," she says softly. "I'll be back in the office full-time next week and I'll miss this so much. We'll get through it, though."

She's right. We've been living in a world of our own—slow mornings, bare skin, quiet laughter.

The outside waits. Work. Pressure. Noise.

When she assures me we'll be fine—voice steady, eyes clear, conviction carved into every word—I won't brace for a crash.

I'll believe her.

Even if I know it isn't true.

Twenty-Seven

A Few Weeks Later

THE APARTMENT'S TOO QUIET.

Not peaceful—lonely.

The silence amplifies everything I've come to miss.

I'm still in the pencil skirt I swore I'd change out of two hours ago, slumped sideways on the couch with my blouse half-unbuttoned and my laptop burning a hole into my thighs.

The only sound is the occasional ping of my inbox, which I ignore at this late hour.

A bag of Thai food sits untouched on the counter. I'm not hungry. It's not fun to eat alone. Not anymore.

It's been several weeks since Seamus and I detonated every last rule we set between us. Two months of eye contact to make my stomach flip. Orgasms that should be illegal. Most of all, intimacy with an incredible man has snuck in the back door and I'll never be the same.

Over the holidays we lived in a suspended state of domesticity. Soft, rainy mornings and long showers. Sex whenever we wanted. Snuggling together like the world didn't exist outside my high-rise. In the new year, he moved in without a conversation. First, his toothbrush and toiletries. Then a selection of hoodies, graphic Ts and jeans. Now piles of scrubs are neatly stacked and tucked into the corner of my closet.

Effortless.

Sadly, the past couple of weeks have been different. Seamus is practically a ghost.

Even though I *thought* I understood the pressure he was under, I was very, very wrong. The neurosurgery program doesn't mess around. His schedule is brutal—lab work for much of the day, as many elective surgeries as he can manage, not to mention coursework, seminars, rounds.

To add to his stress, Caldwell is pretending Seamus doesn't exist. It's been two full months of silent treatment. Punishment, I guess. Abstractly, I figured this would happen when Seamus decided to cooperate with me. And while I don't think he'd change a thing, I feel guilty. His career is in jeopardy because of me.

On top of everything, his brother, Cillian entered rehab a week ago. Seamus carries the weight like it's his fault.

So, yeah. Things feel different. Heavier.

Our bubble sure didn't last long.

What's worse is my schedule isn't any better. A new case has me tangled up in surgical malpractice hell once again. This time a botched facelift has turned into a PR nightmare for a tech billionaire's wife. Her face is not only deformed, it won't move at all. Between the surgeon's gaslighting campaign and her husband spiraling into scary rages, I'm caught between legal firestorms and my own moral compass.

I find myself wondering, is this any way to live?

I glance at the time. Already past ten. Again.

The door clicks. The sound sends something warm through my whole body. He's home.

Seamus walks in like a man at the end of a war—drenched hoodie clinging to him, scrub pants rumpled, hair flattened by a wet beanie. His eyes find mine, bloodshot and exhausted, but there's a flicker.

Every time he looks at me, it feels like a promise whispered across lifetimes.

"Hey." His face lights up as I cross the room before he can take another step.

Seamus drops his bag with a thud and folds into me. His arms slide around my waist and he buries his face in my neck.

I rub my hands up and down his biceps. "You're soaked."

"Ah, it's nothing. You know the drill, we're native. Umbrellas are for wussies." He smirks.

I laugh under my breath. "Seattle: where dreams go to mildew."

We stand there for a long moment, breathing the same air. I hold him a little tighter. He lets me.

"Sixteen hours?" I mutter and scatter kisses on his jaw.

"Yup." He steps back and smooths my hair away from my face. "Caldwell passed me three times today. I could've lit myself on fire and he still wouldn't have looked at me."

I search his face. "Do you want to eat?"

"Yes—I'd like to eat you." He manages a grin.

It should sound cheesy. It doesn't. It sounds honest. Raw. We haven't had sex in a couple days, which seems like weeks considering how much we'd been going at it previously.

Now's probably not the time, though. I guide him to the couch, fingers laced in his. "Sit. I'll get you a towel."

"I love you." He sounds wrecked, like the day sanded him down to the nerve.

Tension bunches in my core as I head toward the bedroom. "Love you too."

I mean it. Every inch of me knows Seamus is the one for me. I also know this—what we're building—isn't easy. It's not going to get easier. Not with the life each of us has chosen.

I return with a towel and crouch in front of him, my knees protesting the position. "Lift," I demand.

Seamus leans forward, eyes half-lidded, and I pull his drenched hoodie over his head. His scrub top sticks to his skin, damp with rain and dried sweat, and I peel it off too.

He doesn't resist, just watches me like I'm his savior. "You gonna undress me every night?"

"Don't tempt me. I'll make a chart and everything."

I towel off his waves gently, raking my fingers through them, and he sighs so deeply it feels like something inside him loosens. The towel drops to his shoulders and I lean in, pressing a kiss to the space above his heart. He's warm, solid, alive.

"You don't have to talk about today," I whisper. "But, you can."

"I'm just so tired." The words are barely audible. "I keep wondering if I made the wrong call. Going back. Pushing through. Acting like it doesn't bother me Caldwell's icing me out while everyone else pretends it's normal."

I crawl into his lap without thinking, straddling him carefully, the towel draping us both like a cloak. My hands frame his face. "You didn't make the wrong call. He's the one being reckless, not you. You're not alone, Seamus. You're not."

There's a war behind his eyes. I kiss his forehead. His nose. His cheek. Then I hold him. Until the shaking stops. Until the shallow breaths even out.

"I hate Caldwell taking up space in your head." I stroke his chest. "After everything."

"I can handle the pressure. I always knew the risk that doing the right thing by Miranda could tank my residency." He palms my lower back and tugs me toward him. "It's a weird vibe at the hospital. I feel like everyone's watching me."

I set down my mug and turn to him. "Because of him?"

He nods, jaw tight. "He's the head of my program. If he wants to ice me out, doors will close. Slowly. Quietly. I'm working with a lot of other surgeons right now, which is normal during research year..." He exhales, frustrated. "I can feel it. Something's shifted."

"Could you switch specialties?" I hate how helpless I sound.

"No. It would be starting over." He shakes his head. "I've come too far. I'm halfway through my residency. I *love* neurosurgery. I can't let this derail my dream."

I struggle to find words. "I'm sorry, baby..."

"Don't. It's not your fault." He puts his finger to my lips. "I made a choice. I'd make it again. I don't know what comes next. I'll fight for what I believe in."

I shift to the side of him, curling one leg under me as I study his face. He's not just tired. He's...worn thin. Like something's slowly eating away at him, and he's been trying to outpace it for weeks. "Could you transfer?

I mean—if Caldwell keeps making things worse, would another school take you?"

He leans his head back and stares up at the ceiling like it holds the answer. "I don't want to leave Seattle. My family's here. You're here. Everything I love is here."

His words should comfort me, right? He doesn't want to leave. He's factoring me into the calculus.

Instead, it makes my mind race.

"Did you ever try to talk to him?" Even though he said it isn't my fault, let's be honest. He's only in this situation because of me. All I want to do is fix the mess I made for him. "You were close before all this happened."

Seamus lets out a sharp, humorless laugh. "Right. March into his office and ask him why he's been treating me like a radioactive threat." He shakes his head sadly. "I used to be one of his favorites, you know? The golden boy. First in, last out. The one my mentors wanted in their OR. Now I walk into a room and it goes quiet. Conversations stop. People watch me like I've got a knife in my coat." His voice drops. "I feel like a snitch. Like I betrayed some unspoken rule."

I place a hand on his thigh, grounding him. "You did it for Miranda."

"I know." He meets my eyes, and the hurt in them punches through me. "Unfortunately, I don't think it matters to any of them. Not in this competitive world. People are scared. Caldwell's got power. Influence. They're protecting themselves."

I reach for his hand and thread my fingers through his.

"I'm with you," I say softly.

I mean it.

Deep down, though, selfish, rotten fear coils tight in my stomach. If things get worse for Seamus—if he has to leave the program, the city, this life—what would it mean for us?

He's younger. Brilliant. Gorgeous. Talented.

His whole future is out in front of him and I don't want to be the reason he walks away from his dream. What if our bubble was temporary? A warm, safe, fragile space meant to be limited. What if it can't possibly hold up now the outside world has seeped back in?

"You've gone quiet." He pulls me closer.

"I'm spacing out," I lie, squeezing his hand tighter. "We'll figure it out. Whatever comes next."

Deep down, I wonder about our timing. If it will find a way to pull us apart.

His arms wind around me tighter, pulling me in until there's no space left between us. We stay pressed together for a while, our bodies heavy, the apartment hushed but humming with quiet tension. Not necessarily bad. The kind when you're both dealing with internal conflicts you're not ready to admit out loud.

Eventually, I coax him off the couch. He follows me into the bedroom, slow and reluctant, like his bones are heavier tonight. He sits on the edge of the bed while I get undressed. When I turn back, he's already peeled off his scrub pants and is sitting in his boxers, elbows on his knees, staring at the floor like it might offer answers.

"You want tea?" I move toward him. "Or whiskey?"

His eyes flick up, and there's a glint of mischief in them, just for a second. "Neither. Get your ass in bed."

"You get in, this is my side." I laugh and tug back the sheets.

He does. Quietly. Easily. Like gravity's stronger between us than anywhere else.

We lie there in the dark, my head on his chest, his fingers lazily tracing the curve of my shoulder. There's nothing sexual about it. Nothing demanding. Just skin and breath and an unspoken promise we're here for each other. Even when life is hard.

At least I hope so.

"I love you." I kiss his chest.

He exhales like I've given him a gift. "I love you so much, Marcella."

We fall asleep wrapped in each other. Two people doing the best we can.

For tonight, it's enough.

Twenty-Eight

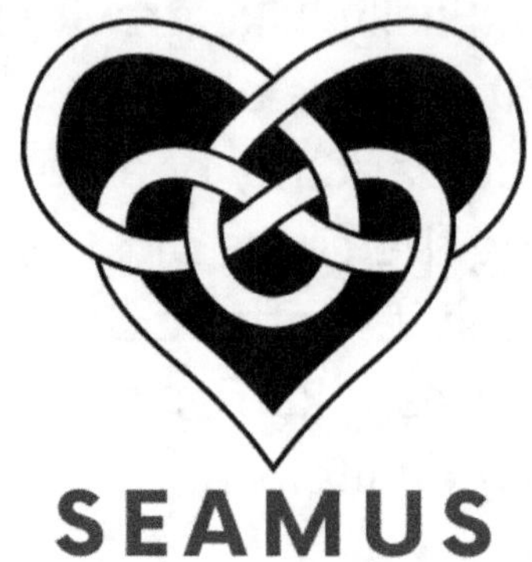

SEAMUS

A Few Weeks Later

Here goes nothing.

I'm about to pitch a study on female sexual response to one of the most respected doctors in the program—while half the hospital still thinks I'm conducting my own trials in the stairwells.

Smart.

Real smart.

I navigate through the maze of tables, my eyes scanning for Dr. Roberta Madison, one of my supervisors during my OBGYN rotation a couple years ago. Spotting her near the window, I make my way over.

The importance of the impending conversation presses down on me.

"Dr. Madison." I attempt a smile as I slide into the seat across from her.

"Seamus," she acknowledges. "It's been a while since we've last talked. What's going on?"

The hum of the hospital cafeteria surrounds me—a low murmur of conversations. Clinking utensils against plates. The occasional burst of laughter. It's a familiar symphony, one I've grown accustomed to over the years.

Today, it feels distant. Background noise in a world slowly shifting underneath my feet.

Dr. Madison sips her coffee, her sharp eyes studying me over the rim of her cup. As my OBGYN mentor, she always had an uncanny ability to see right through me, to peel back the layers and get to the core of whatever's on my mind. It's both comforting and unnerving.

It's also the reason I'm here.

"I've been giving a lot of thought to my upcoming R-5 year and what subspecialty interest I'd like to pursue." I take a deep breath, steadying myself. "I'm interested in neural mechanisms underlying female sexual function."

Her eyebrows lift, a mixture of curiosity and intrigue flashes across her face. "What a fascinating area. Not many venture into that territory."

"Part of the appeal." I offer a slight nod.

She leans back in her chair and crosses her arms. "Alright, Seamus. Walk me through it. What's driving this interest?"

"Over the past few months, I've felt...off." I choose my words carefully. "Not with the work itself—it's the environment. The hospital is tense. Unpredictable. I'm not naïve enough to think people aren't talking."

Dr. Madison crosses one leg over the other, her gaze unreadable. "You're referring to your situation with Caldwell."

"Yeah." I exhale. "I'm sure you've heard what happened. The case. Miranda Black."

"I heard some things," she says evenly. "Rumors, statements. I've read between the lines."

I nod. "He hasn't spoken to me since the settlement. Not a word. No eye contact. No acknowledgment. Honestly, it feels like my name has been quietly circled in red ink. I'm not saying I'm being sabotaged. I'm not getting invited to the table either."

"You're concerned this situation will follow you into R5 and beyond?" She tilts her head.

"Of course it will. Next year I have an opportunity. We're meant to dive deeper into something we care about, right?" My hands are gesturing more than normal because I feel like this is my only chance to salvage things here in Seattle. "The goal is to explore something meaningful to further my studies. Originally I wanted to go into neurosurgery because of my family's history with alcohol. It's not what's driving me anymore."

She leans back, still listening.

"I've worked hard for over a decade. I'm terrified if don't branch out from under Caldwell's shadow—it won't matter what I do. The doors will still be closed." I sigh.

"So?" she prompts.

"I want to design a research track." I meet her eyes. "Neurosurgical implications of female sexual dysfunction. Brain connectivity, arousal response, regional mapping—what we know, what we don't. I want to spend my R5 year working on it. Clinical data, neuroimaging, maybe even collaboration with OBGYN."

I pause. Waiting. I've dangled the carrot.

"Ah." She steeples her fingers, eyes narrowing with curiosity rather than judgment. "Why this subject, Seamus? Why now?"

I hesitate, only for a second. If I want this to work—if I want her to trust me—I have to be real. Even if this is extremely personal.

"I've fallen in love..." Her eyebrows lift, just slightly as I continue, "...with a woman who's never, until me, been with someone who actually understood how to give her pleasure. Without going into the long, sordid history, my interest in this subject started a long time ago. I started reading studies about the neurobiology of female arousal back in med school. It wasn't required, I first stumbled across the research after a class on cortical sensory maps. The variability fascinated me and, as I've been thinking about my future, realize it still does. Humans—mainly men—seem to think sex is a simple binary mechanism. It's not, especially for women and their desire and ability to orgasm."

She holds up a hand. "I didn't expect our conversation to go in this direction."

"Look, I'm not trying to make you uncomfortable. This isn't salacious. It's truly important to me." I shift in my chair because it sucks this topic feels taboo, even in the medical realm. This is part of why I want to tackle it. "Neurosurgery's always been my plan and still is. However, this is a chance to explore how brain function plays into something most people dismiss as emotional or behavioral. I don't want to chase tabloid science. I want to do this with intention. Rigor. Data. Yes, maybe a little fire under my ass, because my back is against the wall right now."

I stop for a moment to gauge her response.

"Go on." Dr. Madison settles back into her chair.

"Sure. I'm struck by how little we understand about the neural mechanisms underlying female sexual function." I decide to lay it all out there. "Especially given the studies indicating specific brain regions—like the medial frontal gyrus, inferior frontal gyrus, putamen, and entorhinal cortex—play roles in sexual desire and arousal. There's still so much uncharted territory to explore."

Dr. Madison's gaze sharpens. "You're referring to the fMRI study on HSDD?"

"For one," I reply, leaning forward. "In that particular study, women with hypoactive sexual desire disorder were shown to exhibit different activation patterns compared to those without the condition. Understanding these differences could be pivotal in developing targeted treatments."

She lifts her chin, contemplating. "Do you believe neurosurgical interventions could play a role in addressing these dysfunctions?"

"Well, it's certainly a possibility worth exploring," I say earnestly. "If I can pinpoint the neural circuits involved, there might be ways to modulate them, either surgically or through neuromodulation techniques."

Dr. Madison's lips curve into a thoughtful smile. "Ambition has never been your shortcoming." Then her brow furrows. "Let me ask again. Why now? Don't give me the poetic answer—give me the practical one."

"Um..." I brace myself. "Despite my situation with Caldwell, I'd rather make something of this moment than sit around waiting for someone to decide my future."

She hums. "What about the stairwells?"

"Excuse me?" I freeze, mortified.

"You've got a reputation," she says plainly. "You're smart. Talented. Too smooth for your own good. Plenty of extracurriculars, from what I've heard."

My face flushes. I tamp it down because this is serious to me, so I hold her gaze. "I'm not going to lie. I've had consensual sexual encounters with a handful of women at the hospital. Nurses and other residents mostly. I can explain. It's not what it probably seems like."

Dr. Madison says nothing—just watches me. Calm. Neutral. A little too quiet.

"It started during med school," I go on, shifting again in the uncomfortable cafeteria chair as I explain what happened with Tara and Priya. "When I started my residency, there was a nurse I worked with who was smart, competent and older than me by a few years. We were on overnights together, and one night, we were standing outside the on-call room waiting for a consult when she kissed me. Told me she'd heard about my 'research' and wanted to participate."

My lips twitch with the memory—how nervous I'd been, how electrified. "We slipped into the stairwell. I used a couple of techniques I'd mastered. Let's just say they worked well. Afterward she told me no man had ever paid attention to her body like I had."

She purses her lips. I keep going. At this point, I might as well.

"She wanted to keep meeting. Once, sometimes twice a week. Same spot, same rhythm. I thought we were building something—this connection, you know?" I think back to when it was happening. "After a month or so, she told me the truth. She had a boyfriend and saw a future with him, and wanted to have a secret relationship. Obviously, I ended it."

I glance down. "She told her friends about me, though. Loose-lipped bragging, I guess. Suddenly, I started getting approached. Women who were curious. Frustrated. Looking for something private, easy, safe. I had more offers than I could keep up with—I never initiated any of this."

"How come you felt compelled to saying yes?" Madison grimaces, not exactly unkindly. More like...pointed.

"Um." I look away for a second. "You have to understand, I was lonely. It was an outlet—a pleasurable one. For me it was clinical. Each woman was different. How they responded. What made them unravel. I was careful—consensual, clear about boundaries, always..."

I trail off, eyes flicking up to meet hers. I sound like a tool. "Look, I didn't realize the reputation I was building. Or the nicknames I was given. I didn't understand or even imagine the women would be confused about my own intentions. Or, how this shit could follow me. Looking back, it was a little fucked up."

Dr. Madison leans back slightly. "Well yes, if you were experimenting with the staff."

"God..." *Fuck*. She's right. I nod again. "I should have had better judgment. With the exception of one incident last year, I stopped over two years ago. It started to feel hollow."

She stares at me, probably in shock.

"For what it's worth, and this may come as a surprise—I was actually a virgin until a few months ago. All of the encounters were...essentially masturbation. Now, I have a serious girlfriend. I see a future with her." I breathe out heavily. "She's the lawyer who represented Miranda's parents."

Dr. Madison presses her fingertips together. "Seamus, this is quite a lot to digest."

"I get it." I try to keep my tone calm and open. "I'm not trying to spin it. You deserve the truth."

She studies me. "Marcella Delgado represented the Blacks."

"Yeah."

"Now you're telling me the two of you are romantically involved."

"Recently," I clarify. "Nothing happened while we were on opposite sides. She convinced me to tell the truth...for Miranda. We were there when they took her off life support and then..."

"You fell for her."

I nod. "Yes. Deeply. She's it for me."

She watches me carefully. "Thank you for being honest, Seamus. All of this is very complicated. Now, let's cut to the chase. What exactly are you asking from me?"

I can see it in her eyes: the needle has moved a little. *Enough.*

"Not for a pass or to ignore what's happened." I begin my actual pitch. "I'm asking to design a research track under your guidance. To give me a chance to dig into something I care about and which could bolster your practice as well. Why not turn what people are whispering about into something useful? Something to actually help women. If I'm going to burn bridges, I want it to be for something that matters."

"Look, I don't support projects driven by personal guilt or romance." She narrows her eyes. "If you can back up your passion with discipline, I'll consider it. You'll need to write a formal proposal. I want an outline of your objectives, your proposed research timeline, and a clear plan for collaboration. I won't go to bat for you unless you come in prepared."

I nod, swallowing down relief. "You'll have it by the end of next week."

"Don't get anything twisted. Even if I agree, I won't be here to offer you sanctuary." Dr. Madison doesn't mince words. "I won't pick sides. If you're serious—and I mean academically serious—then I'll consider it."

My heart pounds. "Thank you. Your expertise makes you an ideal mentor for this endeavor."

Her gaze drifts to the window behind me. For a second, I think we're done. I start to stand.

"*Seamus.*"

I glance at her and lower myself back down. "Yeah?"

She leans in. "You should know, there are serious rumors floating around. You came for Caldwell professionally. Embarrassed him. He expected you to back him and you didn't play ball."

I let the rage simmer just under my ribs. "I didn't play ball because he put the blame on me. He ignored a vessel I flagged. He made the call and killed a twelve-year-old girl. I'd do it again."

"Seamus." Dr. Madison folds her arms and clucks her tongue. "Flagging a vessel and having a different surgical opinion doesn't automatically make him wrong. Surgeons make judgment calls every day. Are you certain it wasn't just a bad outcome?"

Shit. My throat constricts. "I was there. I know what I saw."

"I believe you," she says gently. "You're not just judging the outcome. You're assigning motive. There's a difference."

I stare at the floor, frustration presses down on my chest like a weight I can't lift.

"I think you're in more trouble than you realize." She leans in. "I've heard gossip—Caldwell's not just icing you out. He's started asking around. Quietly gathering names. Nurses, maybe a few residents. The ones you used to see."

My blood runs cold. *"What?"*

"He's building something, Seamus. You know how this works. He won't hit until he's sure the floor will drop out from under you." She tilts her head. "May I ask you a question?"

I nod. "Yeah."

"Marcella pushed you to side with the Blacks and confirm Caldwell's role, didn't she?" Her voice is barely a whisper. "For Miranda?"

I freeze. "She asked me questions in a deposition. I had to answer honestly."

"Did you though?" Her tone isn't accusatory—more reflective. "Entirely? In essence, despite the settlement the Blacks received, you're the one taking the fall professionally. Has it been worth it? Have you asked yourself whether she wanted justice or to close the case with a win?"

I clench my jaw. "Are you insinuating she used me?"

"No. I'm saying it's worth asking her the question." She lifts her chin. "Don't you think? You're in the middle of your research year. Evaluate what's in front of you. Don't let how you feel about her cloud the evidence."

I feel like I'm about to vomit.

Dr. Madsion brings up a valid point. I haven't allowed myself to question any of it. Not the fallout. Not the whispers. Not the shift in the way people look at me.

I've always assumed Marcella was trying to protect me.

What if she wasn't?

What if she was doing her job?

Dr. Madison softens. "You're not naïve, Seamus. You're loyal. Sometimes, the two can get tangled."

I nod. "Thank you for your concern."

She gets up and puts her hand on my shoulder. "You've earned the heads up. Don't waste it. If you can navigate through this, you're going to be a world-class surgeon, doctor."

My pulse stutters.

Because now I'm not just wondering how to salvage my residency.

I'm wondering if I've misread everything with Marcella. Did she really care about me? Or was I just strategy? *Fuck.*
If I can't be sure of her motives...how can I be sure about us?

Twenty-Nine

MARCELLA

Two Days Later

IT'S SATURDAY EVENING AS I pull into the parking garage.

I'm not looking forward to an empty condo.

Seamus has been buried in the hospital all week—long hours, back-to-back cases, late-night rounds.

Some version of us still exists.

Though he didn't text back last night when I went to dinner at my parents' and crashed at Rosa's.

I told myself he was busy. Tired. Distracted.

I'm trying not to read into it.

Which, for me, means I've already drafted a worst-case scenario and three contingency plans I'll never admit to having.

My sister told me not to worry.

Impossible. I'm scared to death. He hasn't been himself—then again, we really haven't known each other long. Maybe this *is* himself.

Anyway, the bloom seems to be off the rose.

So when I open the door to my condo, I don't expect to find Seamus hunched over his laptop at my dining table, surrounded by half-drunk cups of coffee and what looks like a digital graveyard of a hundred open browser tabs.

He's wearing a navy-blue hoodie with sleeves shoved up to his elbows. His hair is its usual mess, like he's been running his hands through it all afternoon. The overhead light casts sharp shadows on his face, highlighting the strain in his jaw.

He looks up when he hears me drop the keys on the counter and for a split second, the corners of his mouth lift. "You're back."

"I didn't expect to see you. I thought you had to work." I set my overnight bag down. Something about the way he doesn't stand and cross the room to kiss me makes my stomach knot up.

He turns his laptop screen toward me. "I swapped out my hospital shifts. I've been putting together an important proposal."

"Proposal?" I blink, trying to catch up. We haven't seen each other in two days. Our texts have been pretty sparse.

"Yeah. For my R5 year." He rubs his eyes. "I'm officially pitching a focused study on the intersection of neurosurgical pathways and female sexual function. Dr. Madison said she'd consider it if I gave her something concrete."

My eyes widen. "Wow."

"I pulled some of the old Stanford studies, plus the fMRI data from the Arnow trials, and I'm mapping a study to incorporate both neurological imaging and surgical case reviews."

He's talking fast—too fast. His words are technically enthusiastic. It's weird, there's no joy behind them. I'm watching someone in full panic mode.

I step closer, placing my hand on the table near his. "Sounds...ambitious."

"It has to be." Seamus's mouth twitches. "If Caldwell's going to continue ignoring me, I have to figure out a way to get through the next three years."

There it is.

"So nothing's changed?" I sink into the chair next to him. He's been so tight-lipped. It's time for him to tell me what's going on.

He shakes his head. "Well, yes. It's worse. People are talking. I can feel it when I walk into the hospital. It's like I've got a target painted on my back." I reach for his hand, but he stands abruptly, pretending not to notice.

"Anyway. This isn't your problem. Did you have a nice visit with your sister?"

His back is to me as he organizes a stack of printouts. The brush-off stings.

Feeling desperate to connect to the man I love, I move behind him, press my chest to his back and slide my arms around his waist. "You've been working nonstop." I trail my fingers along the tensioned line of his shoulder. "Let me take care of you."

He exhales—shaky, uncertain. Doesn't say no.

I shift closer and press a kiss to the back of his neck. I feel the way his entire body tenses then sags slightly. I inch my hands under his sweatshirt, palms warm against his skin, tracing the hard ridges of his abdomen. He shudders when I trail kisses to the spot just behind his ear.

"Come sit," I whisper.

He lets me guide him, pliant but distracted, and lowers himself onto the couch with a soft grunt. I slide between his knees, the hardwood floors beneath mine, and rest my hands on his thighs.

His gaze meets mine. Open. Vulnerable.

I tug at the waistband of his sweats. "Lift up."

He raises his hips and I ease his pants down. His cock is already heavy and half-erect, resting against his abdomen. He watches as I take him in my hand, stroking slow at first then more assertively. His lashes flutter and his mouth parts slightly. Leaning down, I lick him from root to tip before taking him fully into my mouth. His fingers twist into the couch cushion.

There's a beat—one long, suspended moment—where it's just us.

The weight of him on my tongue. The soft, guttural sound he makes when I hollow my cheeks and suck. The way his hand slides to the back of my neck, not pushing, just grounding.

I close my eyes and lose myself in it. In him. In the way his thighs tense under my hands. His salty, musky taste leaking from his crown as it hits the back of my throat. The way my lips barely manage to encompass his thick cock.

Without thinking, Seamus breathes my name like it's a prayer he's not sure he deserves.

His hips move and buck and when he comes, it's with a broken gasp—his whole body bows toward me, one trembling hand fisted in my hair like he's trying to hold on to something real. I swallow everything he gives me, gently licking him clean, not stopping until I feel his fingers relax.

When I do sit back on my heels and glance up—

He's not looking at me anymore.

His head drops into his hands, elbows on his knees, body still shaking. Not from pleasure.

From something else.

My heart squeezes so tightly I can hardly breathe.

"Seamus?" I press my hands over his. "What is it?"

He doesn't lift his head. "I didn't want to fall apart like this."

"Hey." I coax his arms down so I can see his face. His eyes are glassy and unfocused. His mouth turned down in a grimace, like he's holding in something sharp.

"You didn't do anything wrong." His voice cracks. "That was...amazing. You're perfect. It's just—" He breaks off, like the words get caught in his throat.

"What?" The fear still creeps in like smoke under the door.

"I feel like I'm drowning," he rasps. "I've been trying so hard to keep it together for you. For us. The truth is I don't know what the fuck I'm doing anymore. With Caldwell. With work. With everything."

Bracing myself for the worst, I shift up beside him. Pull him into me, winding my arms around his shoulders. His damp forehead presses on my collarbone as he trembles against me. His devastation cracks me open. "Talk to me."

"I met with Dr. Madison. She told me Caldwell..." He squeezes his eyes shut. "He's actively building something against me to push me out."

I feel the air leave the room. "What?"

"Oh, he's doing it. There's no doubt. It all makes sense now." He slumps back against the cushions.

"Because he fucked up and you called him on it?" I'm furious.

He looks at me, broken. "I don't know who I am anymore. I did what I did. Then Miranda...and I don't regret helping you or her family. But Caldwell, the silence, the fucking exile—and now this? I don't think I come back from it."

"You don't have to," I say gently. "It's a bump in the road. There's got to be a way to move forward."

He shakes his head. "I can't even fathom how. Moving forward probably means leaving all of this behind."

"Including me?" I choke out selfishly.

"I don't know." His voice cracks. "I don't want to. I can't promise anything. My professional life is in utter fucking chaos."

I swallow the ache in my chest because I need to put big girl panties on. Shove my own terrified feelings aside and be there for him without worrying how it affects me.

"I'm not going to pressure you, baby. You're the kindest, sweetest, most caring man I've ever known and I'm horrified you're in this position." I cup his cheek. "It's unfair for you to have this hanging over your head and reprehensible for Caldwell to try and destroy you over his own mistake."

He pulls me into his lap, buries his face in my shoulder. "You always make me feel like I'm enough."

"You are." I press my forehead to his.

God. What have I walked into tonight? Even though I knew something was off the second I walked in—I didn't expect this. I have no idea how to help him other than allowing him to work through his complicated situation without me trying to influence him one way or the other.

His arms are still around my waist when I say, "I need to ask you something."

He doesn't flinch. Doesn't speak.

I wait.

"You can be honest. Are you questioning our relationship?" My voice cracks. "Or is this only about Caldwell?"

His head drops to my shoulder. The silence between us is like an icy wind permeating the warmth between our bodies.

"I don't know," Seamus admits. "Maybe both. Maybe they're the same thing."

It hits me like a slap.

I pull away enough to see his face. "Oh?"

"You asked for honesty and the truth is, I wouldn't be questioning this—us—if you hadn't needed me to go against him. Then again, if I hadn't..." he swallows hard, "if I hadn't been in her surgery I wouldn't have spent the last two months wondering whether I destroyed my entire career because I didn't play politics right. On the other hand, I wouldn't have met you and you're the best thing in my life right now."

The lump in my throat threatens to rise. "You testified because it was the right thing to do."

"Was it *entirely* the right thing to do?" Something raw and unguarded flickers behind his eyes.

His words slice through my gut. "What are you saying, Seamus?"

"Marcella, I beat off to your picture every fucking night from the day and hour I saw you. I wanted you desperately, despite the fact you were a threat to my own career. Maybe I was so infatuated with you—what I felt, what I wanted—that I didn't stop to think how my cooperation would play out. Or if you—" He cuts himself off, jaw clenching.

"If I what?" I demand. "If I used you?"

"I'm not saying you did it purposely," he says quickly. "When I told Madison I was in love with you, she brought up something I can't un-hear. She wondered if I was so eager to be your hero I didn't see the full picture. She pointed out the nuances we, as doctors, face every day and asked me if I assumed the worst about Caldwell's intentions because it justified what I wanted to do."

"So, you think I *manipulated* you?" I'm crushed, and not sure I want the answer.

"I think I don't know," he says honestly. "I think I'm trying to make sense of all of it. You're the only person who's ever made me feel seen. Loved. Wanted. I want to believe what we have is real."

I pull my knees up and protectively wrap my arms around them. "I never asked you to lie."

"I didn't lie."

"You told the truth."

"I told *my* truth." He drags a hand through his hair. "I also assigned blame. I wanted Caldwell to be the villain because it was easier to walk away from the part of me that respected him unconditionally. When I started at UW, I wanted to *be* him."

I watch him in silence, aching in places I didn't know were still breakable. "Now?"

"Now I don't know what's worse." He winces. "If I was wrong about him and fucked things up or if I was right and fucked things up."

His words pierce me like dagger, long and jagged. I don't know how to handle this.

So I tell him *my* truth. "I didn't deliberately use you, Seamus."

He looks at me, his eyes brimming with unshed tears.

"I'm not saying I wasn't focused on winning. I was. That's who I am. I never lied to you about Caldwell. I believed then—and still do—what he did to Miranda was reckless." I let out a breath I didn't realize I was holding. "Maybe not malicious. Or intentional. *Reckless*. I proved the legal standard, cut and dry."

Seamus exhales, like my explanation matters.

It should.

It also doesn't fix things.

"At the same time if I had known how deeply I'd end up feeling about you and what your cooperation would cost you professionally..." I trail off. "If I'd known what it would do to *us* over the past few weeks, I might've gone about it differently. Or at least warned you. I couldn't know it at the time. I'm so sorry. I completely understand why you'd question me. I only hope you can feel how much I truly love you and would never intentionally do anything to hurt you."

"I believe you." He nods again, though his eyes are focused on the floor. "Unfortunately, there's more. Apparently Caldwell's legal team is circling a few of the women I was—with."

"What?" My blood goes cold.

"Trying to paint me like some sex-crazed deviant." He meets my eyes. "The worst part? He doesn't have to lie to make me look bad. I gave him the ammunition."

"Bullshit." I'm on my feet now, anger burning up my spine. "You never had power over them. They came to you."

"Marcella, I'm a big, imposing man who used the stairwell like a fucking makeshift motel," he spits out bitterly. "You think anyone's going to care I was technically propositioned in the first place? Believe I never crossed the line into fucking them?"

"I care," I whisper.

"In the beginning *you* questioned my reputation." He scrubs his face with his hand. "It's how he's going to bury me and make it impossible to get hired. The only reason I'm submitting this proposal is Dr. Madison said she'd consider working with me if I can navigate out of this situation. She's not going to take sides."

I nestle into his side and take his hand. "This I can help you with. You fight back. Tell the truth. All of it."

"Even the part where I lost my virginity to the woman who sued my mentor?" His eyebrow quirks.

A small, strangled laugh slips from me. *"Jesus..."*

"It sounds insane."

"Yeah." I squeeze his hand. "It's also our truth. Let's lean in."

He threads his fingers through mine, resting our joined hands on his thigh. "Do you still believe in us?"

I think about it—really think.

About how tired I've been lately. How our days have turned into snatched hours between our professional chaos. How I've spent nights lying awake wishing he were home, wondering if I'd made a mistake by falling too fast. Too hard.

Still...

"I believe in us. I think we're meant to be together."

He whimpers out a breath like he's been hoping this would be my answer.

"I'm scared, baby," I whisper. "If we can't fix this, what if you wake up and realize I'm the one who derailed your dream?"

"You're not." He shakes his head.

I burrow into him. "How can you be sure?"

"Because." His hand curls around mine. "When it comes down to it, you're the only person who makes my dream feel possible."

I let his words wash over me. Allow it to try to undo the shame and self-doubt and fear building inside me for the last thirty minutes of this conversation.

"I'm not great at relationships," I admit. "Historically, I push people away before they can hurt me. I promise not to push you away."

Seamus tugs me back into his lap. "Let's be bad at relationships together."

I press my forehead to his, eyes closed. "I'm not letting you drown in this alone. Caldwell wants to weaponize your past? Let him try. You've got someone protecting *you* now. With everything I have."

"Someone scary as hell in court."

"Damn right."

He chuckles, and for the first time tonight, it doesn't sound hollow.

We sit in silence for a long moment, the weight of everything still real. No longer unbearable.

"You know what's a light in the tunnel about all this?" he finally says.

"What?"

"I think this study...it's feels like the right direction for me, regardless." His eyes light up. "Not just to get out from under Caldwell. It matters. It means something."

I smile. "Then let's make it happen."

Seamus's brow lifts. "Let's?"

"You didn't think I'd let you write a whole-ass research proposal on female sexuality without a little editing finesse, did you?" I kiss his cheek.

His grin breaks wide open. "God, I *love* you."

We're not unscathed. We're not perfect.

We're scarred and stubborn and still here.

This time, we move forward with eyes wide open.
No more running.
Only choosing each other.
Every damn day.

Thirty

SEAMUS

The Next Day

IT'S JUST PAST TEN when I crack an eye open and realize two things:

One, the sun is already blinding.

Two, the woman curled against me has somehow managed to steal all the covers.

Again.

Marcella lets out a sleepy noise and snuggles deeper under the blanket, her thigh sliding over mine. I grin into the pillow.

"You awake?" I murmur against her hair.

She hums. "Barely."

"Good." I kiss her temple.

She nestles against me, slow and decadent, her warm curves pressing into mine with all the familiarity of a woman who knows exactly where she belongs. "What time is it?" she mumbles, voice thick with sleep.

"We've got a couple hours," I murmur, brushing her hair back to kiss her temple. "Plenty of time to be fashionably late to my ma's."

Marcella giggles and buries her face in my chest. "She'll know exactly what we've been up to."

I grin. "Especially if you hoard her brown bread like a dragon. She'll know how we've worked up an appetite."

She snorts, her laugh vibrating through my ribs, and I strengthen my hold around her. It's easy again. Comfortable. Like we've been waking up tangled in each other for years, not just a few short months.

Three and change, to be exact.

Three months of falling hard and fast. Of messy honesty and a couple near implosions. Of figuring out what it means to choose each other when the world's spinning too fast and trying to pull you apart.

We've already had a rough patch. With moments when I wasn't sure we'd find our way back.

We did.

Now it's like we can't get enough of each other. We've been trying to erase the ache of those weeks every time we fuck each other like feral rabbits on a countdown.

We've earned this part—the love. Sex. Ridiculous banter. Our return to something steady. Grounding.

She finally pushes the blanket down and rolls to her back, one slow movement at a time, her body arching, like she's waking from the deepest sleep of her life. The sheets slide off her skin.

My breath catches in my throat. Every. Fucking. Day.

She's bare from head to toe—draped in morning light and nothing else. Her heavy breasts rise and fall with every breath, full and flushed from where I'd already spent the better part of the night worshiping them. Her nipples are dusky and tight, drawing my eyes like a fucking magnet. One leg is bent, the other extended, her hip curves into the mattress like a sin I'm about to commit all over again.

The sleepy smile on her lips?

It wrecks me.

She reaches for me—one slow, inviting curl of her fingers—and I go without hesitation. Crawl over her and brace my forearms on either side of her head like I've done a hundred times before. Sex with her still feels new. Electric. She tilts her face up, and I meet her lips with a tender, reverent kiss, then deepen it into something hungrier.

My cock is already hard again—has been since she woke up. I don't rush, though. I lower my mouth to her neck, dragging my lips across the soft skin just beneath her ear. She shivers and tilts her head to give me more.

"God, Seamus," she breathes.

I hum against her skin, trailing kisses down the slope of her shoulder, over the swell of her breast, and finally closing my mouth over her nipple.
Her back arches like it always does—beautiful and instinctive—and I lick and suck until her fingers are in my hair, tugging, guiding.

"More," she whispers, hips rocking against me. "Please."

I slide my hand down the warm curve of her belly, then lower, until my fingers slip through slick heat.

Fuck.

Always so ready for me.

I stroke her slowly, circling her clit until her legs fall open wider, her thighs trembling as I build her up, up, up. I don't let her come—not yet.

When I finally slide inside her, it's one long, deliberate thrust, so exquisite it punches a hole in my chest. Her breath hitches and her legs wrap around my hips, locking me in place like she can't stand the idea of any space between us.

This isn't a quick fuck. It's not frantic or wild.

It's something else.

It's the way she gasps my name like it's the only word she remembers. The way her nails dig into my back when I angle just right. Slide against the spot that makes her come undone every single time. The way she looks at me—eyes wide, lips parted, makes me feel like I'm giving her something she didn't know she needed.

We move together like we've done this for years. Like we've memorized each other's rhythm in another life and are just falling back into it now.

Her hands frame my face, fingers sliding into my hair, and I brace one arm under her shoulder, the other on her hip, pulling her into each thrust. Her breasts press against my chest, her skin hot and slick with sweat, and every inch of her feels like fucking heaven.

"Harder," she whispers, her voice ragged.

I shift, digging my knees into the mattress and drive into her harder, deeper. Her moan catches in her throat, one hand clinging to my shoulder while the other slides down between us.

"Let me," I pant, and she nods, allowing me take over.

I rub her clit in tight, perfect circles, never breaking rhythm. I can tell her body starts to react by the way her inner muscles grip my cock like a vise.

"Let go." I press my forehead to hers. "Come for me, baby."

She breaks with a cry—low, guttural, desperate. Her body trembles beneath mine, her back arching, mouth open as she falls apart. I ride it out, every flex of her body dragging me closer to the edge.

When she starts to come down, I slow just enough to keep us connected, then shift again—rolling her on top of me in one motion. She blinks down at me, dazed and glowing.

"Ride me." I brush her hair off her face.

Marcella sinks down on me slowly, taking me back in with a shudder. Her mouth drops open. "Fuck…"

She starts to move, her hands braced on my chest, her pace unhurried and delicious. Every roll of her hips is heaven. Watching her like this—hair wild, breasts bouncing, skin flushed, pleasure etched into every line of her face—makes it impossible to last.

I grasp her waist, thrusting up to meet her, losing myself in the rhythm we create. It's raw. Intimate. Holy, even.

"I love you," I breathe.

Her eyes fly open. "Say it again."

"I love you."

She leans down, kissing me so hard it's like she's pouring everything she feels into our kiss. Her hips never stop moving.

"I love you too. Come with me," she whispers against my mouth. "I want to feel you fill me up."

God. I'm already there.

As she requests, I thrust deep and explode. My body shakes, and hers follows, both of us clinging to each other like we'll never let go.

We collapse, breathless and completely spent.

I pull her close, pressing my lips to her shoulder as her breathing evens out.

"Jesus," I murmur into her skin. "You'll be the death of me."

She laughs softly, snuggling into my chest.

Because we both know—this is the kind of death you welcome because it feels like being reborn.

I must doze off for a bit—just long enough for the edges of the morning to blur. When I crack one eye open again, the light in the room has shifted, warmer now, angling through the windows just so. Marcella's head is on my chest, chestnut hair spilled like silk across my ribs.

Her fingers absentmindedly trace the lines of my stomach. "We should probably get up. Your mother's going to guilt me for stealing her son if we're late again."

"We've got time. Plenty." I settle back into position.

She tilts her head up, eyes half-lidded. Playful. "Yeah? Join me in the shower?"

It's all the invitation I need.

She's up before I am, padding across the room with zero concern about being naked—warmth floods my ribs in the best way. Gone are her insecurities. She moves like a curvy queen who knows damn well she's worshiped.

Because she *is*.

I watch her go, letting myself enjoy the view for one long beat before I push off the mattress and follow.

By the time I enter the bathroom, Marcella is standing under the spray, eyes closed, hands running through her wet hair. Water glides over her skin, beading at the tips of her breasts and sliding down the curve of her stomach. She's unreal. A fucking masterpiece.

I step in behind her, wrapping my arms around her waist. She melts back into me like she's been waiting for hours, not minutes.

"Took your time," she teases.

"Worth it," I murmur, brushing her wet hair off her shoulder to kiss the spot just beneath her ear.

She tilts her head, giving me better access, and I trail kisses down her neck and across her shoulder, while my hands slide up her slick skin to cup her breasts. She's already breathing heavier.

Her hips roll back, pressing into me, and when she feels how hard I am, she lets out a low, wicked laugh. "Again?"

"Always."

Marcella turns in my arms and I kiss her before she can say another word. Wet and hungry. I walk her slowly backward until her back is against the tile. Her leg lifts, wrapping around my waist without prompting, and I reach down to guide myself inside her in one slow thrust.

I brace one hand against the wall, the other holding her thigh as I drive into her. She bites her bottom lip, trying to muffle the moan ripping out of her when I pull out and thrust again, harder this time.

The sound of the water, the slap of wet skin, her breathless cries—it's all I can hear as we fuck. When she comes, her head tips back against the tile, and the quiet, broken sound she makes? It undoes me. I follow her over the edge, my hips stuttering, emptying everything I have with a guttural cry pulled from somewhere deeper than my lungs.

We stand there for a long moment after, forehead to forehead, still breathing each other in.

Eventually, she laughs softly. "Okay. Now we really need to get ready."

We step out into the thick bathroom air, grabbing towels and bumping into each other as we move. She shoots me a mock-glare when she realizes her lotion bottle is empty. "You used the last of the good stuff, didn't you?"

"You'll survive." I grin, wrapping my towel low on my hips.

She narrows her eyes. "If you're not careful, I'll hide your razors."

"You wouldn't dare." I chuckle, leaning in to kiss her wet cheek.

We bicker our way back into the bedroom, laughing and towel-drying—our effortless banter is like breathing.

Like routine.

Like *us*.

By two, we're dressed and heading to my parents' house. Marcella's in jeans and a soft black sweater. Her is hair twisted up with pieces falling loose.

I steal a kiss in the elevator down to the garage, and she shakes her head at me, smiling. "What's gotten into you today?"

"I'm happy," I say simply.

She doesn't answer, her hand finds mine and squeezes.

The drive over is full of music and light teasing. Marcella reads me a few text messages from her brother Lucas, who's trying to convince Rosa to put some lamb dish back on the menu. I let her vent about the new witness who just blew a hole in her deposition strategy.

We talk about everything, other than Caldwell. He can wait. I still haven't let anyone from my family in on what's happening. Not until we have our ducks in a row.

Inside, the madness is already in full swing. As usual, Liam and Padraig are in a heated discussion about setlists and gear logistics. Connor's listening, clearly distracted, his curls pulled back and his brow furrowed.

Teagan is balanced on Ronni's hip, babbling nonsense. The twins, Torin and Tristan, are chasing each other around the living room, hopped up on sugar and mischief.

The rest of the afternoon and evening moves in a blur. Marcella plays referee when the twins argue over who gets the last tea cake. She talks music with Liam, legal drama with Ronni, and even gets Rory to laugh when she compliments his vintage flask collection—she knows damn well the house is dry.

When the table is finally set, Ma waves everyone in. We take our usual seats—Marcella beside me, Connor on the opposite side with the twins flanking Ronni, who has Teagan in a high chair next to her.

Across from us, Brennan has a look on his face I don't think I've ever seen before. Not smug. Not calculating.

Content.

Maybe because his girlfriend, Astrid, has changed his life. When she speaks, Brennan leans in close, like her smile is a gravity he can't resist. It hits me hard.

Because for all the ways he's wired differently, and disappears into code and algorithms and neural net mapping—this, right here, is simple. Human. He's in love. It's written all over him.

I glance at Marcella beside me, her eyes shining as she chats with Ronni about some ridiculous *Boyfriend Experiment* theory, and I realize my brothers and I are not very different. Not when it comes to love. We partner for life with women who make us better men.

Dinner is roast lamb with rosemary, buttery mashed potatoes, roasted carrots and parsnips, and the famous brown bread. As always, there's noise and love and way too many stories about someone's embarrassing moment. Cillian's absence is palpable and never spoken about directly.

After the meal, Ronni and Marcella slip off to the living room with Teagan while I catch up with Connor and Brennan. We talk quietly about Cillian. Connor, ever the perceptive older brother, asks how work's going and I give a noncommittal shrug. They don't push. Not yet.

Later, Marcella and I step out onto the porch. The air is crisp, smelling of woodsmoke and pine.

"I love them," she says softly.

"Me too."

She looks at me. There's something vulnerable in her eyes. "You okay?"

"Yeah," I answer honestly. "I'm better. The proposal's in. You're here. We have a plan."

She points to the street. "Then let's go home."

Her fingers thread through mine like she's never letting go.

We head down the stairs, into the future and whatever comes next.

Hope doesn't shout. It settles.

Certain. Steady.

Mine.

Thirty-One

Two Weeks Later

THE PING HITS MY phone midafternoon.

Carlos finally has something.

I should feel relief.

All I feel is dread.

I'm at my desk, with a half-drained coffee and three legal pads fanned out with notes from a deposition prep I'm supposed to be working on for a different case. I haven't touched them.

My inbox is a dumpster fire. My phone's at nine percent. My shoulders ache from being hunched over for hours.

None of this matters if Carlos has something useful.

```
Carlos Soladat: Got something.
You're not gonna like it.
```

I click the attachment without hesitation. It's a brief report, maybe two pages. Nothing formal, the type of summary we usually trade back and forth when a case is too hot for paper trails.

Except this isn't a case. Not officially.

There are five names. All women who work or worked at the hospital. All with a brief note next to them:

- Willing to provide testimony

- Coerced to the stairwell

- Willing to provide testimony

- Used her and threw her in the trash

- Says it was consensual, uncomfortable to work with him

I recoil for a beat, instinctively queasy at how it reads. The woman in me—who's lived in his arms and seen his heart up close—knows better. Seamus isn't a predator.

He's a man who never learned the power he had until it was too late.

Does it matter to me though? I love this man.

It does, goddammit.

Even though he's asked me if it bothered me before and I honestly assured him it didn't, I finally comprehend, suddenly and stupidly, there are more of these women than I can probably count.

I *hate* realizing how many actually came before me. How many came because of him—from the same capable hands, the same talented mouth, the same practiced skill he uses to make me unravel.

I stare at the screen for a full minute, willing the words to change. They don't. So I proceed to the next step. My hands tremble slightly as I reach for the phone and call my colleague, Lucy Dresden.

"Yes?" she answers, clipped and breezy like always.

I suck in a breath. "Hey. It's Marcella. You got ten? I need your brain."

"For you? Always. Shoot." Lucy is always willing to help. It's one of the things I love about her.

"Hypothetically," I say, even though we both know it's not. "Say a surgical resident had consensual sexual encounters with multiple staff members during his early years in the program. Nothing violent. No coercion. Initiated by the women because he got himself a reputation for, um...his technique. Last year, he provided testimony against his mentor, the head of his program. In retaliation, the man is gathering statements from some of these women, likely with the intent to file harassment claims and tank the guy's career."

Silence.

Then a low exhale. "Jesus."

"I need to know how screwed he is." I pinch the bridge of my nose.

"Badly." Lucy whistles through her teeth. "Even if he's innocent, the optics are abysmal. Resident status alone skews the power dynamic. You're talking about someone in a position of medical authority over nurses or techs he's hooking up with. Even if they initiated, it can be reframed. It *will* be."

"So, what? They paint him as a predator?" This is my worst fear come true.

"Well...not necessarily. They won't have to. All it takes is one TikTok. One complaint to HR. One whisper campaign," she advises. "The big problem is the institution. A hospital's at risk for allowing this behavior. To keep their insurance and good standing, they'll pull him from the program so fast his badge will still be swinging on the lanyard."

Pressure coils in my chest. "Even if it was all consensual?"

"Consent isn't a shield in this context. It helps. It probably doesn't eliminate institutional liability. The hospital won't care whether he meant harm. They care whether they can be sued for fostering a hostile work environment." Lucy takes a second before continuing. "If his mentor is trying to retaliate, or get rid of him, this could be his pretext. It won't fall on him if he destroys one of his student's careers."

I pace the office. "What if we can prove it was initiated by the women? Some of the women had partners at the time and still came on to him."

"Won't matter. They'll spin it as emotional manipulation." Lucy's in full lawyer mode now, laying out everything I need to hear. "The moment someone says they felt uncomfortable or pressured, even retroactively, the narrative shifts. Your guy? He'll look like a liability, not a rising star."

I lean against the edge of my desk. "So what's the play?"

"He needs to settle it. Quietly. Directly. With Caldwell." She stops for a second, then adds, "Hire crisis PR to sort out what to do with these women. He may need to preemptively settle with them too."

I squeeze my eyes shut. "Ugh. I was afraid this was the direction."

"Damage control now, or reputation annihilation later. For what it's worth? Even if he survives this, if he doesn't get ahead of it now, it could follow him into private practice. One patient Googles his name and sees something, even half-baked? It'll be game over." She confirms everything I dreaded.

We hang up and my whole body feels ice cold. This is isn't about saving his residency anymore. This is about his future as a man. His entire damn life.

Our life, if we survive. Once he knows the gravity of what he's facing, I wouldn't blame him if he broke things off.

I'm the one who put him here.

I sit for a long time, staring at nothing.

How do I tell him?

Dr. Madison loved his proposal. He has a lifeline because she was impressed and excited to participate. On the other hand, she made it clear—if he wants to pursue this focus on the neuroscience of female sexual response, he needs a clean slate. A solid platform to stand on.

He doesn't have one right now. Not even close.

It's time to face this head-on. The mental toll this is taking has gone on too long.

For months I'm bearing witness to him barely holding it together. It breaks my heart when he insists everything's fine and yet he continues to unravel. Always trying to protect me from the fallout while the ground shifts beneath his feet.

I don't deserve it.

Caldwell's not ignoring him out of pettiness—he's expertly playing the long game to get rid of him while Seamus tries to keep hope alive.

My calendar dings.

A canceled deposition clears the rest of my day.

Good.

I'm done sitting on the sidelines. He's working a split shift today, which means he's probably napping at home. I'm going to him now. To fight. To fix. To love.

Whatever it takes to get him out of this—I'll focus all of my legal skills to give him the best chance.

Fifteen minutes later, I step through the door of my condo, I know he's here. There's music playing softly, it's coming from the kitchen. The air smells of something slightly burnt. Probably toast.

I round the corner and there he is, barefoot in his scrub pants, standing at the stove with an empty plate, a book open beside him and a mug of coffee on the counter.

He turns when he hears me. "Hey."

I cross to him, wrap my arms around his waist and bury my face in the crook of his neck.

"Hey," I whisper.

He stiffens for a half second before melting into my hold. "I didn't think I'd see you before I went back to the hospital."

"*Seamus*." I squeeze him as tightly as I can.

We hug for a long beat. His hands stroke over my back, slow and soothing. "Is everything okay?"

"No. We have a problem." There's no sugar coating this conversation. I owe him complete honesty.

He pulls back just enough to meet my eyes. "What's going on?"

I hesitate. This is hard. The hardest thing I could ever imagine.

He notices.

"Marcella," he says quietly. "Tell me."

So I do.

The report from Carlos. The call with Lucy. The fact five women have seemingly agreed to speak out against him and even if they initiated, he's the one with the most to lose. Caldwell doesn't need to file charges or start a legal process. All he needs to do is whisper the right thing to the right people, and the hospital will gut Seamus's future to avoid liability.

I watch the color drain from his face.

He untangles himself from me and sinks into a chair. "Holy fuck."

"We can get ahead of this." I kneel in front of him and take his hands in mine. "You needed to know what's coming."

His throat bobs as he swallows. "They'll believe it. Because it looks bad. Because I was stupid. Because I didn't think about perception. I thought if it was mutual, it couldn't hurt anyone."

"You *didn't* hurt anyone," I say fiercely. "You do need to protect yourself. Face Caldwell. Make peace, if you can. Or at least make a move before he strikes."

His eyes find mine. "Marcella, are you going to leave me over this?"

"No," I whisper. "Never."

He tilts his head. "Do you think I brought it on myself?"

I hesitate. Then nod. "With the women? We both know you were naïve to your power. You may not have asked for it. You also got something out of it so you didn't stop it right away, either. You'll have to own your part in this if you want to be a man who earns his second chance. You'll have to be willing to face and fix the damage."

He starts to speak but I hold my hand up. "I want to say one more thing. I don't think I've ever taken full accountability for putting you in this position. I pushed you into testifying. I made it about the greater good, about justice without stopping to think about what it would cost you personally. I told myself you were strong enough to handle it, and maybe you are—at the same time, it wasn't right to force my doggedness on you."

His eyes stay locked on mine, searching.

"I'm sorry, Seamus." I squeeze his hand. "I wish I'd protected you better. Not handed you over to a wolf. I may not have meant to use you—doesn't mean I didn't. I hate myself for it. If anyone's going to leave this relationship, it should be you."

He doesn't flinch. Doesn't blink.

Instead, he brings my hand to his mouth and presses a kiss to the inside of my wrist, soft and steady. Like he's grounding us both.

"No." The conviction in his voice makes my breath catch. "Marcella. I know who you are. You're brilliant. Ruthless. Maybe you didn't stop to think through the fallout. I didn't either. I said yes to helping. Eyes open."

Tears prick behind my eyes.

"I know what kind of man I want to be," he continues. "I want to earn back what's mine—my career, my integrity—not by pretending I didn't fuck up. Not by pretending this—us—is some casualty of war."

I press my lips together, trying to keep from falling apart.

"Our love," his hand presses over my heart, "is worth every bit of what we're going through. Even if it's messy. Even if I have to fight tooth and nail to keep it."

He exhales, like he's releasing a truth—or fear—he's long held. "Caldwell or not, my past would've caught up eventually. I'm not stupid—I have three rockstar brothers who've been caught up in scandals before. I should've known one angry nurse, one rejected orderly—it could've all gone sideways. I was arrogant, not naïve. I told myself it was harmless; it was always weird. That's on me."

"As for going against Caldwell, I'd still do it all again for Miranda." He cups my cheek and I lean into it instinctively. "It's time to live clean. Real. I want to fix what I broke. I want to be the man who loves you without hiding."

I can't speak. I just nod as tears spill down my cheeks.

I believe him. I love him. I want the same thing.

Odds are not in our favor, though.

I might lose the only man I'll ever love.

Thirty-Two

A Few Days Later

IT'S NEARLY NINE WHEN we pull up to Connor and Ronni's place.

A waterfront retreat tucked behind evergreens, untouched by noise, judgment, or fallout.

Marcella's hand is in mine. My stomach's a wreck.

If anyone can help me clean this up, it's my brother.

Connor's the one who pulled our family together when our world fell apart after Da's accident. The one who made sure I had shoes that fit. Helped me with my homework. Put food on the table. Comforted me when the house was louder than it should've been—and shielded me from Da's drinking and violent behavior.

I've never approached him for help. Or money. I've managed to hold my own throughout my entire adult life.

Now, I have no choice. My professional life is on the brink of collapse and he might be the only person who can help navigate these fifty-foot waves.

Which means I'm about to admit something to him I never dreamed would come to light.

For years, I let him—all my brothers—believe I was crushing it in the bedroom. Like I had superpowers over the female orgasm or something. I bragged about technique, gave them the play-by-play—how to find the right angles, how to listen for the breathy catch in a woman's throat right before she comes. I made it sound like I had it all figured out.

Control. Precision. Clinical bravado.

The truth?

I wasn't willing to give myself to just anyone. I wasn't waiting for perfection. I was waiting for someone who felt like home.

I was waiting for Marcella.

It's embarrassing. Humbling. Not because I was a virgin by choice...it's the lies I felt compelled to tell.

Unlike my brothers' rockstar antics, my stairwell activities will never be wild stories of my bachelor years. I'm facing an actual reckoning—and I'll have to look my brother in the eye and explain how my stupid reputation may end the career I've sacrificed everything for.

Then there's Ronni.

Brilliant. Fierce. Fearless Ronni Miller.

She knows firsthand what it's like to be on the receiving end of real power abuse—predators hiding behind their titles and contracts and press junkets. I may have never crossed a line or coerced anything not freely offered. Unfortunately, the optics don't always make space for nuance.

If she looks at me differently after tonight—if she thinks, even for a second, I'm anything like the men who hurt her—it might break me.

I've always been comfortable in my own skin. But this? Terrifying.

Connor opens the door before we even knock, like he's been waiting. "You're here. Come in."

Ronni appears behind him in joggers and a hoodie, her hair twisted up. Her bare feet curl against the hardwood as she hugs Marcella like they've been friends for decades.

"Kids are asleep." She motions us to follow her. "We've got all night."

The four of us settle in their whiskey den—dark wood, soft leather chairs facing Lake Washington. A room inviting confessions. Ronni pours red wine for herself and Marcella. Connor cracks open a bottle of sparkling water for me without asking.

He knows. He always knows.

I'll never touch alcohol. Not after witnessing what it's done to my da and to Cillian.

Today I've been trying to hold it together. Working all day while pretending this situation hasn't been eating me alive. The second Connor turns toward me, eyebrows drawn—"Alright, baby brother. Talk to us."—I feel the first thread snap loose.

So I do. I tell them everything.

From our family dinners, they already know about Caldwell and Miranda and the shift I've felt at the hospital after I helped Marcella—the sideways glances, the silence from people who used to seek me out. The sense I'm radioactive.

Tonight it's full confession time about the women. Not in detail. Not everything. Enough to explain Caldwell collecting names, and how he's about to tank my medical career.

Marcella keeps her hand on my thigh through all of it.

When I finish, the silence extends so long I start to think maybe this was a mistake.

Then Ronni speaks. Calm. Unflinching. "You need crisis PR. Immediately."

Marcella nods. "Agreed."

"We've got people." Connor leans forward, elbows on his knees.

Ronni's eyes meet mine. "Say the word and I'll make the call."

I feel like I can breathe for the first time all day.

"You also need to decide if you're going to fight Caldwell or make amends." Connor tips his chin toward me. "You can't do both."

Marcella shifts beside me. "I don't think he wants an apology. He wants leverage."

"This makes him dangerous." Ronni sighs. "It's not about one woman, or even five. It's about perception. A post, a whisper, the right video clip—and suddenly you're not Seamus McGloughlin, gifted neurosurgery resident. You're a predator."

"I'm not—" I start, then catch myself. I know what she means.

Connor's voice is level. "It doesn't matter if you don't get ahead of this. It'll snowball. You think they're gossiping now? Wait until Caldwell feeds it to the board. Or worse, the press."

"You promise me these encounters were all consensual?" Ronni folds her arms and narrows her eyes. "I love you, Seam, I can't bear…"

I hold my hand up and place it over my heart. "On my life, Ronni. I never initiated any of this."

"I believe you." Ronni breathes in. "Okay. this isn't about guilt. It's about damage control. You're young. Gifted. You're in medicine. The standard is higher, Seamus. The blowback will be, too."

"So what's the play?" Marcella reaches for her wine.

Ronni and Connor exchange a look. A whole conversation seems to pass between them in a glance.

"You need to talk to Caldwell." Connor nods.

"What?" My whole body goes taut.

"Aye," Connor says without hesitation. "You give him the chance. Face-to-face. Show your spine. Own your part. Be clear you're not there to grovel—you're there to find a path forward."

Ronni nods beside him. "Powerful people respect people who confront the mess head-on. Especially when the house is already on fire."

"He wants me gone. What if I can't convince him otherwise?" I rake a hand through my hair.

Connor clicks his tongue. "At least you'll know by taking the reins instead of waiting to be tossed off the horse."

"Honestly, Seamus? If you do this right, you might shift the narrative," Ronni adds. "It's best you keep in mind this isn't about guilt or innocence. It's about optics. Intent. If you let someone tell their version long enough it becomes truth. Regardless of the settlement. You need to get your version out there—and not just defensively. Proactively."

My heart pounds in my chest. "So, do I apologize?"

"Not for what you didn't do." Connor's brow furrows. "Not for protecting Miranda. It might be good to play into his ego and apologize for not going to him first. For not showing him you respected the chain of command. A gesture would've mattered."

Marcella shifts beside me. "I haven't encouraged him to go to Caldwell directly because I didn't trust him. I was thinking like a lawyer, not like a girlfriend trying to preserve the man I love's career. When I was negotiating the settlement I pushed Seamus into making a record because it was the correct way to approach it legally." She turns to me, her eyes filled with guilt. "If I hadn't pushed so hard, you might've had a chance to handle it differently. Worked out your differences."

"Where would Miranda's family be then?" I reach for her hand without thinking, our fingers lacing together like they always do when one of us needs grounding. "This is a no-win situation."

Connor watches us, then gives a small nod. "Life deals us all sorts of challenges and we are where we are. I say go in there and own your side of it, Seamus. If he brings up the deposition, don't blame Marcella—acknowledge you'd never been in the situation before. Emphasize the perspective you now have upon reflection. Demonstrate maturity he won't expect."

"Right...because he doesn't know you're aware of what he's doing behind the scenes. He believes you think he's mad at you because of your testimony." Marcella squeezes my hand. "Connor and Ronni have an excellent perspective. You have a window of opportunity to get him to back off."

I sit back and let all of the advice settle like gravel in my stomach. "It's hard for me to kiss his ass. The man fucked up. I told him about the blood vessel. He ignored me. Miranda's dead."

"I know." Connor claps my shoulder and squeezes. "I'm not saying you were wrong. I'm saying there's a difference between being right and being strategic. You need to be both."

Ronni folds her arms across her chest. "Seamus, you're asking him for grace. The only way to get it is to give him something first. Humility. Clarity. A reminder this isn't just about reputations or insurance or settlements—it's about a twelve-year-old girl who isn't here anymore."

"If he doesn't give a shit?" I clench my fist helplessly.

"You walk out with your head high." Connor glances at Ronni and back to me. "Then we move to Plan B."

"Connor and I can work on this in the background until you have the conversation." Ronni leans in. "We'll find the right crisis PR, work on controlled messaging and, if necessary, devise some strategic outreach strategy for the women he's trying to manipulate. It's important you get a list of all the women together, sweetheart."

Shame envelopes me at the thought if this task. My chest feels like it's in a vise although, for the first time since I learned about Caldwell's plan, there's also a flicker of resolve. A blueprint forming.

I glance at Marcella. Her eyes hold mine, steady and sure.

Maybe this is what it means to grow the hell up. Face the fire. Apologize for your blind spots. Fight like hell for your future.

Marcella leans forward, her tone clipped, composed. "What about the women?"

Connor doesn't flinch. "You'll need a strategy for them too."

I brace for what's coming.

"Some may want apologies. Some may want distance. Some might want money." Ronni doesn't sugarcoat.

I blink. "To keep quiet?"

"To walk away," she says simply. "That's how this works, Seamus. The bigger your star, the more leverage people think they have. Especially if Caldwell is whispering into the right ears."

There's a long beat of silence.

Connor turns to me. "How many are we talking about?"

I hesitate. I've been avoiding this number, even in my own head. Now, with all eyes on me—Marcella's especially—I force it out. "Forty, give or take. Realistically, I can't remember all of their names."

Ronni brows hit her hairline.

Marcella doesn't speak. Not at first. She blinks once. Then again. Her lips quiver briefly—I catch it. Her eyes stay trained on the coffee table like she's reading something only she can see.

I want to reassure her, say something. I don't. I get it. If the roles were reversed—if she'd told me she'd blown forty different men in the stairwell to work on technique—I'd be rattled too.

"Okay. Well, could be expensive." Connor exhales, slow and even.

"Yeah," I murmur. "No shit."

Marcella juts out her chin. "We'll figure it out. One by one if we have to."

I hear how hard she's working to keep her voice steady. If it hadn't already before, in this moment it really hits me—not the professional fallout. Not the possible lawsuits or PR blowback. The emotional cost. The way this lands on her. The way it shifts something between us, even if she won't admit it to herself or say it out loud to me.

She's still here. Still on my side. I can see how everything I did before her might make her reconsider our future. All I can do is try to be the man who's worth staying for.

Ronni shifts on the couch, turning slightly toward Marcella. "You know this already, I'm going to say it anyway—Seamus can't use you as his lawyer."

"I know. It's a conflict." Marcella's voice is steady. "Having me involved would weaken his stance, if Caldwell found out especially."

Ronni meets her eyes. "Honestly? It's for the best. You don't want to know the details. Not all of them. He's going to have to remember every interaction, every minute, every stairwell—under the protection of attorney-client privilege."

Relief floods through me like a sudden gust of wind. I didn't want distance from her—didn't want to keep secrets or push her out. The truth is, no one would see her as objective and any move I made would be torn apart. She'd fight like hell for me and her fire would burn us both.

"I can put you in touch with my LA lawyers," Ronni continues. "They're experts in a crisis. They're worth every penny and kept Connor and me afloat during the worst time of our lives. Having them in your corner is the smartest insurance policy you could get."

It's close to midnight. There's a plan. A team. A direction.

When Marcella rises to grab our coats, Ronni gently touches her arm. "Hey—come to lunch with me this week. I've been meaning to talk to you about something. Let me grab my calendar."

I catch the warmth in her tone. An invitation layered with more than scheduling. Marcella follows Ronni into the hallway.

Connor waits a beat. Then turns to me. Before I can say anything, he hauls me into a hug—tight and solid, like he's holding me together with sheer force of will.

"You're my wee baby brother," he mutters. "You're not going through this alone." He pulls back and plants his hands on both my shoulders. "Ronni and I are covering this. Legal, PR, whatever else comes down the line."

"Connor, I can't—"

"You will," he says definitively. "Later. When you're through it. When you're not working sixteen-hour days on a resident's salary and staring down a wall of student loans. You pay me back when you're steady. When you're standing on your own feet."

I nod. Unable to speak.

His expression softens. "You're not the first McGloughlin to weather a scandal, you know."

"Feels different when it's your entire future on the line." I let out a half laugh.

"Aye, True." He doesn't flinch. "You've got us." He looks toward the hall, where Marcella's deep in conversation with Ronni. "Marcella. Having her by your side matters."

"It does," I agree. "*She* does."

Connor gives me one last pat on the back. "Then let's make sure you come out of this with everything intact."

I nod again, firmer this time. "Yeah. Let's do it."

For the first time since I found out what Caldwell was planning, I believe I might actually have a chance.

I'm not alone in this. Not anymore.

Marcella. Connor. My family. My future.

Caldwell can come for me—he'll find all of us.

I feel empowered to reclaim everything Caldwell tried to steal.

I've never felt stronger.

Thirty-Three

MARCELLA

"LET'S STEAL A MINUTE?"

Ronni's hand touches my arm—light, but purposeful.

It's phrased like an invitation. I know better.

She's offering something—wisdom, maybe a lifeline.

I'd be a fool not to take it.

I follow her out of the sitting room, taking a glance back at Seamus who is talking to his brother, Connor. They're angled slightly away from us now. Seamus is nodding, his expression tight, like he's forcing composure he doesn't actually feel. His hand grips the armrest like he might crack it. Whatever Connor's saying, it's hitting deep.

My man is unraveling, quietly and with restraint. I feel helpless.

Ronni gives my arm a small tug, leading me through the open doorway and into the kitchen, polished and warmly lit. There's purpose behind her unhurried steps. This isn't small talk. She wanted me away from Seamus for a reason.

Or, more likely, she wanted to give the brothers space for a one-on-one. Older brother to younger.

Ronni stops by one of her kitchen islands and leans back against it, arms folded loosely across her chest. Her posture is relaxed yet her eyes are sharp. "Tell me the truth. Are you okay?"

"Define okay." I face her and slump against the opposite island.

Her lips curve. "Yeah. That's what I thought."

"Honestly? I hadn't let myself...uh. *Shit*. I'm trying to process the sheer volume of it all. Forty women, Ronni. Forty." I wince, picturing my boyfriend in the fucking stairwell with other women—thinner, more beautiful, younger...

"You love him." She nods, slow and steady.

It's not a question. "I do. So much it scares the hell out of me."

"Then I'm going to tell you the same thing my therapist told me the first time a tabloid published a rumor about Connor's sex life after they found out we were a couple."

She glances at me sideways. "You don't get to rewrite the past. Only the present and the future."

I exhale, eyes trained on the edge of the counter. "My head knows it. My heart tells me it's different when it's your person. I hate knowing those women felt the type of pleasure he gives me. Physically at least. It messes with your head."

"Of course it does." Ronni's voice softens. "You're human. You need to remember you have something they didn't. Seamus didn't just open his body to you, Marcella. He's given you the part of himself no one else has. The *best* part."

I swallow hard.

Ronni steps toward me and tucks a piece of hair behind my ear in a gesture so motherly and intimate it nearly undoes me. "Don't let shame write the script. You have every right to feel hurt, or confused, or even angry. If it's any consolation, I've known Seamus a long time. He's kind. Loyal. Complicated, yeah. He's got a steady heart. He needs you to hold steady, too."

I press my lips together, holding back tears.

Ronni smiles, then opens a drawer and rummages around until she finds what she's looking for. A business card, which she hands to me. "This is the firm I recommend. You should vet them. If there is any doubt, we'll regroup."

"Okay. Thank you." I stare down at the card, the weight of it heavier than the cardstock should allow.

"Connor is going to help his brother financially," she adds. "For what it's worth, Seamus needs to handle this. As a man. With you at his side, not in front of him with a shield."

"I get it," I whisper. "I just hate feeling like I can't fix it for him."

"You can't," she says gently. "You can only stand beside him while he cleans his own house. You're not alone, Marcella. We're here for you too." She pulls me in for a brief, fierce hug. "I mean it."

After a moment I'm able to steel myself and we make our way back into the den.

Seamus is waiting with my car keys in hand. He's smiling at something Connor said. The moment he sees me, the smile falters. Not entirely—enough.

The ride home is quiet, humming with everything unsaid. I rest my hand on his thigh, and he covers it with his own. Our fingers interlace without thought.

He's thinking about the women. I know it. About the money. The fallout. The way I looked at him when Ronni said "forty." I didn't mean to recoil. I couldn't help it, the number hit me in a way I wasn't prepared for.

We don't talk until we're inside my condo. He kicks off his shoes and hesitates like he's waiting for me to say something.

Instead, I grab his hand and lead him to the bedroom.

He pulls me back again. "You're not...angry?"

"I'm furious," I correct him. "Not at you. Not really. I'm angry you have to carry this. Even more pissed the truth might not be enough."

His face falters for a second. The quiet devastation nearly guts me. Before the weight of it can drag him under, I kiss him—soft and deliberate. Then deeper, until we're breathing each other in like the only air we need lives between us.

His hands come to my waist, tentative at first. Then certain.

He breaks the kiss with a gravelly whisper, "I don't deserve you."

"Maybe not," I tug his sweatshirt over his head, "you have me anyway."

"I want to rewrite it all." I unbutton and unzip his pants and he lets me. Doesn't speak, doesn't rush. Watches me like I'm something holy. "All those women who only wanted a piece of you in a stairwell—all the ones who took what you gave without seeing the man underneath? I want to erase them. I want to be the one who rewrites those memories—with love, with depth, with forever."

"You already have." His voice breaks. "Marcella. You're all I ever wanted. All I ever dreamed about—even when I didn't think someone like you was real."

We move in sync—quiet and slow—stripping down as we make our way to the bedroom, discarding the day piece by piece. I pull back the covers and climb in first. He follows a beat later, warm and solid, sliding up behind me until our bodies are flush.

He wraps around me, draping his hand low over the curve of my belly. He buries his face against the back of my neck like he's anchoring himself there. "I love you," he murmurs against my skin. "You've changed me."

"Say it again." I reach back and run my fingers through his hair, guiding him closer.

"I love you," he repeats. "Not just in an I-want-you way. Not just in bed. I love your mind. Your fire. Your mouth, even when it terrifies people in the courtroom."

He shifts, pressing himself inside me in one smooth, reverent stroke. I gasp, and clutch his forearm, holding him against me as he begins to move. Slow. Deep. Each thrust an unspoken vow.

"I didn't know I could ever feel like this," he says against my shoulder. "I thought I understood desire, pleasure, connection. I didn't know a damn thing. Not until you."

His rhythm doesn't change—it's steady, like he's savoring the feel of me around him. Letting it burn through every layer of fear and doubt still clinging to him. "I want to give you everything. Not just orgasms. Or weekends and weeknights and whatever's left after the hospital grinds me down."

He wraps his arm tighter around me, his hand slipping between my legs, finding my clit with the ease of a man who's mapped my every nerve ending. "I want to build a life with you. Marry you. Have babies with you, if you want them. I want to fall asleep with my cock buried inside of you every fucking night. I want holidays and bad reality TV and your hair in my sink. I want it all."

"Seamus..." I arch against him, trembling, undone from the inside out.

His hand moves in tandem with his body and my whole world sharpens into white heat. I come with a breathless cry, his name on my lips. He follows, pulsing deep inside me.

Afterward, he holds me so tight I can feel his heartbeat in every part of me.

We don't speak again for a long time. We don't need to.

No words. No doubts.

This is what it feels like to belong to someone—completely and irrevocably.

He's mine. I'm his.

Whatever comes, we face it as one.

Thirty-Four

SEAMUS

Ten Days Later

I'VE REHEARSED THIS MOMENT a dozen different ways.

Crisis PR says stay calm. Legal says stay neutral.

My gut says don't let him see you bleed.

None of those voices matter when I'm standing outside Caldwell's office, palms slick against my jeans. My heart punching slow, heavy beats into my ribs.

I knock twice. Sharp. Controlled. Like it's any other day.

His voice is muffled. "Come in."

The door creaks open and there he is—behind the same desk where I sat across from him for my interview years ago. When I was still wide-eyed and determined. When I thought the rules were fixed and fairness was something you could count on in medicine.

Now?

I know better.

Caldwell doesn't stand. He looks up from a chart like I'm one more resident interrupting his day. Undeterred, I step inside, close the door, and take the seat across from him without waiting to be told.

Silence.

"Clearly you're not here for feedback on your last assist." A few minutes later, he goes back to writing up a chart without glancing at me. His pen glides across the page.

I let the quiet linger a beat longer before answering, "No, sir."

"So?" He sets the pen down, folds his hands. His eyes—cold and sharp—land on mine.

I straighten in my chair. "I wanted to speak to you directly. About everything."

"Everything. Quite a narrow category." He leans back, arms crossed.

"I recognize it's been a complicated year." I lean forward and clasp my hands. "For you. For the program. For me."

A muscle in his jaw ticks. "Complicated is one word for it."

"I'm not here to debate Miranda Black. What happened to her was devastating. I made the choice I did because I believed it was the right thing to do." I do not break eye contact.

His nostrils flare.

"What I realize is I should've come to you first," I continue. "Out of respect. You were my boss. My mentor. I was caught up in my emotions and I could have handled things differently with you. Been honest and not blindsided you."

"You think an apology makes this right?" Caldwell lets out a sharp exhale of disbelief as he leans back in his chair, shaking his head slowly. "You come skulking in here with a half-baked apology and expect me to pat your head like some wounded intern. It's far too late, McGloughlin. We've barely spoken all year. You've dodged me, undermined me, and everyone around this hospital knows you tried to sink my career. Do you seriously want to pretend this is salvageable?"

"I'm not pretending anything," I say quietly. Firmly.

"Sure." He laughs again—hollow this time. "You thought I didn't care. You really thought I walked into the OR and gambled with her life for my ego."

I flinch. His words hit me hard.

He doesn't wait for my answer.

"I've lost patients before. You don't do this job—this specific job—for decades and walk away clean. Every one of them stays with you. But Miranda?" He shakes his head slowly, like he's still stuck in the loop. "She was a child. Twelve. I've replayed her surgery in my mind every damn night. I've second-guessed every clamp, every suction, every decision."

He continues, his eyes glinting with something raw. "Losing her took something from me and then my star pupil turned on me and thought the worst. Yet I still showed up. I kept going. I held this department together despite it all."

The air feels tight between us. Like it can't carry both of our truths at the same time.

Here's mine: He's not wrong.

Today, I came here thinking if I took some hits—apologized, played contrite—I might get what I needed. Maybe save my career. Get my name off the chopping block.

I certainly didn't come in here to hang out with him. Not really.

My focus was so narrow, I never gave him the benefit of the doubt. I didn't once ask how he was doing after she died. Never wondered how Miranda's death carved into him. Instead, I just saw the mistakes. Assumed the power imbalance. Hated his arrogance, which could have been masking grief.

In this moment, I realize how flawed all of us truly are. How life isn't always black and white. Why forgiveness and redemption matter.

I sit straight up. "I came to take responsibility."

This stops him cold.

My hands rest in my lap, fingers laced so I don't start shaking. "I was scared." I struggle to keep my composure. "Not just of the fallout. After your deposition, it seemed clear where the blame was headed, and I panicked. It felt like I was going to lose everything I've worked for—my license, my future—and I was angry. I didn't trust the system to protect me and I didn't think you would either."

His expression doesn't change, his posture does—slightly, subtly. The tiniest shift of weight.

"So, no. I wasn't ready to face you," I say. "After a few weeks passed, I told myself I was too busy. Then, when the litigation was happening, decided you owed me an apology. In retrospect? I keep coming back to the notion I should have come to you instead of avoiding you."

Tension is a taut wire between us. I don't break eye contact. I want him to see this isn't rehearsed. This is me. Raw. Tired. Honest.

"To answer your question, I don't think this apology makes it right," I add. "I think it matters. Because I mean it. Continuing to avoid you would be another mistake."

Caldwell exhales sharply through his nose, then rubs the bridge of his nose like he's warding off a headache. "Jesus Christ," he mutters, not with venom this time. Exhaustion. Weariness. Maybe even recognition.

He leans forward slightly. "Worked for, huh? You think you've been working?"

"Sir?" I blink.

"You walk into this program with a name and more cockiness than your rockstar brothers. You're a brilliant student and try to sabotage yourself by fucking half the hospital staff. Then, when the going gets as rough as it can be, you waltz into a deposition like it's your turn on stage. Do you really think I believe you've learned something?" His voice cuts sharp. "You're not as charming as you think, McGloughlin."

My fingers twitch against my thigh. "I'm not proud of everything I've done."

"You shouldn't be," he snaps. "One thing you are good at? Covering your ass."

I inhale slowly. "I'm not here to cover. I'm here to make amends, if possible."

"Why now?" He doesn't blink.

"I've always needed this program. You know as well as I do I need your support to finish my residency. I didn't come here to manipulate you." I glance past him, briefly. The window behind his desk shows nothing but gray sky. "I came because I want to stay and earn my place in neurosurgery."

His laugh remains humorless. "You selfish little fuck. Do you really think this is about you?"

My stomach seizes.

"This program has a reputation to uphold," he continues. "When a resident behaves recklessly—whether in the OR, or in a stairwell—it reflects on all of us."

There it is.

The veiled threat.

"I haven't broken any hospital policies," I reply evenly.

"Are you sure?" His brow arches.

I bite the inside of my cheek. *Don't react.* I've been prepared by my team for this. "I've followed professional protocol to the letter since day one. Every personal interaction I've had was consensual."

"Professional my ass." He leans back, studying me. "You had a reputation, you know. Before Miranda. Before the lawsuit."

I say nothing.

They all signed.

Every single one.

The crisis attorneys called me two nights ago—NDA after NDA. Some typed statements, some handwritten notes. None of them accusing. All of them clear.

Every woman said the same thing, in their own way: *he never made me feel small.*

Even Cecily. She was the only one who hesitated. But Tara and Priya—thank God—talked to her. Told her I wasn't the problem. Told her I helped them realize they deserved more than stolen moments in stairwells.

It wasn't love. It wasn't even intimacy.

But it was never cruel.

Still, I know now—that's not enough.

Not for who I want to be. Not for Marcella. Not for the man I'm trying to become.

That chapter's closed. Quietly. Cleanly. And I'm never opening it again.

Caldwell doesn't know this, though.

"I had nurses and orderlies clamoring to get on your service. Not because of your surgical skill—which is a goddamn shame because you have the talent— they wanted their shot at the legend. Dr. Orgasm or whatever the fuck they call you. You turned my goddamn hospital into your personal playground. You built a brand on pleasure and pretense, and now you want to cry foul because the spotlight's too hot? Understand this—I turned a blind eye to the bullshit because of your talent. I knew those women were seeking you out and gave you the benefit of the doubt. Tried to subtly steer you away from fucking up your career. Got ahold of them after the fact to make sure they didn't fuck things up for you."

Shit. Shit. *Shit*. I recall his words. I've heard the gossip. Interpreted all of it as another threat.

Was I wrong? Were we all wrong?

"I didn't realize…"

He narrows his eyes. "I've been around the block a few times. Knowledge doesn't matter. Perception does."

A long silence falls. He lets it settle, lets it stew.

"Do you know how many phone calls I fielded from colleagues after the Black case?" he asks quietly. "How many whispers I heard in the halls about how I killed a little girl? I bet you didn't know I had to face the hospital board to keep my position here."

I meet his gaze. "I couldn't lie under oath."

"Betrayal of the man who has the power to crush your career." He raises an eyebrow.

I take a breath. "I didn't betray you. I spoke my truth."

"The truth according to a bitch lawyer who wanted a win at any cost." His eyes gleam.

It takes everything I have not to defend my girlfriend. She prepared me for this too. I say nothing and force my expression to stay neutral. If I get through this, he and I are going to have a heart to heart about how he speaks about women. "She was Black's attorney. She asked for my opinion. I gave it."

He snorts. "Is that what we're calling it?"

I don't take the bait.

He leans forward again. "Let me be clear, McGloughlin. I'm not here to debate the past. I'm here to determine your future. Right now? Trust me. It's hanging by a thread."

I nod once, resisting all urges to bite back. "I understand."

"You've got three more years." He regards me as if I'm a specimen under a microscope. "Three years of grueling hours, pressure, and scrutiny. Assuming I keep you here."

I wait.

"Why should I? Keep you here." He squints.

I lean forward. "Because neurosurgery is what I'm meant to do. Because I came here alone. I'm not hiding from what happened. I could've transferred. I didn't."

Silence. Then, "You're not out of the woods."

"I didn't expect to be." The first waves of relief wash over me. Did I pull this off?

"You'll be watched," he adds. "More than ever before."

"I understand."

"If you make even one misstep—" He cuts himself off. "You'll be gone."

I shake my head. "I won't give you a reason."

He considers me for a long moment, then finally pushes back from his desk. Stands. Walks to the window.

"Do you love it?" he asks, almost absently.

"Sir?"

"This field. This work. Neurosurgery. Do you love it?"

I don't hesitate. "With everything I have."

"Fuck." He's quiet a moment.

"I've been thinking about all of it. About what kind of surgeon I want to be," I go on. "I'm hoping to work with Dr. Madison this year—for my R5 research. Studying the neural mechanisms of female sexual function. It's niche, I know. It's the first time I've felt inspired again. Like I'm building something, not trying to solve my own family's dysfunction."

I meet his eyes. "Dr. Madison didn't take my side. She challenged me to see this whole thing in shades, not absolutes. Conditioned her support on me facing you. She was right. Our conversation changed everything for me."

"How so?" He regards me carefully.

"I don't want to coast through the next three years. I want to be better. Smarter. Different. I can't accomplish anything if I don't face the ways I got this wrong—including how I treated you." I swallow the last bit of my pride. "I want to be the best."

"Then act like it. Starting now." He doesn't tell me I'm safe. Doesn't tell me I'm forgiven. At least the heat in his glare is gone. Replaced by something harder. Cooler. Not indifferent. "I'll see you back in the OR."

"Yes, sir." I rise. It's time to get the fuck out of here before he changes his mind.

I make it to the door before he says, "Don't make me regret this."

I glance back. "I won't."

This isn't redemption. It's accountability.

Dr. Madison gave me a second chance. Caldwell gave me a lifeline.

I give myself a mission.

No more excuses. No more drifting.

This is my shot.

I'm not wasting it.

Thirty-Five

MARCELLA

A Few Weeks Later

THE ELEVATOR HUMS BENEATH us as it climbs, the faint buzz filling the space between us.

Seamus leans against the wall, one knee bent, hands deep in the pockets of his jacket. The collar's turned up, more habit than style.

He doesn't say anything, just watches me out of the corner of his eye like he's waiting for a signal.

"What?" I finally ask, lifting a brow.

He points to my chest, slow and casual. "You got sauce on your cardigan."

I glance down to see the faintest speck of tomato right in the middle of my boob. "The only reason you noticed is because of the placement."

"What can I say?" He smirks.

My chest does this funny little flutter thing, like my heart's trying to stutter-step out of time. Six months in and I still feel like I'm in junior high around him.

When we step into the condo, I drop my clutch on the counter, kick off my shoes with a sigh of relief and tug my sweater over my head. Seamus trails in behind me, shrugging out of his jacket and laying it over the back of the couch.

He doesn't say anything. I turn and catch him watching me again.

"What now?" I ask, teasing this time.

He tilts his head, lazy, amused. "You know, you get this look of contentment after spending time with your family."

"Oh yeah?" I cross my arms over my tank top, grinning.

"*Yeah*." He moves closer, closing the space between us in slow, deliberate steps. "You're all soft around the edges. Like you might let someone kiss you if they're lucky enough."

I roll my eyes. "Don't get used to it."

"Oh, I'm already addicted." He's in front of me now, warm and close. When his hands find my hips, I don't stop him. I don't want to.

"They love you," I murmur. "Even Rosa. Which honestly makes me suspicious."

He nuzzles my neck. "She told me if I ever hurt you, she'd bury me in a paella pan."

"That tracks…" I bite my lip. "Because it doesn't make a lick of sense."

His mouth curves into something sly and knowing. "Right? Then she gave me a second helping of *arroz negro* and called me *mijo*, so I think I passed whatever convoluted test it was."

"She's ruthless," I whisper, curling a finger into the collar of his T-shirt. "And very, very invested in my love life."

"I noticed." He kisses the edge of my jaw, soft and slow. "I think they're all trying to will a wedding into existence with every course."

"At my age, I'm trying not to take it personally." My voice comes out breathier than I intend.

He pulls back just enough to look at me. "Marriage doesn't scare me."

"Oh?" I lift a brow. "Even though I'm ancient? Or, I could crush you with a well-placed motion in limine?"

He leans back in, lips brushing mine as he murmurs, "I want things with you I never thought about before."

I go still, his words winding around something fragile and unspoken inside me.

"Don't act like you're not into it." He doesn't give me time to overthink it before he kisses me again, deeper this time. Familiar. A promise and a question all in one.

I slide my hands under his shirt, fingers skating over the smooth lines of his back. "I plead the Fifth."

"So..." He tugs me against him. "You think I'm worth keeping around forever?"

I look up at him. His face is too close. Too beautiful. I nod.

"*Yeah.*"

"Good." He kisses my forehead and leads me to the couch. "Before I fuck you until dawn, do you want to talk about it?"

I tuck myself into his side. "About what?"

"You got real quiet after dessert." He gives me a look. "Your mom kept glancing between us like she knew something I don't."

I wince. "She means well."

"I know she does. Something's on your mind. I can feel it." He pulls me against him, my back to his front. I tuck my legs under me and stare out the window at the lights of the city.

"It's not one thing," I admit after a long moment. "It's a lot of things."

His arm bands around my shoulder. "Start somewhere."

"Your meeting with Caldwell changed something for me." I lean against him.

He goes still.

"Not in a bad way," I say quickly. "It made me realize how I've spent the last fifteen years looking at the world in absolutes. Right and wrong. Justice and revenge.

Maybe that perspective served me in the courtroom. In life it's messier."

Seamus nods slowly. "Yeah. It is."

"You're still here. Still standing." I look up at him. "You didn't run from any of it."

He laughs, low and soft. "I wanted to. More than once. I guess I realized saving my career meant figuring out who I want to be."

"And?"

Something in his eyes pulls at a thread I didn't know was unraveling. "I want to be someone who wakes up beside the woman he loves and doesn't ever question if he deserves her. I want to be a surgeon who sees the people behind the scans. I want to be a man who learns from his mistakes instead of hiding behind them."

I squeeze my eyes shut for a second before looking back at him.

"You definitely sound like someone I want to keep around forever." I kiss the bottom of his chin

We sit in silence for a moment, letting the truth settle around us like dust.

"There's something else." I thread my fingers through his.

He rests his head on mine. "Yeah?"

"I've been thinking about my career. The kind of lawyer I am. These past few months have been...after everything with Miranda, and Caldwell..." I swallow hard. "I don't know if I can keep doing what I'm doing. At least not in the same way."

He flutters kisses into my hair. He never rushes me.

So I say it. "I've spent the last decade feeling pretty fucking altruistic. Giving families a voice. Holding people accountable. Lately I wonder if I've been so focused on winning I stopped thinking about the collateral damage."

His fingers still.

My thoughts whoosh out unfiltered. "I've been rethinking everything. Who I help. Why I help them. If the good I do is enough to justify the hurt I sometimes leave behind."

"Do you think you want to quit?" Seamus squeezes his arms around me.

I shake my head, eyes fixed on the grain of the coffee table. "No. Maybe pivot. I don't know to what. Something quieter. I'd rather build than tear down."

"The woman who stands in court and cuts through bullshit with a glance and makes grown men quake in thousand-dollar suits doesn't need to go away." His hand slides up, until it rests below my heart. "If you want to grow, I think it's brave. Allowable."

I turn slightly, craning to look at him. "Really?"

"Yes." He nuzzles my temple. "The mess with Caldwell made me question everything about this neurosurgery program. It's so demanding."

"You're telling me."

He lifts a shoulder. "I don't want to be a guy who wakes up at forty with a white coat and a nameplate with no life. No home of my own with no wife and kids to come home to."

His words settle into the hollow behind my ribs. I blink, already a little breathless from the idea he's referring to me. Our children.

"I want a future, baby," he says softly. "I want all of it—with you."

I swallow hard. My fingers tighten around his forearm. "Seamus…"

He doesn't let me interrupt. "I know the next two years are going to be hell and if you're willing to stick by me, when I'm done and I can finally breathe again, I want us to get married and get to work on some kids."

"I'll be forty." My chest twists.

"Yeah." His thumb brushes slow circles over my lip. "I've been thinking. Not in a panicked way. Would you want to talk to Dr. Madison about fertility options? Not alone, I mean. We'd do it together."

My eyes sting suddenly. Until Seamus, I'd given up hope to have my own kids. "Really?"

"Of course." He sighs happily. "If it helps us get a head start on a future we both want, I'm all in."

I turn my face into his arm. Breathe him in. His scent. His promise. His everything. "You mean it?"

"With all of my heart."

We sit there in the quiet for a while. Then, he speaks again, a little rougher. "There's something else I've been thinking about."

"What?" I twist enough to glance at him over my shoulder.

His eyes meet mine. "Going public."

"But, Caldwell..." My heart skips. "Are you sure?"

He nods. "We have ceasefire. I'm tired of pretending I'm not in love with you."

I can't speak. This is huge.

"I want people to know who you are to me," he says. "Marcella Delgado. My girlfriend. My partner. The woman I love. Who stood by me when it would've been easier to walk away."

His expression is open, earnest. No fear. No regret.

"I'd like that." I press my lips to his. "I'd really like that."

His mouth brushes mine, gentle and firm. "Good. Because I'm done hiding."

"So am I." My fingers slide through his hair as I pull him closer.

His voice drops to a hush. "We're going to figure this out. All of it. You and me."

"I know," I whisper back. "We already are."

We sit for a while longer, curled up together. Eventually, he moves me off his lap and stands. "Come to bed with me."

I follow him into the bedroom, shedding clothes like old skin, the last of the day slipping off my shoulders. He lifts the covers and I slide in, back to his front, his chest pressed warm against my spine like the most natural thing in the world. The way we fall asleep every single night.

His arm wraps around my waist. A sigh against my neck. "I love you."

It's not a declaration anymore. It's a heartbeat. I thread my fingers through his, settling our joined hands against my stomach. "I love you too."

He kisses the back of my shoulder, then my neck, then rests there—breathing me in like I'm oxygen.

No vows. No fireworks.

Only the soft weight of his arm, the press of his chest, the warmth of his body.

Love isn't loud in this room.

It's steady.

It's ours.

Thirty-Six

Six Months Later

IT'S FUCKING COLD.

Boston's a frozen postcard—too bright, too clean, too cheery.

Marcella tugs her red knit hat over her ears and loops her arm through mine like we belong here.

Maybe we do.

The icy air nips at my face when we step out of the hotel, our breath visible with every exhale. It's December and the city's wrapped in an end-of-year hum—twinkling lights in the trees, street musicians playing jazz near the corner of Harvard Square, a kid trying to juggle while wearing mittens.

I'm still riding the high from my presentation this morning at Harvard Medical School to neurosurgical staff. I'm not sure what I expected.

Definitely not a packed room.

Instead of awkward silence or schoolboy snickering—which, let's be honest, I half expected after presenting a neuroanatomical breakdown of the female orgasm—I got a standing ovation. A few muffled chuckles, sure. A flushed med student or two ducking their heads. Mostly? Serious questions. Respectful curiosity. Three different professors asked if I'd consider coming back to teach or taking on a full-time research fellowship.

At Harvard *Fucking* Medical School.

Marcella was in the back row, grinning like she knew something the rest of the room hadn't figured out yet. Well, I guess she does because she's the beneficiary of most of my research. Seriously, though, she's always told me I'd be great at public speaking. Her support gave me confidence.

I can't wipe the grin off my face when I look at her. The kind of love we share really does something to you.

"You gonna tell me what you're smiling about or gape at me like a psychopath?" Marcella bumps my hip with hers as we pass a bookstore window full of leather-bound journals and expensive, pretentious pens no one actually uses.

I laugh. "If things work out, I'm wondering how we're gonna explain my profession to our moms."

"Oh God." Marcella stops and puts her gloved hands up to her mouth. "I never thought about it."

I shake my head and wince. "Your mom will be like, 'What kind of fellowship is it, Seamus?' I'll say, 'Female sexual response in relation to neuroanatomical stimulation and cortical response mapping,' and she'll faint."

"She's Spanish. She won't faint. She'll pour you a sangria and pray for your soul." Marcella mimics a prayer. "I'm more interested in what you're going to tell your brothers."

I make a pinching motion with my fingers. "I'll say I'm mapping the clitoris. I'll be a hero."

She swats my face with the fluffy end of the scarf.

"Seriously." I laugh. "I love surgery. This research is a game changer. I've spent so long trying to prove to Caldwell I deserve to be in the OR. With Madison and this work, I'm creating something of my own instead of trying to measure up."

I smile to myself at the thought of Caldwell. It's funny, he didn't blow up when he found out Marcella and I were a couple a few months ago. No threats, no terse warnings—only a long, tired sigh and a dry, "Well, I guess it explains some things."

He hasn't mentioned it since. Things are...fine. Neutral. Every now and then I catch a look in his eyes—less judgment, more resignation. He knows who I am. Who he is.

Now who we are.

She beams. "I love you so much."

"So, business as usual, then?" We stop at the edge of the sidewalk, waiting for the walk signal. She shivers slightly, and I tug her closer. "Still cold?"

"I seem to always be cold right now." Marcella puts her hand in my coat pocket.

With my free hand, I tug my scarf loose and wind it around her neck. "We could go back inside where I could warm you up properly."

"Save it for after pizza. I'm starving." She arches a brow.

We find a cozy spot off Brattle Street, an old-world place with brick walls and a wood-burning oven. We're seated in five minutes.

"You know, if this law thing doesn't work out," I pick up the menu, "you could have a career in managing problematic neurosurgeons."

"Only if they're as hot as you...*Orgasm Whisperer*." She reaches for my hand across the table.

I thread my fingers between hers. "Today was the first time in months I didn't feel like the guy who almost got kicked out of his program."

"You were *never* that guy." She tilts her head.

I boop her nose. "I *was*. For a while. It's behind us now."

Our waitress brings wine, pizza, and some saucy dish smelling of garlic and heaven. We eat like we haven't in days—hands brushing as we reach for another slice, mouths full, eyes lazy with heat and Chianti.

After dinner, we walk. Harvard Square at night is magic. Bookstores glowing like lanterns, buskers performing half-frozen versions of 90s ballads, the sound of late-night coffee orders drifting from a nearby café. There's laughter in the air, floating over cobblestone and making the cold feel romantic instead of cruel.

She tugs me into a narrow alley lit by fairy lights strung overhead, the bulbs glowing amber against the dark. It's quiet here, tucked away from the city hum. She wraps her arms around my neck and kisses me like she's starving. Like she's missed me, even though I've been beside her all night.

"I'm proud of you," she whispers, voice warm against my lips. "You were incredible today."

I cup her cheeks, brushing my thumbs beneath her eyes. "Yeah?"

"Yeah," she says, and it's so certain I feel it in my bones. "Even with the tie slightly askew and the nervous lip twitch."

I gripe. "The lip twitch is genetic. Blame Rory."

"It was hot. Made you human. You're usually so—" She laughs as her hands slide to my chest. *Perfect.*

I kiss her again, slower this time. Promising her everything—later, always, forever. "You're my favorite person,"

On the way back to the hotel, we pause at a coffee cart, the scent of espresso rising in clouds of steam. She orders a hot chocolate. I get tea.

"Dr. Madison was right, you know," Marcella adds, blowing over the cup. "About making amends. About choosing to see the gray."

Marcella had the fertility consult with her a couple months ago. I'm glad I pushed for it, if I'm honest. We're not ready. Soon, though, and improving our odds of starting a family when my residency is behind me is a massive priority.

Instead, I say, "She's the reason this project exists. The reason I want to continue this full-time when I'm done."

Marcella nudges me with her shoulder, like she's holding something back.

"What?" I squint at her over the rim of my cup.

She bites her lip. "Speaking of full-time…I didn't want to bug you when you were preparing for the presentation. Remember last week when I had lunch with Zoey Pearson? The thing is…I applied for something."

My brows lift. At first I thought it was strange she was having lunch with Connor's bandmate's wife, until I remembered they worked at the same law firm once upon a time. I didn't even think to ask how it went.

"Zoey is the Chair of the Board for the Rainier Foundation." She gives a small, excited smile. "Next week, I'm meeting her again with their CEO, Shay Andrews. They're looking to hire an in-house General Counsel."

This shocks me to my core. Marcella hasn't mentioned wanting to leave the firm for months. "You applied?"

"I'm pretty sure the job is mine if I want it. It's very different than what I'm used to. A big opportunity nonetheless." She bites her lip. "Arts in schools, equity work, all of it. The foundation's exploded in the last year. I think I could really do something good there. It pays well and would reduce my stress level considerably."

"You'd crush it," I say, no hesitation. "They'd be lucky to have you."

She blushes and glances away. I catch the little smile she can't hold back.

What an excellent, wonderful day.

We head back to the hotel, fingers laced. Once we're inside, we throw our coats on the couch and kick off our boots.

The room's bathed in amber light, cast from the antique sconces along the walls and the soft glow of the city below. Harvard Square sprawls out beneath us, a living painting—shop lights flickering, students rushing through cold air, the occasional flash of headlights from a passing bus.

Marcella stands in front of the floor-to-ceiling window, her reflection mirrored back at us in the glass. She watches me as she strips down to her bra and panties, curves illuminated in the glass like some goddess only I get to touch. She's not posing, not trying. She's glorious and real, the woman I'd do anything for.

I come up behind her, wrapping my arms around her waist. My hands skim the softness of her belly, the dip of her hips. I rest my chin on her shoulder.

"You see?" I murmur against her neck, nodding toward the window where Harvard Square is still buzzing. "I want to fuck you against this window while all those people are oblivious below."

She hums, arching her back slightly into my chest. "Can they see us?"

"If they can, lucky them. They'll see how much you turn me on." I kiss her neck. "How much my cock loves being inside you."

Her laugh is low and rich, and I feel it in my chest.

I kiss down the slope of her shoulder, then lower the straps of her bra. She watches us in the window as I trail my fingers along her sides, slowly, reverently, easing her out of the last of her clothes. Her reflection flushes with color, and mine—tall, broad, utterly wrapped around her like a stormfront.

When I sink to my knees behind her, she gasps, one hand reaching up to brace against the glass. I spread her open and taste her slowly, deliberately, until her thighs are shaking and her voice catches in her throat. *"Seamus—"*

I rise again, covering her body with mine. She's so warm, so soft, and I'm already hard, pressing into the small of her back. I nudge her legs apart with my knee and yank her ass toward me. Press myself against her entrance. The first thrust has both of us moaning.

Her hands flatten against the glass as I slide in and out of her from behind, slow and deep. I hold her hips steady, watching us reflected together—the way she arches, the flush on her cheeks, the way her breasts bounce with every motion.

I've never seen anything more erotic than us, right here, right now.

"This okay?" I whisper against her neck.

She nods, breathless. "Oh, yeah."

I clutch her tightly, my rhythm steady. Hungry. We move together, bodies slapping in sync, pleasure curling around us like the night air outside. She watches herself, biting her lip as I drive into her again and again, never breaking eye contact with our reflection. It's not about dominance or power—it's intimacy. Raw and real.

Us.

"I love you so fucking much," I grunt. "You hear me, Marcella? I love fucking every inch of you. Every sound you make when I fuck you. Every damn part of your body."

She cries out when she comes, her whole body trembling against the glass, and the sound undoes me. I follow her over the edge, teeth at her shoulder, arms wrapped tight like I can anchor us both there forever.

When we finally still, the city keeps moving beneath us—horns, footsteps, the hum of life not pausing for anyone. Up here, it's her and me. Breathless. Joined. Whole.

In the quiet that follows and the way she melts back into my arms, I hear it—the ache of something rare and lasting. A wistful whisper of everything we almost lost, and everything we still get to build.

Ours.

Always.

Forever.

MARCELLA

Christmas Day

Life is funny.

A year ago, I was cross-examining a cardiac surgeon so ruthlessly the court reporter needed a break.

Today, I'm pregnant, in my much-younger-boyfriend's oversized hoodie, riding shotgun to a family dinner where I get to tell my parents they're about to become *abuelos*.

I'm giddy. I'm terrified.

I've never been happier.

This wasn't the plan.

Turns out, I don't miss the plan at all.

After spending a few hours at the McGloughlins, my hand is tangled in Seamus's on our way to Tacoma. He drives like he's got nowhere to be but next to me. One hand on the wheel, the other brushing slow circles against my knuckles like he can feel every neuron firing beneath the skin.

The air inside the car is warm. Calm. Outside, the trees blur past like watercolor—pine-tipped, wrapped in sleepy holiday lights. We're both still buzzing, and I'm not talking about coffee—obviously.

We fucked each other blind all morning.

Not lazy, half-asleep sex either. I mean full-throttle, hand-over-mouth, can't-stop-coming sex.

He worships my soft, ripe body like it's holy ground. My breasts are heavier, my hips wider, my belly already starting to pop around the baby we didn't plan but already love—and none of it seems to scare him.

If anything, he's more obsessed than ever.

"I crave you," he whispered against my skin under the covers when he pushed into me from behind. "You drive me mad."

I know it's true. I feel it. His hands on me constantly, possessive and gentle. Reverent. Like he's cataloging every change. Every inch of soft new curves.

I crave him too. I'm insatiable for my man. Pregnancy hormones have turned me into some sort of touch-starved Siren, and thank God I'm with the one man on earth who's both relentlessly good at sex and delighted to be used like a personal vibrator.

My own personal Orgasm Whisperer.

We barely made it to his parents' house. On our way out the door, I yanked him back into the bedroom and pushed him onto the edge of the bed. Then I climbed on and rode him slow in front of the mirror—my eyes locked on his, his hands controlling my hips so his cock hit me just so—until I came so hard I saw stars.

It wasn't enough, I'm embarrassed to say.

A few hours later, his mom was putting out scones and coffee after the gifts were opened, and he walked past me, stopping to give me a kiss on the temple. Instant hormonal surge.

I gave Seamus the "look." He tracked my meaning and motioned for me to follow him upstairs.

"We'll be right back." I tried to sound innocent, already halfway out of my chair.

Everyone was on to us. I mean, duh.

I saw the way his brothers exchanged glances. Ronni, Astrid, and Ivy all smirked. Maureen didn't even look up as we made our way past her.

In his childhood bedroom, the moment the door clicked shut behind us, I pushed him against it.

Hands under his shirt. Tongue in his mouth. Desperate and completely unapologetic.

"Jesus, Marcella," he groaned.

I pulled his pants down. "Quick, fuck me so they don't get suspicious."

"They already know exactly what's happening." He spun me around, pressed me against the door, and dragged my leggings and underwear down in one motion. My palms braced on the wood as he slid inside. One of his hands covered my mouth, the other splayed over the curve of my belly.

We made it back downstairs ten minutes later, hair slightly tousled, cheeks flushed, pretending like we weren't christening his childhood bedroom.

Connor raised one brow. "You're glowing, Doc."

"Hope the door didn't splinter." Padraig took a long sip of coffee.

Astrid hid a smile behind her hand and Ronni rolled her eyes.

Maureen seemed unfazed. She slid a plate of eggs in front of me, then patted my shoulder. "Eat up, love. You'll need your strength."

Seamus's eyes caught mine from across the table. He winked.

God, I love his family.

When it came to telling them, we didn't make a big speech. There was no dramatic pause, no clink of a glass. Just a natural lull in the conversation—one of those rare silences you don't see coming until it lands—and Seamus gave my hand a squeeze under the table and said, "We have news."

He looked at me. I nodded.

"We're having a baby." Simple. Clear.

For a second, no one moved.

Then Maureen cried. Not a polite dab at the eyes either—*cried* cried. Hand to her heart, reaching for Ronni like she needed to physically anchor herself. Connor made an awkward joke about shotgun weddings until Ronni elbowed him so hard he nearly spilled his drink. Cillian's face lit up. Brennan and Astrid gazed at each other lovingly. Liam and Padraig exchanged a long, unreadable look I still haven't deciphered. Rory raised his glass and said, "Good. The world needs more of you."

"We didn't plan this. I had to stop birth control to prep for egg freezing," I explained. "Dr. Madison told me the older I get, the lower my odds. So I went off the pill, planning to start the cycle."

Cillian deadpanned. "Well, if a few minutes ago is any indication of how often you guys are together..."

"You're one to talk." Brennan slugged him in the arm.

Ronni choked on her wine. Maureen fanned herself like she was about to faint.

"We're grateful," I said quickly. "Really grateful. We've got a healthy baby on the way."

Through all of it, Seamus never let go of my hand.

Now we're heading to my family's restaurant, and my nerves are pulsing with a vengeance. It's not the same kind of nerves—not performance anxiety or dread. More like I'm walking into a room I've been in a hundred times before, only this time I'm carrying something no one else can see yet.

To my family, maybe it looks like I've gained ten pounds. My body's changing. My life is changing. I don't know what they'll say when I tell them it's not a phase or a craving or the holidays.

Seamus and I are having a baby. It's real.

"You okay?" Seamus asks as we exit the freeway, heading toward the waterfront.

I fib, "I'm fine."

He smirks. "Which means you've been replaying every past Christmas dinner in your head and bracing for a fresh round of sibling interrogation—only this time, it's your sister's turn to grill us instead of my brothers."

"I have not," I say. Then sigh. "Okay, maybe a little. Mostly reliving their faces when we came back downstairs."

We smile at each other.

He covers my hand with his. "Want to run one of your arguments by me?"

"Do you think they'll be weird about this?" I panic a little.

He laughs and pulls my hand to his thigh. "We don't have to tell them tonight, you know. We could...eat, smile, and lie."

I give him a look.

"Right," he says. "You don't lie."

"Not well." I scrunch my nose.

He raises a brow. "Or, not at all."

"It's time." I turn my hand over and let his fingers lace through mine. "If I don't say something tonight, my mom's going to say it for me. She kept staring at my boobs last Friday at dinner."

"Hard not to," Seamus says under his breath.

My mouth drops open dramatically. *"Seamus."*

"I'm just saying. There's a very obvious growth curve." He licks his lips.

I swat him gently with our laced hands. "Do not say 'growth curve' while discussing my pregnancy symptoms. You're a scientist, not a frat boy."

"You say it like the two are mutually exclusive," he says as we pull up in front of the restaurant. He leans across the console, presses a kiss to my temple. "Let's go, Mama."

Twinkling lights dance behind fogged windows. Inside, the noise hits first. My family doesn't do quiet holidays. Someone's baby is crying—probably my cousin Lucia's. My dad is laughing like a man who's had two glasses of wine and plans on having seven more. The smell of garlic and chorizo makes my mouth water—and the caramelized cinnamon wafts from a giant bowl Rosa is setting on the table. *Arroz con leche.* My comfort food.

My mom looks up from behind the bar and immediately points at me.

"Late," she calls, smiling.

"It's Christmas," I protest. "Time is a construct in an Irish household."

Seamus chuckles behind me. "She reminds me every time we leave my family's house."

"Chellie." My mom makes her way around the bar, pulling me into a hug and holding me for a beat longer than usual. "You look tired."

"I'm fine."

She pulls back, narrows her eyes. "Are you?"

I don't answer.

Seamus distracts her by kissing her cheek. "Merry Christmas, Mrs. Delgado."

"You're too handsome." She swats him with a towel. "You make us all suspicious. Go sit before I get out my rosary."

Lucas emerges from the office, scrolling his phone. "Why are you glowing? Either you're getting married or you're pregnant."

I choke on air.

Seamus slides into his seat like this is the most normal night of his life. "Can't it be both?"

Lucas lowers his phone and stares at me. At Seamus. Back at me.

"What did you say?" Rosa appears at his side, wooden spoon in hand.

"Nothing," I croak.

"Definitely something," my dad says, appearing with a bottle of wine and five glasses. "She has the 'I'm about to make an announcement and ruin dinner' face."

I cross my arms. "I do not."

"You do," Rosa says. "You always have."

"Chellie?" My mother's voice is soft now. Her eyes are wide.

I glance at Seamus. He nods, like this is one more thing we do together. Like telling my family I'm pregnant is no more terrifying than making tea or choosing a name or holding my hair back while I throw up every other morning.

"Fine. I'm pregnant," I say.

For a second, the room doesn't move.

Then my mom gasps and says, "I knew it," while my dad shouts something in Spanish I think loosely translates to "buy more wine."

Lucas chokes on his drink.

Rosa leans against the wall and grins. "You're glowing."

"What?" I narrow my eyes.

"Kidding." She gestures to my glass. "You're drinking sparkling water with lemon. Could you be more obvious?"

Lucas raises his glass. "To the next generation of chaos."

"You're sure? You're happy?" my mother asks, wiping at her eyes.

I nod, unable to speak. My throat is tight and my heart's too full to form words, so I hold her gaze and hope she can see it—how much I mean it.

She smiles like she does.

The conversation starts to flow again in gentle waves—softer now, like the intensity has passed and left only the glow. Plates are half-finished. Wine refilled. Bit by bit, laughter returns to the edges of the room.

Eventually dinner winds down. Wine glasses are half-full. Plates scraped clean. My mom's leaning against the back of her chair, flushed from Rioja and joy. Rosa's still seated—finally off her feet, watching everyone like she's trying to memorize the scene before it shifts. My dad is retelling a story he's told at least three Christmases in a row. No one interrupts because no one minds.

The energy is soft. Wistful, even. Like we're all suspended in a beautiful evening we don't want to end.

Then Seamus stands.

Not abruptly. Or dramatically.

Purposefully.

I look up. "What are you doing?"

"Something important." He leans down, presses his mouth to my hair, and murmurs, "Trust me."

Then he turns to my dad. "Mr. Delgado?"

"Yes, Seamus?" My father's head tilts slightly.

"I'd like to ask for your blessing," he asks earnestly.

Every fork stills. My breath stills.

"I love your daughter," Seamus says. "Not because of this baby, or because our lives collided at the wrong time in all the right ways. I love her because when she walked into my world—demanding, brilliant, impossible—everything shifted."

He breathes in. Steadies. "She didn't make it easy and I'm glad because nothing worth it ever is. She challenged me. Called me on my bullshit. Made me question every rule I thought I had to follow. From the second I saw her there was something between us. Even when we were on opposite sides."

His voice catches—slightly—and Rosa reaches over and gently touches my mother's arm.

"She makes me better. Not by fixing me. By *seeing* me. Completely. Loving me anyway."

No one moves.

"I know things are happening fast. I also know what matters. So does Marcella. She's it for me. The loud moments, the quiet ones, the way she whispers 'I love you' when she thinks I'm asleep. The way she holds our future like it's fragile and fierce all at once."

He looks at my dad, steady. Strong. "I want to marry her. Not because we're supposed to. Not to make anything right. I want to marry her because she's the only life I want."

Silence folds over us, full and still and reverent.

My dad stands, walks around the table, and stops in front of Seamus.

"You love her," he says quietly. "I believe you know what that means to me."

"I do."

My father places a hand on his shoulder, nods once. "Then you have my blessing."

He pulls Seamus in for a brief, firm hug.

My throat burns. My heart pounds. I don't even realize I'm crying until Rosa hands me a napkin across the table and says, "You always act so tough and you're the softest one here."

Tonight, maybe I am.

Seamus returns to his seat beside me and takes my hand under the table, thumb stroking mine.

"Are you ready for forever?" I whisper, quiet enough for only him.

He turns to me, steady and soft. "I've never wanted anything more."

Everything's happening out of order.

A baby first. A proposal in a crowded restaurant. A future we didn't anticipate.

None of it feels wrong.

Seamus is the right choice—no matter how and when he showed up.

I'm saying yes to all of it.

SEAMUS

Epilogue - One Year Later

Family dinner is always organized chaos.

Christmas at the McGloughlin household is a sensory overload of the highest order.

Especially now the clan is expanding exponentially.

Elias, snug against my chest in his wrap, lets out a long, suspiciously timed sigh. It sounds judgmental, honestly. Which is fair. His entire family is here, both my side and Marcella's—and, as the newest member, he's the center of attention.

He best get used to it. This is what his life is going to look like—too many people talking at once, someone always trying to feed him, and cousins who will absolutely teach him how to swear in Gaelic, English, and Spanish before preschool.

The front door's wide open. No one's bothered to close it in hours. Liam and Padraig are staging a Nerf war in the hallway. Connor's got Teagan tugging on his shirt, wearing glitter antlers and no socks, like a feral elf. Cillian's in the kitchen with his new wife, pretending to help while sneaking bites off a *jamón* platter Rosa told him not to touch.

Marcella is perched next to Ronni on the window seat, glasses of Rioja in one hand. Her other hand rests absently over her belly like she hasn't stopped protecting the space—even though he's here in the world now. Her hair is loose. Her cheeks are flushed. She's barefoot, glowing, and impossibly beautiful.

When she looks up and catches my eye, she mouths, "You okay?"

I nod, shifting Elias against my chest silently communicating, *More than*.

We got married last February at City Hall. The two of us and our parents and Elias in the form of a bump. Marcella wore white. No veil. Just her, wrapped in something soft and strong and stunning. There was no pressure. Her hand in mine and dinner with the entire clan at The Metropolitan Grill afterward.

For our honeymoon, we disappeared for a long weekend on Whidbey Island—three nights of stormy windows, warm tea, and her falling asleep on my chest while Elias shifted inside her like he had opinions.

Our son arrived in August. Seven pounds. Long fingers. All eyes.

Connor and Ronni brought him a miniature leather jacket with LTZ embroidered on the back. Liam and Padraig wrote him a lullaby. Cillian built his crib and set up his entire nursery. Brennan sent us a baby monitor with more features than my research lab, and Marcella's family loaded us up with every gadget known to man.

Marcella's mom and Ma now operate as a unit. They take turns showing up to "help" and have somehow merged into a two-woman holiday-planning task force no one dares interrupt. They cook, clean, fuss, and argue over nap schedules like it's a team sport.

We need the help. I'm halfway through R6, one last long obstacle before this doctor life becomes mine on my own terms. The hours are still brutal. When I get home at 2 a.m., exhausted and wired and thinking I've got nothing left to give, I find Marcella asleep with Elias curled against her chest—I realize I'm the luckiest man on earth.

Marcella's back to work—General Counsel at the Rainier Foundation. It's different from the world she used to command. No courtroom battles. No cross-examinations. Strategy. Operations. Leadership. She's thriving. She still runs on ambition and caffeine, with a softness now. A steadiness.

She's letting herself have joy without guilt.

Like today. Joy personified.

The entire house smells like someone opened a spice market in the middle of a bakery—Ma's brown-butter carrots and soda bread, Rosa's *arroz con pollo*, garlic and saffron and thyme all layered on top of the familiar tang of something delicious roasting in the oven.

I'm wedged between Brennan and my dad, one leg propped up on the hearth, Elias's pacifier tucked in my hoodie pocket like a secret weapon. He'll need it soon.

Marcella crosses the room, acutely aware of our son getting fussy. She leans over the back of the couch and brushes her lips over Elias's head. "I'm going to feed him before dinner."

"Want me to help?" I ask as I hand him up to her.

She shakes her head. "Nah, we've got a system."

Of course they do.

I watch her leave the room, soft and sure, Elias pressed to her shoulder. The others barely notice her departure, already rolling into a debate over which family member first tried to mix cinnamon into Ma's roast potatoes. (It was Padraig. It was definitely Padraig.)

The music's low in the background, something jazzy and instrumental, loud enough to catch when the voices dip. The table's already set—Ma's best white tablecloth, Rosa's insistence on proper chargers. It's longer than usual this year. Two tables pushed together. Lucas brought folding chairs from the restaurant. There's a bench against the far wall with a pillow from the living room thrown on top. It works.

Ma appears in the doorway, wiping her hands on a towel. "Dinner's ready."

People move. Voices rise. The familiar swell of chairs scraping and silverware shifting and holiday dinner settling into motion. The dining room hums like a living thing.

Rosa and Ma flow in and out of the kitchen, each trip bringing a new wave of color, scent, and barely disguised competitiveness. There's a carved lamb roast with a glistening crust, flanked by a golden-crackled leg of *jamón ibérico*.

Saffron rice glows under curls of seared lemon, tucked beside bowls of garlicky gambas and slow-roasted *patatas bravas*. A massive paella pan holds pride of place, scattered with mussels and bright-red peppers.

Next to it, Ma's creamy *colcannon* is mounded high beside steaming trays of roasted parsnips and honeyed carrots with fresh thyme. There's brown bread still warm from the oven, sliced thick and set out with curls of Kerrygold butter, and a dish of cranberry-orange compote she insists "rounds things out."

Croquetas—crispy, molten, perfect—are lined up like soldiers next to a basket of sausage rolls wrapped in puff pastry so flaky the edges shatter when you breathe near them.

Dishes fill the table. Hands pass plates. Laughter starts to echo over the clatter of silverware. Marcella reenters as everyone begins to sit, Elias already dozing again, seemingly completely uninterested in the fanfare.

She settles beside me, Elias tucked snug in his wrap against her chest, his tiny hand peeking out near her collarbone. She exhales as she eases into the chair, eyes scanning the table, already full of conversation.

"You made me a plate?" She spots it in front of her.

"Of course." I slide it closer. "You didn't think I'd let you go hungry, did you?"

Her lips curve. "How very husbandly of you."

"Careful." I smirk. "I might start setting expectations."

She takes a bite, then rests her elbow on the table and leans in slightly, voice low, meant only for me.

"This is good," she says. "All of it."

"Yeah." I rest my hand on her thigh under the table. "It really is."

It takes a while to settle—like it always does when this many people are packed around one table. Someone forgets their drink, someone else needs a spoon, a napkin falls, a chair creaks. It's all part of the music.

I glance around the table—Connor and Ronni wrangling their three kids, Lucas and Brennan in deep debate about AI, Rafael and my da are deep into a conversation about woodworking, something about restoring an old wine rack. Liam corrects Padraig's retelling of how their band almost opened for U2. Astrid and Ivy lament not being able to eat sushi. Cillian sits listening, quietly content, next to his wife.

Ma and Rosa watch everything. Not judging—keeping track. Like the whole thing only works because they see all the pieces and let them move.

I catch Marcella watching, too. The way her eyes scan the table, her fingers gently brushing the edge of her water glass, Elias's sleepy weight resting on her shoulder. Her father laughs at something Ma says, and Lucas leans in to correct whatever it was.

She glows.

Not in a glowy-mom way people always reduce her to now. In the way she's always glowed when she's right where she's supposed to be—even if it took her longer to believe the space existed.

"You did this, you know." She leans toward me.

I tilt my head. "Did what?"

"This." She gestures loosely around the table. "You made this life real for me. If you'd never convinced me to come back to the abandoned hospital room…"

I don't know what to say, so I don't. I merely look at her, take in the curve of her mouth, the light in her eyes, the soft curl of Elias's hand peeking out of the blanket tucked against her chest—and I let myself feel it.

All of it.

The fullness. The noise. The warmth.

The knowing there's no going back.

Dessert appears with no warning. Aromas bloom from the kitchen and Rosa steps back in with a tray of *Basque* cheesecake, a bowl of sherry whipped cream, and a look saying, *don't you dare ask for substitutions.* Ma brings in her annual apple tart, with a lattice top and crust so flaky it's almost delicate.

"Small pieces," Rosa says as she starts slicing. "A suggestion, not a request."

"Too late," Lucas calls, already helping himself to a giant helping.

I cut a piece of each for Marcella and I to share. Elias stirs in Marcella's arms but doesn't wake.

Marcella smiles and kisses the top of his head. "If he sleeps through dessert, he's officially invited back next year."

Eventually, people start peeling away from the table—some toward the living room, some toward the kitchen to "help" clean up (which really means snacking until Ma kicks them out). Rosa collects plates with military efficiency. Connor's kids run laps around the coffee table.

I slip outside.

For a breath.

The porch light spills onto the steps. It's cold—sharp and clean—quiet in a way the inside never is. My lungs stretch. My thoughts ease. I hear the door creak behind me. Marcella.

She wraps my coat around her shoulders and steps onto the porch beside me, Elias tucked against her chest, his breath fogging lightly against the fleece of the wrap. The cold is sharp, not cruel.

"I've been thinking about next year," she says softly.

I glance over.

"I rescheduled the egg retrieval. January."

I nod once. "Okay. Seems about right."

"I need to know you're still in this." She shifts her weight, watching me. "Do you still want more kids? It'll get harder."

I reach over and brush my thumb over my son's tiny forehead. "I'm going to finish this thing, Residency. Research. All of it."

"I know."

"I want to keep going. Past R7. Full-time." I continue, "I want to stay in it. Teach. Build something lasting."

"I figured." She leans against me. "It's why I'm asking."

"None of it will mean anything without you—and our children. Retrieve the eggs. We're adding to our family one way or another, there's no question in my mind." I pull her against me.

We stand there for a long moment—our son sleeping between us, my parents' house glowing behind us, the quiet finally catching up.

We're about to head back inside when we hear footsteps.

Not rushed. Just steady. Confident, even. All the way up the stone steps like they've done it a hundred times before.

Marcella shifts beside me and she appears.

Stevie.

Bounding toward the door, her coat unzipped, hair swept up, face bare. Her expression is unreadable. Her presence is too familiar to be strange. She's been in and out of this house since we were kids. Padraig's best friend. His once-girlfriend. The one we all thought would always be around.

I smile without thinking. "Stevie?"

"Hi, Shaymie." Stevie stops at the foot of the porch.

"It's good to see you." I open the front door. "Come in—it's freezing."

She follows Marcella and I into the warmth.

It all happens in a blur.

We're halfway inside, coats halfway off, when Padraig looks up from the kitchen doorway—and freezes.

Everyone else keeps talking.

He doesn't move.

Not one step.

Stevie pauses near the entry, suddenly still. Like she feels what's coming before anyone else notices.

Padraig's voice cuts through the noise, loud and sharp. "You shouldn't be here."

The room stops breathing.

Connor glances between them. Liam's brows go up.

Marcella straightens beside me. "What—?"

"I don't know." I shake my head.

Stevie doesn't flinch. She meets his eyes and says, steadily, "I know."

The air fractures with something unfinished.

Everyone watches Stevie. No one says a word.

Padraig's footsteps vanish down the hallway, but the wreckage stays behind.

Suddenly, we're not celebrating anything anymore.

A story for another day...

Want one more moment with Seamus and Marcella?
Read the bonus scene here.

Loved their story? A quick review goes a long way—thank you for supporting indie romance!

Padraig let Stevie go once. But this time? He'll burn it all down to keep her. Preorder Forever Flames

Behind the Scenes

Something about Seamus called to me. The youngest of the McGloughlin clan first showed up way back in Fearless as a teen. Even then, I knew he had something special. His official "grown-up" debut came in Limitless Encore (get it below!), when he helped Jace through Alex's terrifying medical crisis. From that moment, I knew Seamus would be a worthy leading man. The only question left was: who could possibly match him?

Enter Marcella.

There's a little bit of me—or my closest friends—in every heroine I write, but Marcella? We share more than most. We're both lawyers (different fields, same energy). We've both fallen for younger men (my husband is four years younger!). Most of all, we've both navigated the complex world of body image as curvy women.

Weight has been part of my personal journey forever. I've been thin, heavy, and everywhere in between. For many of us, body image is always present. There are so many assumptions people make—that we're lazy, don't care about what we eat, or couldn't possibly keep up. None of it is true. I'd bet most curvy women know more about food, nutrition, and dieting than the average person. We've lived it. It's constant. It's complicated.

I wanted Marcella to reflect that truth. She has dealt with the microaggressions, the dating double standards, the internal doubts. The harsh moments she experiences in Wistful Whispers might be dramatized (because, well... it's a romance novel!), but they come from a very real place. When Seamus sees her exactly as she is, loves her for who she is, and makes her believe she deserves that kind of love? She falls hard. She questions whether it's him or the validation she craves (spoiler: it's him—I mean, come on). I hope her journey resonates with anyone who has ever struggled with their weight and self-worth.

Now... let's talk about Seamus and the stairwells.

For someone so brilliant, how did he let it spiral so badly?

In my head, this traces back to Seamus' upbringing. His three older brothers are literal rock stars. His father, though loving, was absent due to his health struggles. Connor stepped up but eventually left to chase music. Liam and Padraig had each other. Brennan and Cillian were older, but still kids themselves. Seamus grew up watching the McGloughlin men navigate fame and attention, so of course he equated desirability with validation. Add in his natural shyness and academic tunnel vision, and he truly didn't understand the emotional impact of his actions.

Marcella was right to call him out. He listened. He learned. He changed. That, to me, makes him a worthy hero. No man fully understands what women go through—but the good ones try.

Writing Wistful Whispers felt like wrapping my arms around two of my most complicated, lovable characters and letting them finally breathe. Seamus and Marcella were a joy to create—messy, flawed, passionate, real. I could've happily stayed in their cozy bubble forever… except this family isn't done with me yet. Not even close.

Next up? The rockstar twins.

Padraig and Liam McGloughlin are about to take center stage.

You've met them. You've felt the energy crackle when they walk into a room. You know these two are fiercely loyal, wildly talented, and stubborn as hell. What you haven't seen yet is how hard they'll fall—or how much damage their hearts will take on the way down.

First comes Padraig in his second-chance romance. The one who walked away from the girl he never stopped loving… only to be blindsided by a devastating secret that could tear them apart for good.

Then Liam. Oh, Liam. The quiet one. The protector. The man with an explosive career and a private life spiraling wildly out of control. The only thing harder than living in the shadows of his family's fame will be choosing whether to stay hidden… or finally risk it all for love.

Both books are an emotional rollercoaster of family, fame, friendship, and the raw, messy kind of love that leaves scars in the best possible way.

I can't wait for you to meet them the way I have.

Buckle up.

Limitless Encore

Maureen McGloughlin's
Famous Irish Stew

Feeds 12, or 6 if the
boys are hungry

INGREDIENTS

- 1½ pounds boneless leg of lamb, cut into chunks
- 1½ pounds boneless chuck roast, cut into chunks
- 1 (10-ounce) bone-in lamb shoulder chop
- 1 teaspoon kosher salt
- 1 teaspoon freshly ground black pepper
- 2 medium yellow onions, thinly sliced
- 1 tablespoon vegetable oil
- Guinness Irish Stout (I use Guinness non-alcoholic)
- 1 large russet potato, peeled and sliced (for thickening)
- 8 large carrots, thick-sliced
- 2 large parsnips, peeled and cut into chunks
- 4 sprigs fresh thyme
- 1 bay leaf
- 2 to 3 cups good lamb or beef broth (homemade if you've got it)
- 1 pound Yukon Gold potatoes, cut into chunks
- Worcestershire sauce, to taste

DIRECTIONS

Buy Good Meat. I use a mix of lamb and beef because not everyone at this table appreciates the gamey flavor of lamb, and the chuck balances it nicely. I always throw in a lamb shoulder chop, bone-in, for depth. Never buy pre-cut stew meat. It's lazy, and you don't know what you're getting.

Brown the Meat. Start by browning your meat in a heavy Dutch oven. Heat the oil until it's just shy of smoking. Work in batches and don't crowd the pot—we're building flavor here, not steaming socks. Salt and pepper the meat, turn it every couple of minutes until it's got a nice crust, then set it aside.

Cook the Veggies. In the same pot, drop in your onions. Let them go slow and sweet—don't you dare rush them. This is where the magic happens. When they're soft and golden, toss in the carrots, russet potato and parsnips. Scrape the bottom of the pot like your grandmother's watching.

Pour in the Guinness. Let it foam up, breathe deep, and remember this is how a real Irish house smells in winter. Add the broth, bay leaf, and thyme. Nestle in the lamb and beef. Line the base of the pot with your thin-sliced russets—they'll dissolve and give the stew its heart.

Slow Cook. Lid on, oven set to 325°F, and let it bake for 90 minutes. No peeking.

Add Potatoes. After that, skim the fat (you'll thank me later), then toss in the Yukon Golds. Put the lid back on, this time a bit askew, and let it go another 30–40 minutes until the meat falls apart under a fork and the potatoes are buttery and soft.

Final step: remove the bay leaf, give it a stir, taste it. Add a dash or two of Worcestershire if it needs rounding out. Maybe a touch more salt. Maybe not.

Ladle it into bowls, top with a sprig of fresh thyme if you're feeling fancy, and serve it with thick slices of warm soda bread and a smile.

Tip: If anyone tells you it needs more salt, hand them the shaker and tell them to hush. This stew's fed generations. It'll do just fine.

Rosa's Rioja–Braised Short Ribs

Ingredients:

1 tablespoon olive oil
1 pound beef short ribs (about 2 ribs, cut in half)
1 medium yellow onion, diced
1 medium carrot, peeled and diced
1 small red bell pepper, finely diced
2 cloves garlic, minced
½ teaspoon smoked paprika (pimencon)
¼ cup Risja (or other dry red wine—don't you dare use cooking wine)
1 cup beef stock
½ cup diced tomatoes
½ teaspoon kosher salt
1 bay leaf
¼ cup pitted Kalamata or Nicuse olives
½ cup fresh parsley leaves, chopped (for serving)

You start with real meat. Two meaty short ribs, bone in. Ask your butcher to cut them in half—you want structure and tenderness.

In a Dutch oven, heat a good glug of olive oil until it's hot enough to make your ribs sing when they hit the pan. Brown them—two minutes per side. No poking. Let them crust up. Pull them out and let them rest while you build the base.

Lower the heat. Add diced onion and carrot—basic sofrito moves. Stir until they soften, about five minutes. Then in go the bell pepper, garlic, and smoked paprika. Stir again. Let the heat wake everything up.

Pour in the Rioja. Scrape the bottom—every bit of flavor clings there. Add beef stock, tomatoes, salt, and a bay leaf. Give it a stir. Nestle the short ribs back into the pot like they never left.

Cover and transfer to a 300" F oven for 2½ hours. Halfway through, turn the ribs. This uint a set-it-and-ferget-it dish. It's an act of dcision.

To serve: ladle into wide bowls, spoon sauce generously, and finish with a scatter of fresh parsley.

Then wait for silence.

Acknowledgments

COVER/GRAPHIC DESIGNER/FINDER OF HOTTIES: Regina Wamba

Editor: Grace Bradley Editing, LLC

Proofreading: Letitia Delan & Anna Theurer

Formatting: Willow Yanarella

PR: Dani Sanchez, Wildfire Marketing

Literary Agent: Stephanie Phillips, SBR Media

Website Maven: Sherri Kiarsis, Ruby Moon Designs

My Right Hand: Willow Yanarella

YAY to KAYLENE'S KREW!!!

A special thank you to Julia Barnes, for her expertise, wisdom and 40 years of friendship.

Dedication

To my husband Gareth. There's nothing like being part of a big, feisty, passionate, hardworking Irish clan, I hope the McGloughlin's capture the love and loyalty I've experienced in my found family.
Also, all of the first responders and medical workers who selflessly work to make our lives better.

About the Author

KAYLENE WINTER IS A best-selling author of steamy, contemporary romance.

Each character-driven novel is filled with snappy dialogue, pop-culture references and enough steam to make you fan yourself. Kaylene weaves authenticity, emotion and angst into a turbulent rollercoaster ride of love, passion and soul-searing romance always ending with a delicious HEA.

Kaylene lives in Seattle with her amazing Irish husband and her Pomsky, Phalen. She loves creating art of all kinds.

Other Titles

Find Me Everywhere

9 781963 545241